FROM ACHILLES' HEEL
TO ZEUS'S SHIELD

FROM
ACHILLES' HEEL,
TO
ZEUS'S SHIELD

Dale Corey Dibbley

FAWCETT COLUMBINE

NEW YORK

A Fawcett Columbine Book
Published by Ballantine Books

Library of Congress Catalog Card Number: 92-97336

ISBN: 0-449-90735-X

Cover design by Dale Fiorillo
Text design by Debby Jay

Manufactured in the United States of America
First Edition: August 1993
10 9 8 7 6 5 4 3 2 1

For my mother

ACKNOWLEDGMENTS

I owe my first debt of gratitude to Regula Noetzli. It was she who realized the need for a work that brought together, in one volume, all our linguistic references to mythology, and it was she who first brought the idea to Ballantine Books.

When Regula was looking for someone to write this book, I was recommended to her by Szilvia Szmuk. There is no way I can ever express my gratitude to Szilvia for recommending me and for sharing her expertise as a professional librarian and teacher of research methods. The only things more valuable to me during this project, as they have been for the past thirty-two years, were her constant friendship and moral support.

I would also like to thank my editor, Julie Merberg, for her ongoing encouragement, and the staffs of the Jervis Library in Rome, New York; the Frank J. Basloe Library in Herkimer, New York; and the Utica Public and Utica College Libraries in Utica, New York, for their assistance.

Finally, more than thirty years after he first introduced me to the Greek gods, I would like to thank my high-school English teacher, Mr. Milton Novak. It was his unbridled enthusiasm for Homer and the Greek tragedians that inspired my lifelong interest in mythology. He was truly my "mentor," both in literature and in life.

INTRODUCTION

You wake up early on a *Thursday* in *June. Venus,* the morning star, is still visible in the sky. A glance at the thermometer outside your bedroom window shows that the *mercury* has already risen into the seventies.

You go downstairs and turn on the TV, then fix yourself a bowl of *cereal.* The morning news includes a report of a *volcanic* eruption in the South Pacific and a retrospective on the *Apollo* and *Gemini* space programs. After eating breakfast, you pack your lunch, which includes some *ambrosia* salad and a *nectarine.*

At 7:00 A.M. you get in your car and drive to the new gas station at the end of the street, where you fill your tank. You pay the attendant and receive a free *atlas* as part of the station's Grand Opening promotion. Back on the road, you hear the sound of a *siren* behind you and pull over to let an ambulance pass. You turn on the radio, hoping for some soothing *music,* but it's time for the weather report, and they're predicting that it will be over one hundred degrees in *Phoenix,* Arizona, today.

The atmosphere at the office is anything but *jovial.* The boss is in a terrible mood, and no one has a *clue* as to why. He calls you into his office and berates you for not having finished the *herculean* task he gave you just yesterday. What he says *rankles,* but rather than protest and open up a *Pandora's box,* you meekly accept his criticism and return to your desk, muttering under your breath that the man is nothing but a *narcissistic* slave driver.

You try to finish the project, but the air conditioner is on the fritz and it's already *hot as Hades.* The windows of your modern office building are *hermetically* sealed, so it's impossible to let in any fresh air. You're *lethargic,* but you work until lunchtime. At noon you eat in the cafeteria with your friend *Iris,* then do a little window shopping. The stores are filled with *tantalizing* things, but you don't get paid until *Friday,* so you have no *money* to spare.

After lunch you work like a *demon,* then ask your secretary to type up your notes as soon as possible. "How do you expect me to read this *mumbo jumbo*?" is the reply. When it's almost quitting time and the report's not ready, you start to *panic.* You ask what's taking so long, and the response is *a look that could turn you to stone.* Inside, you're going *berserk,* but you withdraw into your office and try to wait patiently. The report is on the *ogre*'s desk just before quitting time.

After a *chaotic* day you get into a car that's an *inferno.* You can see lightning and hear *thunder* in the distance, and soon there's so much wind and rain you think you're in a *hurricane* or *typhoon.* You can't wait to get home. All you want to do is sit like a *zombie* in front of the TV and watch some silly horror movie—about *werewolves* or *vampires*—until you drop off to sleep.

Chances are you've had days very similar to the one described above. And you've probably talked about them the same way, using most of the forty-one italicized words and phrases. Although they're all part of our everyday vocabulary, at first glance these nouns, adjectives, verbs, and figures of speech don't seem to have much in common—that is, unless you are familiar with world mythology. For each of these English words and phrases has its origin in ancient religious beliefs, legends, or folklore. Most are derived from the myths of Greece and Rome, but some can be traced to Africa, Central America, Scandinavia, and Eastern Europe.

For example, the mercury in our thermometers is named after Mercury, the Roman messenger of the gods, while the cereal in our breakfast bowls honors Ceres, the Roman goddess of agriculture and grain. The sirens attached to modern emergency vehicles bear the name of a group of mythical Greek temptresses whose singing lured sailors to their death. *Tantalizing* is an adjective that can also be traced to Greek mythology:

Tantalus was a sinner who was doomed to spend eternity with food and drink in sight, but just outside his reach. The ancient Egyptians believed in a mythical bird who, every five hundred years, was reborn from its own ashes; the city of Phoenix, Arizona, is named for that legendary creature. In another part of Africa, on the Senegal River, priests of the god Mama Dyambo made horrible noises to frighten away evil spirits; their meaningless ravings became English *mumbo jumbo.* From the Norse tales of frenzied warriors who fought to the death clad only in bearskins came the word *berserk,* while the tropical storms we call hurricanes are named after Hurakán, the Quiché god of thunder and lightning. The other thirty-three italicized expressions have equally surprising and fascinating origins, as do hundreds of others that we "borrowed" from world mythology.

English as we speak it today has been evolving for over fifteen hundred years. Our language owes its unparalleled richness of vocabulary and colorful figures of speech to the fact that each time English-speaking peoples came into contact with a new culture, they found a new source of words and expressions, which they did not hesitate to incorporate into their writing and speech.

The history of the English language begins with the Angles, Saxons, Jutes, and other Germanic tribes who conquered the British Isles sometime after the middle of the fifth century A.D. By that time Britain had been cut off from the rest of the Roman Empire for at least a generation, and although Latin was perhaps still spoken in the larger towns, most of the inhabitants of the rural areas had reverted to the indigenous Celtic language. The various dialects spoken by the German invaders came from Primitive Germanic, or Teutonic, which had also spawned the Scandinavian languages. The Anglo-Saxons shared more than a common linguistic heritage with the Norsemen, however. They also worshiped many of the same gods, albeit under slightly different names. The leader of the Norse pantheon or *Aesir* was Odin; to the Germanic peoples he was known as Woden. Tyr, the Norse god of war, was called

Tiw by the Germans. Thunor was the Germanic name for Thor, the Scandinavian god of thunder. English-speaking people still refer to these ancient gods at least four days out of every week, since Tuesday, Wednesday, Thursday, and Friday are named for Tiw, Woden, Thunor, and Woden's wife, Frige, respectively.

From the fifth to the eighth century, the Anglo-Saxons expanded their territories, overcoming the resistance of the Celtic-speaking Britons. By the time the Vikings began their raids at the end of the eighth century, several Anglo-Saxon dialects flourished in Britain. A century later, however, only the kingdom of Wessex remained independent of the Scandinavian invaders. Eventually, in the tenth century, it fell to the kings of Wessex to reclaim Britain and to establish their own West Saxon dialect as that of the new nation. During the period of the Danelaw many new English words had been formed from the language of the invaders. The islanders had also heard more tales of Scandinavian gods and heroes, and from these they had borrowed more words and expressions with which to enrich their developing language.

The real milestone in the development of English came, however, with the Norman Conquest of 1066. The Frenchmen who followed William the Conqueror to Britain brought with them a whole new language. While the study of Latin and Greek had continued in the monasteries, after the departure of the Romans the lay population of the British Isles had had little or no contact with either of these languages or the classical literature written in them. Now, for the first time, Englishmen were exposed to the thousands of French words and expressions that had, in turn, come from Latin. In the years after the conquest, contact with the mainland expanded and the islanders became familiar with other European languages as well. During this period, not only did Englishmen hear and adopt hundreds of words of Latin and Greek origin, but they began to hear exciting tales of ancient gods and heroes.

In the following centuries, as writers like Chaucer, Spenser, Marlowe, Shakespeare, and Milton created English literature, they often turned to classical Greek and Roman writers, especially Homer and Virgil, for inspiration. And, as they popularized classical literature, words and phrases relating to the old myths began to be used in everyday speech.

Once the floodgates of Greek and Roman culture were opened, there was no end in sight. References to the ancient myths now abound in English. Half our months commemorate mythological figures, January through June still bearing the names of the gods with which the Romans christened them. Besides appearing on our calendars, the gods of Greece and Rome live on in many aspects of modern life. In particular, scientific terminology is replete with references to the gods, as well as to legendary heroes and monsters. What is now the science of astronomy dates back to at least 3000 B.C., when the early peoples of Mesopotamia identified seven moving bodies in the night sky: the sun, the moon, and five planets. Believing each to be a god, they named them for their major deities. The Greeks continued this tradition, renaming the planets for the Olympian gods; later, the Romans did the same for their pantheon. English adopted this system of classical nomenclature, and as modern scientists discovered additional planets these too were given the names of Roman gods. (A Norse goddess, Jord, who was known to the Germanic peoples as Erda, gave her name to our own planet.) In addition, of the eighty-eight constellations recognized by modern astronomers, over half commemorate characters and events in Greek mythology, although most bear the Latin names for these.

Astronomy is not the only branch of science to draw its inspiration from mythology. Many of the elements discovered by chemists reminded them of mythical beings. The silver-gray, magnetic element that played tricks on miners, leading them to believe they had found a more precious metal, was named cobalt after the Germanic kobolds—mischievous underground spirits who made a habit of tricking people. The iridescence of another element's solutions and the various colors of its compounds led its discoverers to call it iridium, after Iris, the Greek goddess of the rainbow. A heavy, gray, radioactive element discovered in 1828 was named thorium because it called to mind Thor, the formidable and ominous Norse god of thunder.

Botanists and zoologists also drew heavily on resemblances to legendary creatures when classifying plants and animals. A genus of small East Indian fish, which have horselike faces and fins resembling wings, reminded zoologists of Pegasus, the winged steed of Greek mythology, and was thus named after him. The Arachnida—the class of invertebrates that includes spiders—are named for Arachne, a Greek maiden who challenged Athena to a weaving contest and was turned into a spider. Pythons, the largest snakes known to man, bear the name of a mythical serpent that lived on Mount Parnassus and was slain by Apollo. Multicolored irises are named for the goddess of the rainbow; hyacinths and narcissuses commemorate characters in Greek myths; and peonies, once believed to have healing properties, are fittingly named after Paean, the physician of the Greek gods. The list goes on and on.

Early men developed myths to explain the world around them: its creation; natural phenomena such as thunder and lightning, floods, and the seasons; the topographical features of their land. Many of the words we use every day can be traced back to these primal myths. The Germanic peoples believed the god Thunor voiced his displeasure by sending thunder and lightning through the sky; the Greeks explained echoes as the voice of a disembodied nymph named Echo, who could only repeat what others said; the Romans thought volcanoes were the underground forges of the smith god, Vulcanus.

The gods were also believed to have great power over human emotions and reactions. We still use terminology from ancient myths when describing the most fundamental human emotions: love and aggression. The adjective *venereal* and the noun *aphrodisiac* come from the names of Venus and Aphrodite, the Roman and Greek goddesses of love. The martial arts and martial law are named after Mars, the Roman god of war. Psychologists have studied the myths of Oedipus and Electra and extrapolated them into "complexes"—disturbances of the human psyche (which, by the way, was named for Psyche, the maiden who symbolized the human soul in the Roman allegory of Cupid and Psyche).

Most of us have grown up hearing and using such expressions as "the Midas touch," "Achilles' heel," "Pandora's box," "a Trojan horse," etc. These and many other metaphors have been adopted from classical mythology. They have been in use for so long that in many cases their literal meaning has been lost, and it is only by going back to the original myths that we see how they came to mean what they do.

Many of the ancient tales that are retold in this book are remarkable for the light they shed on the character of the people who made them up. Different peoples had very different concepts of their gods, and their myths reflect this. In general, the gods of the Egyptians, the Germanic peoples, and the Norsemen were a much sterner, more awe-inspiring lot than those of the Greeks (and, by extension, the Romans, since they adopted most of the Greek deities and their legends). Yes, Zeus did get angry and hurl his thunderbolt from time to time, and his wife, Hera, often took cruel revenge on the "corespondents" in his extramarital affairs. But the gods that the Greeks created were often as human as their creators. They were jealous, petty, self-centered, thoughtless—in short, they were just like us. The same is true of the mortal heroes and heroines of Greek mythology.

These all-too-human characteristics are what make the tales of the gods' exploits so lively and amusing. It is no wonder that the figures of speech that come from them are equally colorful. The mischievous Roman boy god, who fired his arrows on unsuspecting passers-by, gave us the wonderful phrase "struck by Cupid's arrow," to describe someone who has fallen head over heels in love. We call a vigilant person "Argus-eyed" after the hundred-eyed sentry that the Greek goddess Hera posted to watch over her philandering husband and one of his paramours. Oversexed males and females are called "satyromaniacs" and "nymphomaniacs," respectively, in remembrance of the wild cavorting of the Greek nature spirits called nymphs with the satyrs, followers of the god Pan.

Other cultures have given us expressions that, although not as numerous as those from Greece and Rome, are every bit as colorful. From the West Indian belief that dead men can be made to walk and carry out the orders of the living we borrowed the word *zombie* to refer to a person who moves as though in a trance. From the Islamic belief that there are seven separate heavens, one above the other, we took the phrase "in seventh heaven" to mean "as happy as can be." Because they believed Hindus frequently threw themselves under a gigantic wheeled statue of Vishnu that was called Jagannath, Englishmen coined the term *juggernaut* for an inexorable force that crushes anything in its path. From the Celtic legends of King Arthur and his knights we speak of a perfect gentleman as a "Sir Galahad" and an idealistic quest as a "search for the Holy Grail."

*   *   *

While I have no doubt missed a few, I have tried to include all the best-known words and phrases that English has borrowed from world mythology. It is my hope that you will find the stories behind these expressions as captivating as I do. As you read through them, you may find that you have heard a different version of a myth, or have run across another story to explain a word's origin. While researching this book I sometimes felt as though there were as many versions of certain myths as there are words in the English language. In general, I have related the best-known version of each tale, while mentioning that others exist. In the case of particularly colorful variations, or where there are several well-known tales, I have recounted as many of these as made sense within the context of the individual entry. In those cases where there are multiple theories as to the origin of a word or phrase, I have included as much information as was available in support of each.

Working with material in translation presents a unique set of problems, particularly when the translation is from one alphabet to another. Certain Greek sounds are rendered into the

Latin alphabet differently by different translators. For example, the Greek name *Uranus* is often written *Ouranos; Cronus* frequently appears as *Cronos* or *Kronos; Dionysus* is sometimes written *Dionysos.* In nearly all cases, I have used the *-us* ending, simply because it is more common. Many feminine names, such as *Athena* and *Hera,* are often transcribed with an *e* rather than an *a* at the end (*Athene, Here,* etc.). I believe most readers of English are more familiar with the *-a* ending, which comes closer to our pronunciation, so I have chosen to follow that model. I have also used the letter *c* rather than *k* for the hard sound in names such as *Bacchus* and *Cronus,* for the same reason. In names such as *Penthesilea* and *Tiresias,* which are often written as *Penthesileia* and *Teiresias,* I have generally opted for the simpler spelling and reduced the number of vowels accordingly.

Capitalization is another area in which there are no hard-and-fast rules and one must exercise one's own judgment. Many English words were formed from proper names. Some of these, like *Cassandra,* are always written with a capital initial letter. Others, like *mentor,* always begin with a lowercase letter. Still others may begin with either a lowercase or a capital letter: *Antaean/antaean, Circean/circean, Herculean/herculean,* etc. In these cases, as in all those where there are variant spellings, I have listed the options, separated by a slash.

Some readers may be new to Greek and Roman mythology. Most of the Greek gods were adopted by the Romans, who associated them with their own indigenous Italian gods. To make the relationship between the two sets of gods clearer, I have included a side-by-side list of the major Greek and Roman divinities.

—*Dale Corey Dibbley*

THE CLASSICAL DEITIES

GREEK		ROMAN
Aphrodite	Goddess of love	Venus
Apollo	God of light, medicine, poetry	Apollo
Ares	God of war	Mars
Artemis	Goddess of hunting	Diana
Athena	Goddess of wisdom	Minerva
Cronus	One of the Titans, father of Zeus	Saturn
Demeter	Goddess of growing things, agriculture	Ceres
Dionysus	God of wine	Bacchus
Eros	God of love	Cupid
Hades	God of the Underworld	Pluto
Hephaestus	God of fire, metalworking	Vulcanus
Hera	Goddess of women, wife of Zeus/Jupiter	Juno
Hermes	Messenger of the gods	Mercury
Poseidon	God of the sea	Neptune
Zeus	Ruler of the gods	Jupiter/Jove

FROM ACHILLES' HEEL
TO ZEUS'S SHIELD

A

(faithful) Achates: a bosom friend; a companion through thick and thin

Of the exiles who fled the burning city of Troy with Aeneas, none was more devoted to their new chieftain than Achates. Virgil uses several other adjectives—*brave, valiant, stalwart*—to describe him, but the epithet most associated with his name is *faithful*. He was Aeneas's second in command, riding alongside him in the vanguard as they approached new allies and enemies. He was entrusted with the most important messages and missions and never failed to carry out Aeneas's orders. But the two men were more than a leader and a follower. Virgil tells us that after they heard the terrifying prophecies of the Cumean Sibyl, Aeneas walked "sad-faced with downcast eyes," and Achates "walked beside him, keeping step in sympathy with him."

Achates wasn't permitted to accompany Aeneas on the perilous journey to the Underworld, but readers of the *Aeneid* have no doubt he gladly would have gone, and it's this certainty that made them, over the centuries, turn his name into a synonym for undying friendship and devotion.

Achilles' heel: a vulnerable spot

There are many Greek myths about heroes or demigods. Born of the union between a god or goddess and a mortal, these beings possessed many superhuman traits but, unfortunately, did not inherit the immortality of their divine parent. Achilles is one of the best known of these heroes. He was the son of Peleus, king of the Myrmidons, and the sea nymph Thetis. When he was a baby his mother dipped him into the river Styx in an effort to make him immortal. In a tragic oversight, she kept hold of him by one heel and the magical waters weren't able to flow over it, leaving him only partially protected. Achilles fought on the Greek side in the Trojan War, while the god Apollo favored Troy. Knowing of Thetis's oversight, Apollo directed Paris's poisoned arrow straight to Achilles' heel. (In another version of the myth, Apollo assumed the guise of Paris and fired the deadly arrow himself.) In either case, Achilles succumbed, and his heel became a lasting metaphor for a vulnerable spot.

Anatomists also had in mind the image of Thetis dipping her son into the river when they named the tendon that joins the calf muscles to the heel the *Achilles tendon.*

Achilles' wrath was the subject of the *Iliad,* and Homer's recounting of the hero's refusal to leave his tent and fight because Agamemnon took away his concubine gave rise to the phrase "a sulking Achilles" to describe someone who is pouting and being unreasonably stubborn.

These and other stories about Achilles have given us the adjective *Achillean,* meaning great in strength and invincibility, or in wrath.

Adonis: a handsome man

When we say a man is an *Adonis,* we are comparing him to a youth who was so handsome that he captured the heart of the goddess of love herself, Aphrodite.

In the most popular of the Greek myths about Adonis, Aphrodite found him as a newborn and gave him to Persephone, Queen of the Underworld, for safekeeping. But when Aphrodite went to Hades to reclaim him, Persephone, who had also fallen in love with the youth, refused to let him go. Zeus mediated the dispute and decreed that Adonis was to spend half the year on earth with Aphrodite and the other half with Persephone in Hades. When Aphrodite persuaded Adonis to violate the agreement, Persephone took revenge. She went to Ares—Aphrodite's lover of long standing, and told him the goddess now preferred a mere mortal to him. Enraged,

Ares took the form of a wild boar and fatally gored his young rival. Or, as the story was sometimes told, Adonis simply overestimated his skill in the hunt and died as a result of his boldness. As he lay dying, the blood from his wounds turned to bright red anemones that continue to bloom every spring, commemorating his beauty and Aphrodite's love for him.

(The story of Adonis is a Greek adaptation of earlier Semitic myths related to the yearly death and regeneration of vegetation. In Babylonia, Adon [Lord] Tammuz was the god of agriculture. As lover of the mother goddess Ishtar, he spent half the year above ground with her and the other half in the Underworld. In Syria his counterpart was the god Baal; in Egypt, Osiris; in Phrygia, Attis. This last, consort of Cybele, was also slain by a boar, and violets grew from his blood, just as anemones grew from that of Adonis.)

See also: anemone (under "Plants"), Mother Earth/Mother Nature

aegis/egis: protection; sponsorship

Zeus, the most powerful of the Olympian gods, carried a shield of this name, forged by Hephaestus. When he shook it, thunder reverberated throughout the world. On it was the head of the snake-haired Gorgon Medusa, whose glance instantly turned all who beheld her to stone. In the *Iliad* the aegis is described as a mantle or cloak, rather than a shield. Some say that the word *aegis* originally meant "goatskin," and that the shield was covered by (or the mantle was made of) the skin of the goat that suckled Zeus in infancy. Zeus often entrusted the aegis to his daughter Athena, who kept a veil over the Gorgon's head when she wasn't facing her enemies.

Today, when we say an individual is acting "under the aegis of" another person or agency, we mean that they have that party's sponsorship or power behind them, in the same way that Zeus's protection extended to all who carried his shield.

Aeolian/aeolian: giving a moaning or sighing sound, like the wind; carried or produced by the wind

When Zeus defeated the Titans and became leader of the Olympian gods, it fell to him to devise a way of controlling the winds so they wouldn't sweep away the earth and the sea. At his wife Hera's suggestion, he made Aeolus god of the winds. Aeolus lived in the mythical island kingdom of Aeolia, where he kept the winds imprisoned in a cave, letting them out only at his own discretion or at the request of the Olympians. The association of his name with wind was so strong that two adjectives were created from it: *aeolian,* which describes a windlike sound or anything carried or produced by the wind, such as aeolian rock sculpture or aeolian sand; and *aeolistic,* meaning long-winded in speech.

Scientists and musicologists also remembered the myth when they gave names to various inventions and instruments that depend on air currents for their operation. Musical terms that commemorate Aeolus include: an aeolian attachment to intensify a piano's sound; the aeolian harp, which is placed in an open window so the wind can blow over its strings and produce harmonious sounds; the Aeolian minor scale; the Aeolian mode; an aeoline, which is both a musical stop and a mouth harmonica. The prefix *aeolo* is used in music to denote a wind instrument (aeolodicon, aeolomelodicon, aeolopantalon, etc.).

Among inventors, Hero of Alexandria, who lived in the first century A.D., called a contraption that has since been referred to as the first steam engine—an *aeolipile* or *aeolipyle* ("ball of Aeolus" or "doorway of Aeolus").

alma mater: *See: Mother Earth/Mother Nature*

Althaea's brand: an object on which a person's life or reputation depends

When Meleager was born, his mother heard the Fates say that he would live only until the brand—the piece of wood—that burned on her hearth was consumed by fire. In an attempt to prolong her son's life, Althaea snatched up the smoldering brand and hid it. The young man grew to manhood, and all was well until the Hunt for the Calydonian Boar.

Artemis had sent a wild boar to ravage the lands of the king of Calydonia, and Meleager put together an expedition of heroes to stop the beast. Among those who joined in the adventure was the beautiful huntress Atalanta, and Meleager fell in love with her instantly. When he succeeded in killing the boar, he skinned it and presented the skin to his beloved. His mother's brothers, who had also stalked the boar, challenged their nephew's right to give away the spoils of the hunt. Carried away by his passion for Atalanta, Meleager drew his sword and killed them. When Althaea learned that her son had murdered his uncles, she was overcome with rage and grief. She removed the brand from its hiding place and threw it back into the fire. As the Fates had predicted years before, Meleager died as the wood turned to ashes.

From this Greek myth we get the term *Althaea's brand*, which is used for an object on which a person's life or reputation depends, and which has the power to destroy him.

amazon: a large, strong, masculine woman

While modern editions of the *Iliad* end with the funeral of Hector, poets after Homer continued the tale with the arrival of the queen of the Amazons, Penthesilea, who comes to Priam's aid and is killed by Achilles. Another queen of the Amazons, Hippolyta, was supposedly killed by Heracles, whose ninth Labor was to procure her girdle. According to Greek myth, these and other queens ruled a race of female warriors said to live in Scythia, in Asia Minor. Fierce and man-hating, they often invaded other kingdoms. It was said that they periodically sought foreign men with whom to mate, afterwards killing their male offspring and raising their daughters to fight. The original myths were later embellished, and it was said that every Amazon cut off her right breast at puberty so she could handle a bow more easily. This detail was no doubt added to try to establish the etymology of the word *Amazon* as a combination of *a* (without) and *mazos* (breast). In fact, the word is of uncertain origin. Robert Graves, author of *The Greek Myths,* has suggested that it is an Armenian word meaning "moon-women," and that the original Amazons may have been priestesses of the moon goddess, who lived on the shores of the Black Sea and bore arms.

Wherever the name Amazon originated, it is now applied— often pejoratively—to any large, strong woman who exhibits masculine traits.

The Amazon River was also named for the Amazons of Greek mythology; while traveling on it, Spanish explorer Francisco de Orellana was attacked by a band of skirted Indians whom he believed to be female warriors.

ambrosia: *See: nectar and ambrosia*

ammonia: a pungent, gaseous alkaline compound; the modern cleaning agent "ammonia water"

Who would think that the name of a common cleaning product comes from that of a god? Such is the case with ammonia, which is named for the Egyptian god Ammon (also spelled Amon, Amen, or Amun).

During the New Kingdom, Ammon became the principal god of Egypt, identified by the Greeks with Zeus and by the Romans with Jupiter. There was a famous temple and oracle of the god in the Siwah oasis of the Libyan desert, already well known in the time of Herodotus and consulted by Alexander the Great. At the same time, ammonium chloride was an article of commerce. The Egyptians distilled it from organic material containing nitrogen by heating either camel dung or a mixture of salt and urine. When the Greeks saw the compound being prepared in the vicinity of Ammon's temple, they dubbed it *Ammoniakos,* meaning "of Ammon." The Romans called it *sal ammoniacus.* The word *ammonia* was adopted into English around 1799.

amphitryon: a generous host; one who entertains lavishly

The most famous hero of Greek mythology was Heracles, whose superhuman strength and cunning were inherited from his father, Zeus. Heracles was only half divine, however, being the fruit of the union of the great god and a mortal woman, Alcmena. Alcmena was the wife of Amphitryon, and she was never unfaithful to her husband—at least as far as she knew! But, in fact, unbeknownst to her, she had lain with Zeus one night and conceived Heracles by him.

This is how it happened: Alcmena's brothers had been murdered, and she refused to consummate her marriage with Amphitryon until he avenged them. He went off and succeeded in killing their assassins, but Zeus arrived at his home before he returned. Taking the form of Amphitryon, Zeus announced his victory and exercised his conjugal rights. When the real Amphitryon arrived, his wife's reaction to him was strange, to say the least. She chided him for repeating the story of his vengeance, when he had already told her all about it the night before, and she made reference to the many hours they had already spent making love. Puzzled, he consulted the seer Tiresias and learned that Zeus had possessed his wife before he did and that one of the "twins" she was carrying was the son of the god. Nine months later, Heracles and Iphicles were born. Amphitryon raised them both as his sons, but Heracles' semidivine attributes manifested themselves while he was still in the cradle, and Amphitryon knew that it was he who had been conceived during Alcmena's first session of lovemaking with her "husband."

The story of Amphitryon's cuckolding has been immensely popular over the centuries, with some thirty-eight versions of it appearing in literature. One of the most popular of these was a play by Molière that was first presented in 1668. In it, Amphitryon returns home unexpectedly and finds the god Jupiter ensconced in his home, pretending to be him. Jupiter offers to give proofs of his identity to an assembly of nobles and, while awaiting them, invites all present to dine. Amphitryon's servant, Sosia, who is really the god Mercury in disguise, announces that this offer puts an end to all doubt, saying, "the real Amphitryon is the Amphitryon who gives dinners." This remark led to the French use of the word *amphitryon* to denote a generous host, one who offers fine food to those who visit his home. The word entered English during the nineteenth century and is still used when referring to a person who has a reputation for providing lavishly for his guests, particularly in the area of food and drink.

ANIMALS

For centuries, laymen have given the names of mythological creatures to living animals that resemble these fantastic beings. The scientists who set out to classify the animal kingdom often followed this example, so that much of our popular and scientific nomenclature for animals comes from classical mythology. It would be impossible to include all of the zoological references to the ancient myths but here are some of the most interesting ones.

Amphisbaena: a genus of limbless tropical lizards

With their concealed eyes and ears and short, blunt tails, these lizards resemble the Amphisbaena, a two-headed serpent of Greek mythology. Its name means "going in both directions," which the fabled creature reputedly could do with ease. It could also put one head inside the mouth of the other, forming a circle, and roll along from one place to another.

arachnid: one of the class of invertebrates that includes spiders, scorpions, mites, and ticks

The Arachnida are named after Arachne, a Greek maiden who challenged the goddess Athena to a weaving contest. Although Arachne's work was flawless, it depicted the gods in rather compromising positions, which angered Athena. She destroyed the offending tapestry and struck Arachne. Chastised, the girl hanged herself, and Athena transformed her into a spider—the first arachnid.

argus pheasant: an East Indian pheasant that resembles the peacock

The peacock was the favorite bird of the Greek goddess Hera. It was said to have once been Argus, a monster with one hundred eyes who was sent by Hera to guard Zeus's paramour, Ino. On Zeus's orders, Hermes killed Argus and released Ino. The grief-stricken Hera then turned Argus into a peacock, setting his hundred eyes into his tail. The pheasant that looks like a peacock is named for him, as is the argusfish, with its many spots, and the argus tortoise beetle—a reddish beetle spotted with black.

See also: Argus-eyed

echidna: the porcupine anteater, found in Australia, Tasmania, and New Guinea

Echidna is the name of a horrible monster of Greek mythology. Half woman, half serpent, she was the mother of many hideous creatures, including the Sphinx, the Hydra, the Chimera, and the Nemean Lion. The spiny, or porcupine, anteater is covered with hair (and spines) like a mammal but lays eggs like a reptile. This unusual combination of traits reminded zoologists of the hybrid Echidna, and they gave the animal her name.

Gorgonia: a genus of coral

The Gorgonia is a genus of coral that becomes rock-hard in air. The allusion is clear: a look from one of the Gorgons of Greek mythology could turn a person to stone. One of the species of Gorgonia—*Gorgonia flabellum*—is a fan-shaped coral commonly known as Venus's-fan.

harpy eagle: a large, double-crested eagle of northern South and Central America; a large eagle of the Philippines

Both these birds have remarkably strong bills and claws. They were named for the Harpies, the rapacious, long-clawed bird-women of Greek mythology. The Harpies tormented Phineus by fouling his food each time he tried to eat. They were finally driven off by the sons of Boreas.

Hydra: a genus of freshwater polyps

Hydras have a simple tubular body, and their mouths are encircled by tentacles with which they catch their prey. Because of their regenerative powers—they can be cut into pieces and each piece will become a new animal—they were named for the Hydra of Greek mythology who, when one of its heads was cut off, grew two more in its place.

See also: Hydra (under "Constellations"), hydra-headed

Junonia: a genus of peacock butterflies

A popular name for the peacock has long been "Juno's bird," because the handsome creature with the "eyes" in its tail was sacred to the Roman goddess. The peacock butterflies of eastern North American have also been named for Juno, because their spots resemble the eyes of a peacock's tail.

lemur: an arboreal mammal of Madagascar

The lemurs take their name from the Roman *lemures*—evil spirits of the dead that haunted the living, striking them with madness. They were spirits that appeared at night, akin to the Greek *lamia;* hence these nocturnal mammals were named after them.

medusa: a type of jellyfish

Medusa was the best known of the Gorgons, a trio of female monsters whose name means "the grim ones." They were covered with scales, their hands were made of bronze, and their teeth protruded like tusks. The long tentacles of this jellyfish bear a strong resemblance to the masses of writhing snakes that made up the hair of Medusa and her sisters, so the marine creature was christened for her.

See also: (a) look that could turn you to stone

Neptune's-cup: a large sponge

Neptune was the Roman name for the god of the sea. Two varieties of large, cup-shaped sponges that grow in the ocean have been given his name. Neptune's-cups can grow as tall as four feet, a height that makes them worthy to bear the name of the king of the sea.

nymph: the immature stage of an insect

The nymphs of Greek mythology were eternally young and beautiful. Their name became a synonym for a young girl and is also used by zoologists to denote the immature stage of an insect. Many insects, such as moths and butterflies, begin life as larvae, metamorphose to pupae or nymphs, and then emerge as adults.

Pegasus: a "winged" fish

Pegasus is the name of a genus of small East Indian marine fish. They have a long snout, and their body is covered with bony plates. Their horselike face, coupled with pectoral fins that spread horizontally like a pair of wings, reminded zoologists of the winged steed of Greek mythology, and they christened the genus after him.

Polyphemus moth: a large American silkworm moth

The Polyphemus moth is unusually large and has a single, eyelike spot on each of its hind wings. The Cyclops of Homer's

Odyssey, who terrorized Odysseus and his crew, was a one-eyed giant. Zoologists were struck by the coincidence and named this colorful moth *Antheraea polyphemus.*

Python: a genus of snakes that includes the largest known to man

The original Python was a mythological serpent that lived in the caves of Mount Parnassus, in Greece. It was slain by the god Apollo, who took over its oracle at Delphi, and henceforth its priestess, the Pythia, delivered Apollo's messages to questioners. This mythological serpent reputedly was enormous, so it made sense to name the largest snakes in the world after it.

Rhesus monkey: the Indian macaque (*Macaca rhesus*)

Rhesus was a mythical king of Thrace and an ally of the Trojans during their war with the Greeks. His horses protected the city of Troy until they were stolen by Diomedes and Odysseus. The Indian macaque was named after Rhesus at the beginning of the nineteenth century. There was no apparent reason for the appellation, except a trend among scientists of that era to use names from classical mythology for their discoveries. (The Rh factor was discovered and named after the monkey in 1941.)

Stentor: a protozoan with a trumpet-shaped body

Stentor was the herald of the Greek army during the Trojan War. He could easily be heard throughout the entire camp, his voice being equal to that of fifty men. Zoologists named a genus of trumpet-shaped protozoans that have their mouth at the large end after him.

vampire bat: any of several species of Central and South American bats that live on the blood of animals

Many bats of Central and South America actually suck the blood of animals in order to maintain their existence, just as the vampires of central European mythology sucked the blood of humans. Their sharp teeth are well suited to slit the skin of their victims, and their digestive system is not designed to handle food other than blood. The term *vampire bat* is also applied, loosely and erroneously, to many other small bats that are mistakenly believed to feed on blood.

See also: vampire

Venus's-flower-basket: a tubular sponge found on the ocean floor

Also known as Venus's-purse, this ocean creature belongs to the genus Euplectella. Its skeleton consists of glassy, siliceous fibers, and it stands erect at the bottom of the sea. Its elegant tubular or cornucopia shape brings to mind a flower basket or vase. Venus's-flower-basket is native to the East Indies and the eastern coast of Asia.

Venus's-girdle: a long, belt-shaped ctenophore

The ctenophora are jellyfishlike marine animals, more or less ellipsoidal in shape. The Venus's-girdle is elongated, like the belt or ribbon the Roman goddess of love might have fastened around her waist.

Antaean/antaean: having superhuman strength; invincible

Antaeus was a Greek giant, son of Poseidon (Sea) and Gaea (Earth). He was invincible as long as he remained in contact with his mother, the earth, who continually renewed his strength. It was said that he forced all who passed through his land to wrestle with him, and, when they inevitably lost, he killed them. Superhuman strength and prowess, such as Antaeus possessed, are described by the adjective *Antaean*.

In the end, it took another superman to defeat the cruel Antaeus. Heracles used a combination of his own great power and his wits to succeed where all others had failed. Holding Antaeus in midair, where he could not touch the earth and renew his strength, Heracles strangled the weakened giant, ending his reign of terror once and for all.

antediluvian: ancient; antiquated

The word *antediluvian,* both as an adjective and as a noun, comes from the Latin *ante* (before) and *diluvium* (deluge). It refers, of course, to the time before the Great Flood that is described in the Book of Genesis. In popular speech, we call something antediluvian when we want to stress its great age or how outmoded it is. Teenagers always think their parents' ideas about dating and curfews are carryovers from "before the Flood," and calling the older generation antediluvians is a polite way of saying they're old fogies.

What many people who know the Bible story don't realize is that it is but one version of a flood myth common to peoples of many parts of the world. The basic premise of all these stories is the same: The supreme deity, angered by the wickedness of mankind, sends floodwaters to cover the earth. One righteous man—with his family and some animals—is spared by the deity, who assists him in building a boat that will carry him to safety. When the floodwaters finally recede, it is this man who founds a new race of men to repeople the earth.

The oldest known story of the Great Flood is inscribed on a clay tablet found at Nippur, in what was once ancient Sumeria. It dates from the nineteenth or twentieth century B.C. and its hero is Ziusudra, a priest of the Sumerian god Enki. When the other gods decided to destroy mankind by sending a deluge to cover the earth, Enki rewarded Ziusudra's faithful service by surreptitiously warning him. Like Noah, Ziusudra rode out the storm in a ship he built after being instructed by Enki. Unfortunately, the details of how he constructed it and who sailed with him were lost when the tablet was broken. The remaining portions of the tablet go on to say that the Flood lasted seven days and seven nights, and that when it was over Ziusudra offered sacrifices to the gods and was made immortal.

The same story, with only a few minor changes, was later incorporated into the well-known *Epic of Gilgamesh.* An Assyrian text of this work, on cuneiform tablets, was found at Nineveh, in the library of King Ashurbanipal (seventh century

B.C.). It relates how Utnapishtim received the gift of eternal life from the gods after surviving the Great Flood. He too was warned by one of the gods, in this case Ea, Lord of the Waters.

Very similar myths were told in India and Greece as well. In the ancient Hindu treatise the *Satapatha Brahmana,* the hero Manu is warned of the impending deluge by a fish. When the floodwaters recede, he offers dairy products to the gods, and out of these they create a woman with whom Manu is able to repeople the earth. In the Greek version, Deucalion's ark comes to rest on Mount Parnassus after weathering a storm sent by Zeus. (As in the Near Eastern myths, the gods had decided to wipe man off the face of the earth because of his wickedness.) Deucalion and Pyrrha then throw stones over their shoulders, and the stones become a new race of men. In a late version of Deucalion's story, which was no doubt influenced by the Mesopotamian tales, the Greek hero, like Noah, is instructed to bring two of each animal into the ship with him.

From archeological evidence it is apparent that Mesopotamia suffered flood damage many times, when the Tigris and the Euphrates rivers overflowed their banks. Most likely, one of these floods (around 3000 B.C.) was worse than the others, and the memory of that disaster may have inspired the legends that later proliferated throughout the Indo-European world. It is interesting to note that no such flood myths exist in Egypt or the rest of Africa. Oddly, though, legends about angry gods sending a deluge to wipe out mankind, with one virtuous man surviving, also exist in Burma and other parts of southern Asia, in Australia and New Zealand, in New Guinea and the Pacific Islands, and in the Americas.

While areas of western Europe—in particular, the British Isles—have many legends about lands that were lost (i.e., flooded over), none of these tell of universal destruction, and they seem to be related to actual small-scale disasters that occurred throughout the centuries. They do, however, often reprise the theme of one good man escaping from the floodwaters that swallow up his neighbors.

There are also flood myths in China, but they are entirely different from those that gave us the story of Noah and the word *antediluvian*. In Chinese mythology, the deluge was represented not as a punishment sent by the gods to wipe out evil men, but rather as the primordial state of the universe. The best-known Chinese myth is that of Yu and the Deluge, in which the hero spends many years trying to get the waters that cover the earth to recede. By dint of hard labor and with help from many water animals and spirits, Yu finally channels the water into the great sea and becomes "the Tamer of the Flood." Thanks to his heroic efforts, crops can be sown and animals raised. Civilization arrives, and mankind enters a new age.

aphrodisiac: that which induces sexual desire

The gods of the ancient Greeks were definitely not purely spiritual beings. They possessed the same lust for life, and for the flesh, as their worshipers—perhaps none more so than Aphrodite, goddess of love. While she was said to inspire all feelings of love and devotion in mankind, she specialized in stirring up sexual desire, and she practiced what she preached! Although Zeus gave her in marriage to Hephaestus, the Greek myths are full of tales of her liaisons with other Olympians, and with many mortals as well.

Given her association with the physical act of love, it was natural for her name to be given to the many love potions men and women have concocted through the centuries. The adjective *aphrodisiac* is used to describe any substance that supposedly increases sexual desire and potency.

See also: erotic, Venus

Apollonian: harmonious; balanced; ordered (opposite of Dionysian)

The Greek god Apollo was the son of Zeus and the Titaness Leto. He was the god of the intellect, of the arts, and of healing.

He was called Phoebus (shining) Apollo and was associated with the sun and light. Apollo personified order and rationality, the bright side of the universe and of man.

We use the adjective *Apollonian* to describe that which is harmonious, balanced, and under control of the rational mind. The attributes of Apollo are often contrasted with those of Dionysus, god of wine and revelry, under whose influence men became anything but rational and orderly!

See also: *bacchanal, Dionysian*

argonaut: an adventurer engaged in a quest

Said to have made its famous voyage a generation before the Trojan War, the *Argo,* according to some accounts, was the first ship. The goddess Athena helped the Greeks to build it, fashioning its prow from part of Zeus's sacred talking oak, which made several prophecies to the sailors during their long voyage. The crew were called Argonauts, and in their ranks were some of the most famous heroes of Greek mythology, among them Heracles, Orpheus, Castor and Pollux, Peleus, and others who agreed to sail with Jason in his quest for the Golden Fleece.

The great courage shown by the Argonauts in signing on for this voyage and the many perils they overcame—the fierce Harpies, the Clashing Rocks, Scylla and Charybdis, to name but a few—have given us the term *argonaut* for a bold, daring adventurer who goes off to face the unknown in high spirits. The term became popular in the U.S. when thousands of fortune seekers dropped everything to join the Gold Rush of 1848–49—modern-day argonauts in search of California's equivalent of the Golden Fleece.

See also: *harpy, (between) Scylla and Charybdis*

Argus-eyed: vigilantly observant

Anyone with one hundred eyes is bound to make a good watchman. That's why Hera, Zeus's wife, chose Argus to guard the maiden Io and prevent Zeus from resuming his adulterous affair with her. The greatest—and most lecherous—of the Greek gods, Zeus hid himself and Io in a dark, thick cloud while he possessed her. Hera immediately became suspicious and went looking for him under the cloud. When she found him, he was standing beside a lovely white heifer, which he claimed had just sprung from the earth. Knowing he could not refuse her with good reason, Hera asked him to give her the animal and quickly engaged Argus, who could sleep with some of his eyes closed and keep watch with others, to assure that the heifer remained a heifer. Totally frustrated, Zeus went to his son Hermes, who was known for his cleverness, and told him he must find a way to kill Argus and release Io. Hermes sped off to the pasture where Argus kept his vigil, and either played on his pipe or told endless stories until all one hundred eyes were finally lulled to sleep.

Hermes killed Argus, but Hera took the latter's eyes and set them in the tail of the peacock, her sacred bird. While they didn't improve the peacock's sight, a person who is *Argus-eyed* is an ever-vigilant, keen observer of the world around him.

ass-eared: having no ear for music

King Midas is best known for his lack of foresight in asking for the golden touch that turned out to be a colossal curse. There is another story about him, which reveals his lack of judgment in other areas as well, and which gave us the unusual epithet *ass-eared* for someone who has no appreciation of music.

In this Greek myth the god Apollo, who enchanted gods and men alike when he played on his lyre, took part in a musical competition with Pan. To everyone else who listened, the simple, rustic tune the latter played on his reed pipe was no match for the exquisite notes of the great god's lyre, but Midas preferred Pan's music and was foolish enough to say so. In fury, Apollo gave Midas the ears of an ass, which from then on served as a constant reminder of his lack of taste and his indiscretion.

See also: Midas touch

atheneum: a building in which books are kept; a literary or scientific association

By most accounts the Greek goddess Athena was the offspring of Zeus alone, and sprang from his head full-grown and fully armed. In at least one account, however, she had a mother: the Titaness Metis, who was the personification of wisdom and prudence. When Metis became pregnant by Zeus, an oracle foretold that she would give birth to a girl, but that her next offspring would be a boy who would depose his father. Zeus immediately swallowed the pregnant Metis, ending once and for all any threat her children might pose to his sovereignty. A while later he developed a terrible headache. His son Hermes persuaded either Hephaestus or Prometheus to split open Zeus's skull, and out came Athena. She soon became his favorite child, the one he entrusted to carry his aegis into battle.

Athena may have inherited her father's bravery, but in her many other attributes she was definitely Metis's child. She was the goddess of law and jurisprudence, of the arts and culture, and of learning. It was she who taught mankind to make musical instruments, ploughs, chariots, and ships. The Romans also revered Athena (whom they called Minerva) as the goddess of wisdom, and the emperor Hadrian's famous Atheneum—a school of oratory, philosophy, jurisprudence, and poetry—flourished in Rome until the fifth century A.D. Modern-day literary or scientific associations and clubs have followed Hadrian's example, referring to themselves as *atheneums*. Buildings that house libraries and other repositories of the knowledge Athena so generously shared are also named after her.

atlas: one who carries a heavy burden; a bound book of maps

Atlas was one of the Greek Titans who, when Zeus rebelled against his father, came to Cronus's aid, fought the Olympians, and were defeated. Most of them were banished by Zeus to Tartarus, the lowest section of the Underworld. Atlas, however, received a worse punishment: He was condemned to bear forever the weight of the heavens on his shoulders, holding the sky apart from the earth. In later versions of the myth, he was said to have held up the world itself. Hence the use of his name to symbolize someone who is saddled with a heavy burden, either physical or emotional (one who "bears the weight of the world on his shoulders").

The ancient Greeks did not know that the earth was round, and it was only after Columbus's voyages that illustrators depicted Atlas holding a globe on his back. One such illustration was used as a frontispiece by Gerardus Mercator in his sixteenth-century *Atlas; or a Geographic Description of the World,* and it was because of this that subsequent collections of maps have been called *atlases.*

The image of the Titan holding up the globe also inspired anatomists to name the topmost vertebra in the neck, which supports the sphere of the head, the atlas.

In another reference to Atlas's weight-bearing abilities, classical architects created *atlantes* (plural of Atlas), male counterparts of the female caryatids, used as columns to support an entablature.

atropine: a drug made from belladonna (deadly nightshade)

The ancient Greeks believed that at every child's birth three invisible old women were present. They were the Morae, or Fates. Clotho was the one who spun the thread of life. Her sister, Lachesis, measured it out, determining its length at the moment of birth. The name of the third Fate, Atropos, means one who cannot be turned, and no one—not even Zeus—

could stop her from cutting the thread of life when the time came.

Her appearance, with her "abhorred shears" in hand, meant certain death—just as partaking of the belladonna or deadly nightshade plant usually meant death for those foolhardy enough to try it. In small doses, this poisonous herb is used to relieve pain and spasms, dilate the pupil of the eye, and diminish bodily secretions. Its potentially fatal effects, however, led botanists to create the genus Atropa for it and other related poisonous plants. Following their example, pharmacologists named the alkaloid that is extracted from these plants *atropine*.

(clean the) Augean stables: accomplish an extremely formidable task; clear away massive corruption

One of the Labors of the Greek hero Heracles was to clean the stables of King Augeus. It doesn't sound like such a difficult task—until you learn that the king had three thousand oxen and hadn't bothered to clean their stalls for thirty years! It's no wonder the Augean stables have become a metaphor for both a formidable task and great corruption. Likewise, cleaning them out is used as a figure of speech for clearing up a mess or carrying out reforms, especially in government or politics.

How *did* Heracles perform this seemingly impossible task? Operating on the principle that drastic problems require drastic solutions, he temporarily diverted two rivers from their beds, allowing the rushing waters to sweep through the stables and wash away the years of accumulated filth.

See also: Herculean

aurora: dawn; a beginning; an early period

The Greeks personified dawn as the goddess Eos, and the Romans gave her the name Aurora. Homer described her as "rosy-fingered," and she was believed to lie down each night in the bed of her lover, Tithonus. On rising, she would join her brother, the sun, in his chariot, and the two would ride across the sky from east to west, spreading light over the world. Aurora's name has become a synonym both for daybreak—the time when the sun rises in the east—and, in a figurative sense, for the early stages of any period or endeavor.

Tithonus was a Trojan prince on whom Zeus conferred immortality. By him, Aurora gave birth to a son, Memnon, who was killed by Achilles during the Trojan War. The dew that covers the earth each morning was said to be Aurora's tears, shed when she woke up and remembered her dead child.

Aurora's other children were immortal, being born of her union with her husband, the Titan Astraeus. They were the four winds, and the Greeks called them Boreas (north), Notus (south/southwest), Eurus (east), and Zephyrus (west). To the Romans they were, respectively, Aquilo, Auster, Eurus, and Favonius. Boreas's name was combined with that of his mother in the term *aurora borealis,* which describes the electromagnetic phenomenon of "northern lights." In the Southern Hemisphere these fantastic waves of color and light, which spread across the night sky like dawn's rosy fingers, are referred to as the *aurora australis* after the goddess and her southern son, Auster.

See also: zephyr

avatar: the embodiment of a concept or philosophy

There are three gods in the Hindu triad: Brahma, the creator; Vishnu, the preserver; and Shiva, the destroyer. The stories the ancient Hindus told about these gods include many in which Vishnu comes down to earth to fight evil and restore the power of the righteous. To do this, he is incarnated in the form of a human or an animal. The form he assumes is called an *avatar,* from the Sanskrit *ava* (down) and *tarati* (he passes or crosses over). According to Hindu scripture, the avatars of Vishnu on earth included a fish, a tortoise, a boar, a man-lion, a dwarf, and many others. His two most important incarnations, around which substantial cults have grown, were those of Rama and Krishna.

The word *avatar* has been adopted into English to describe someone who embodies an idea or concept, who is its personification. Thus, Hitler has often been referred to as "the avatar of evil," meaning he was evil incarnate. Conversely, Florence Nightingale and Mother Theresa could be said to be avatars of goodness in their acts of compassion toward the sick and dying.

B

bacchanal: a wild party; an orgy

Bacchus was an alternate name for Dionysus, the Greek god of vegetation, fertility, and—especially—wine. While the origin of the name Dionysus is unknown, the name Bacchus is of Thracian origin, and the god was first worshiped under that name in Asia Minor. The cult of Dionysus/Bacchus became widespread in Greece and, later, in the Roman Empire. The Romans adopted the earlier, Thracian form of the god's name when they took him into their pantheon.

The devotees of Bacchus believed they could best commune with the god after having partaken liberally of his favorite beverage. As a result, their "religious" observances were less than decorous, to say the least. Inhibitions were thrown to the wind, and unrestrained revelry prevailed. There is evidence that both in Asia Minor and in Greece the worship of Bacchus included the consumption of the raw flesh of sacrificial victims—both animal and human. While murder does not seem to have been part of the Roman Bacchanalia—the Latin name for the rites of Bacchus—these too were characterized by extreme debauchery and orgiastic activity. At first they were attended only by women, who carried on the tradition of the Asiatic and Greek Bacchantes, or Maenads. Later, however, men joined in the rites and, as might have been expected, the debauchery increased. Evidently the gatherings also became a forum in which all kinds of crimes and political conspiracies were planned.

The Bacchanalia became so notorious that in 186 B.C. the Roman Senate outlawed them. Although violators of the decree were punished severely, clandestine rites of Bacchus continued to be held for several centuries. Nor were the senators able to prevent the followers of the god from leaving their linguistic legacy. The words *bacchanal* and *bacchanalia* are often used today to refer to wild parties where the celebration gets more than a little out of hand. The revelers may be called *bacchanals* or *bacchants*. The name of the god of wine and revelry has been transformed into the adjectives *bacchic, bacchian, bacchanalian,* and several other variations.

See also: Apollonian, Dionysian

banshee: a loud, out-of-control person, especially a female

When someone is out of control, screaming or crying loudly, we say they are "wailing like a banshee," relating their screeches to those of a mythical spirit in which Celtic peoples believed for centuries.

The word *banshee* is from the Old Irish *ben side,* meaning "woman of the fairies." Although usually depicted as beautiful women, banshees were associated with death by the Irish. A banshee stationed herself outside the house of a person who was about to die and let out ear-piercing shrieks to warn the family of their impending loss. It was said that only families of pure Irish descent were thus visited. If death was to come to a very holy or very great person, several banshees might appear at once, keening in chorus beneath his windows.

The Irish practice of keening (*caione*) at a funeral is believed by some to have originated as an imitation of the wails of the banshees.

berserk: frenzied; irrational; reckless

The myths of the Norsemen are full of wild beasts and wild men. In the Norse legends, *berserkrs* were warriors who wore bearskin coats (*bjorn* meant "bear" and *serkr* meant "shirt" in Old Norse). So brave (or mad) were they, and so convinced of their invulnerability, that they refused to put on the traditional coat of mail for protection and went into battle clad only in fur. Believing they were protected by the god Odin, they fought as furiously as wild beasts.

It's easy to see why the word *berserk* has come down to us with the connotation of "recklessly defiant" and "frenzied," and why we say people have "gone berserk" when they have lost their sense of reason and do foolhardy things.

Briarean: complicated; many-faceted

According to Hesiod's *Theogony,* after Gaea (Earth) gave birth to the Titans and the Giants, she and Uranus became the parents of the Hundred-Handed Ones: three huge, powerful sons. They were named Cottus, Briareus, and Gyes. Each had "a hundred intolerably strong arms bursting out of his shoulders, and on the shoulders of each grew fifty heads, above their massive bodies." Hesiod goes on to say that of all of Earth's children they were the most terrible, and that they hated their father, the Sky, from the beginning. Uranus hated them as well, and tried to prevent them from being born. He imprisoned them deep inside Gaea's womb, i.e., inside the earth, where they were unable to see the light of day. There they remained, in great agony, until the war between the Titans and the Olympians. When Zeus rebelled against his father and the other Titans, the Hundred-Handed Ones joined the battle on Zeus's side, and "from their powerful hands they volleyed three hundred boulders one after another, and their missile flights overwhelmed the Titans. . . ."

Hesiod's descriptions and other Greek myths about Briareus and his brothers inspired the creation of the adjective *Briarean.* Some situations are so complicated, and force us to deal with so many issues at once, that we feel completely overwhelmed, like the fired-upon Titans. A Briarean problem winds itself around us, just like the tentacles of an octopus or the arms of a hundred-handed giant.

Brownie: the youngest level of Girl Scouts

Girls between eleven and sixteen years of age can join the green-uniformed Girl Scouts of America or the Girl Guides of

Great Britain. Before that, they are eligible to be Brownies: girls from seven and a half to eleven, who dress in brown and take an oath to help people every day, especially at home. Sir Robert Baden-Powell founded the Boy Scouts in England in 1908 and the Girl Guides in 1910. When he decided to set up troops of younger girls, he borrowed the name *Brownie* from Celtic mythology, and it is a very fitting one.

The people of the British Isles have long believed in the existence of "little people." These supernatural beings come in many forms, one of which is the brownie. A small, brown-cloaked and hooded fairy, the brownie attaches itself to a household and becomes a sort of guardian spirit. Although brownies occasionally play tricks on the families they have adopted, they are generally kind and industrious. Rarely seen, they often can be heard cleaning and performing other domestic chores while the family sleeps.

Taking their Brownie oath, therefore, little British and American girls promise to emulate the helpful household spirits who many believe still people the British Isles.

See also: fairyland, leprechaun, pixie-led

C

Cadmean victory: *See: (to sow) dragon's teeth*

caduceus: a winged staff with serpents entwined around it, symbol of the medical profession

A Greek herald was called a *keryx,* and carried a staff of office called a *kerykeion.* The Romans referred to such a staff as a *caduceum,* and it is from Latin that we got the English word *caduceus.*

The most famous herald of Greek mythology was, of course, the god Hermes. When Zeus selected Hermes to be his messenger, he gave him a special cap to protect him from the elements and a pair of winged sandals to speed him on his way. A wooden kerykeion, from which white ribbons fluttered, served as Hermes' badge of office, and Zeus ordered all gods and men to respect it as the symbol of his emissary. (The inviolability of the white-ribboned herald's staff is very likely behind the tradition of the white flag carried by troops calling for a truce or wanting to surrender.)

There are many conflicting stories about how the caduceus's ribbons became snakes. One version is that Hermes once threw his staff at two snakes that were fighting on the ground. They became entangled in its ribbons and remained there. It has also been suggested that the snakes were added to the Greek and Roman caduceus in imitation of Oriental objects of a similar shape, since magic sticks or staves with serpents entwined around them appear as a motif in Indian and Mesopotamian art. The Mesopotamians evidently believed the serpent-entwined staff to be the symbol of the god who cures all illness.

Because of this, and confusion with a similar staff carried by

Asclepius, the famous healer of Greek mythology, Hermes' *kerykeion* was transformed into the symbol of the medical profession. The Greeks believed snakes to be symbols of healing due to their ability to shed their old skins and replace them with new ones. Asclepius was associated with serpents in several myths, including one in which he was said to have learned how to raise people from the dead, using magical herbs, by seeing one snake revive another in this manner. Thus, Asclepius was often represented in art as a bearded man holding a staff with a serpent coiled around it. Somehow, the staff of Asclepius and the *kerykeion* of Hermes became confused over the centuries, and the medical profession wound up adopting the messenger's staff as its symbol. (The wings on top of the staff were added in later Greek and Roman art.)

See also: Ophiucus (under "Constellations"), magic wand

calliope: *See: muse*

Camelot: a splendid political/social world

The most romantic figure in Celtic mythology is, without doubt, King Arthur. While debate still rages as to whether or not he actually lived and reigned in Britain, he has left a legacy far greater than many of Britain's historical kings.

As early as the tenth century, poems were being written about Arthur's superhuman exploits. In the early Celtic stories, he is surrounded by a large retinue, including some of the old Celtic gods transformed into humans, and a few of the knights of the Round Table. The first complete account of Arthur's life, written by Geoffrey of Monmouth around 1135, says the hero was conceived in Tintagel Castle in Cornwall and crowned at Silchester. Neither Geoffrey nor any of the earlier storytellers mention Camelot by name, however. The fabled town first appears as the site of King Arthur's court in *Lancelot,* a French romance written by Chrétien de Troyes between 1160 and 1180. In Malory's fourteenth-century *Morte d'Artur,* Camelot became the capital of Arthur's realm, where he and his knights sat at the legendary Round Table. Malory and later writers depicted Camelot as the center of courtly love and chivalry, where beautiful, exquisitely dressed women would look on as their favorite knights jousted for them, wearing their colors. The latest trends in fashion, sport, and the arts were set in Camelot by Arthur and his entourage and spread from there throughout the land. It is from these literary portraits that Camelot came to represent a brilliant social/political center, and the twentieth-century news media popularized this image when they applied it to Washington, D.C., during the administration of John Fitzgerald Kennedy.

Going on the assumption that there is some historical basis to the legends of King Arthur, scholars have proposed several sites for Camelot, including Colchester, called Camulodunum by the Romans; the area around the River Camel and Camelford, near Tintagel; Caerleon-upon-Usk in Wales; and the vicinity of Winchester. The place with the strongest claim seems to be Cadbury Castle in Somerset, which is the site of a large, pre-Roman fort and which is near the village of Queen Camel (once called simply Camel). John Leland, writing during the reign of Henry VIII, related that the inhabitants of the area around the fort still referred to it as Camalat and as the home of King Arthur—"the once and future king."

(to) carry water in a sieve: do a futile task, make no progress

In Judeo-Christian hell, the punishment meted out to sinners usually consists of some form of physical torture. The ancient Greeks, evidently, found the prospect of eternal *psychological* torment far more dismaying. Their equivalent of hell—Tartarus—was peopled with numerous penitents who were made to pay for their earthly transgressions by performing tasks of endless frustration. Among these miserable souls were the Danaïds: forty-nine of the fifty daughters of Danaüs.

Danaüs was a mythical king, whose name means "dweller by

the Nile," and who had a twin brother named Aegyptus. Danaüs had fifty daughters and Aegyptus had fifty sons. The brothers quarreled, and although Aegyptus suggested they end their feud by marrying their children to one another, Danaüs remained suspicious. He and his daughters fled from Egypt to Greece, where they found temporary sanctuary. The storytellers are unclear as to how, but eventually Danaüs was forced to give his daughters in marriage to their cousins.

On the wedding day, he put a dagger into each girl's hand and told her she must kill her new husband that night. Forty-nine of the young women obeyed their father's orders, plunging their daggers into the hearts of their sleeping spouses. Only one, Hypermnestra, could not bear to kill the young man who slept so peacefully beside her, and she woke him and helped him flee. When her father found out the next day, she was put into prison for her disobedience. The myths do not tell us how long she was kept there, but even a life sentence would have been preferable to sharing her sisters' fate. Like Sisyphus, who never succeeded in rolling his rock to the top of the hill, their punishment was never ending. They were forced to spend eternity on a riverbank, filling jars with water. The jars, however, were riddled with holes, so that no sooner did the Danaïds fill them than the water ran out and they had to begin their chore over again.

The labors of both Sisyphus and the Danaïds are commonly used by us to symbolize tasks that seem pointless and futile. Thus, to "carry water in a sieve" is to experience the endless frustration of never seeing any results from one's labors, no matter how hard one works.

See also: Sisyphean labor

Cassandra: a person who foretells dire events; a pessimist

Cassandra was a Trojan princess, the daughter of Hecuba and Priam, and her first appearance in Greek mythology is in the *Iliad*. Homer says she is "beautiful as Golden Aphrodite," and later writers relate the way in which this beauty led to her tragic gift. The most common tale is that the god Apollo saw the lovely princess in his temple and was filled with desire for her. He appeared and promised to give her the gift of prescience in return for her love. Cassandra accepted and became a prophetess, but when Apollo tried to consummate their union, she changed her mind and refused him her favors. Unable to take back his gift, the most the furious god could do was insure that no one would ever believe Cassandra's predictions. Thus, when she tried to warn the Trojans that there were armed Greeks inside the Wooden Horse, they ignored her and brought it into their citadel. When Agamemnon brought her home as his concubine, she foresaw both their deaths at the hands of his wife, but there was nothing she could do to avert the tragedy.

A *Cassandra* is, therefore, someone who predicts dire events. In modern usage, the name is given to anyone who is constantly making pessimistic statements about the future, whether or not they are believed.

See also: Trojan horse

catamite: a young boy used in pederasty

The term *catamite* is a direct translation of the Latin name Catamitus. This, in turn, was a translation of the Greek name Ganymedes. Ganymedes, or Ganymede, as he is called in English, was a young Trojan prince; some say he was the most beautiful boy in the world. One day, while he was out watching his father's sheep, Zeus spied him and fell in love instantly. The great god either disguised himself as an eagle or sent one of his sacred eagles down to earth to carry the boy off. In either case, Ganymede was brought up to Olympus, where he became Zeus's lover and cupbearer to the gods.

The myth of Ganymede was extremely popular in Greece and Rome, where it was used to justify the common practice, by adult males, of taking young boys as lovers. During the

Middle Ages, *Ganymede* became a term for a homosexual. A young boy engaged by an older male for the purposes of pederasty is still called a catamite in our language.

(give a sop to) Cerberus: give someone a bribe to get out of a hazardous situation

In Greek mythology, Cerberus was the dog that stood guard at the entrance to the Underworld. He wasn't your run-of-the-mill poodle or schnauzer. The myths don't specify his breed, but they do tell us he had three heads and a dragon's tail. It wasn't easy to get past him, but he did have one weakness: cake. Psyche distracted him with a piece of cake, which kept him happy while she went down into Hades to obtain some of Persephone's beauty. Later on, in the *Aeneid,* the Sibyl who led Aeneas to his father carried some cake for Cerberus so he would permit them to enter unmolested.

The ancient Greeks took the legend of Cerberus and that of the ferryman Charon so seriously that, when a loved one died, they put a cake soaked in honey and poppy juice in his hands and a gold coin in his mouth. The cake was for the dog and the coin for the man, to insure the deceased's safe passage.

The expression "give a sop to Cerberus" came to be used to describe the giving of a bribe to someone to get out of an awkward or dangerous plight.

See also: hell, Stygian

cereal: a grain product, commonly a breakfast food

What do oatmeal, corn flakes, and shredded wheat have in common with a Roman goddess?

The answer is that they are all cereals and, as such, are named after the Roman goddess of grain and agriculture, Ceres. Known to the Greeks as Demeter, Ceres was the great mother goddess who assured fertile crops and a good harvest. One day, while her daughter Proserpine (Kore or Persephone to the Greeks) was on earth picking flowers, Pluto came up from the Underworld and abducted her. When Ceres learned that the god of the dead had taken her child, she refused to return to Olympus and, on earth, forbade the crops to grow and the trees to yield fruit. Seeing that mankind's existence was threatened, Jupiter was forced to intervene, and he convinced Pluto to send the girl back to her mother. Unfortunately, during her stay in the Underworld, Proserpine had eaten a few pomegranate seeds—the food of the dead—and, therefore, could not return to the living. Finally, a compromise was reached, and for each seed Proserpine had eaten she was sentenced to spend one month of the year below ground. (The number of seeds varies from three to seven, depending on which version of the myth you read.) Every autumn since then she has descended to Pluto's dark realm, and Ceres, who goes into mourning each time, allows the earth's vegetation to wither and die until her daughter's reemergence in the spring.

Before Ceres returned to Olympus, she was said to have given mankind corn and other grains, along with instructions on how to cultivate them. The word *cereal* came into English through the Latin *Cerealis* (pertaining to Ceres). Our ancestors used it to refer to the edible grasses and grains they cultivated, which we now process and package in the millions of little boxes that line supermarket shelves all over the world.

See also: Mother Earth

chaos: disorder; confusion

The ancient Greeks developed numerous, conflicting myths about the creation of the universe. In one, Eurynome, the goddess of all things, rose out of Chaos and proceeded to divide the sea from the sky. She then laid the Universal Egg, out of which came the sun, moon, planets, and all living things. Another Greek myth says that Mother Earth emerged from Chaos and bore Uranus (Sky). Her son then impregnated her with rain, and she gave birth to all the world's plants and animals. In a myth borrowed from the Babylonian story of the Creation, it was stated that the god of all things rose from Chaos and separated earth from the heavens, water from earth, etc. This unknown god set the world as we know it into motion and peopled it with all living things.

The one element common to all these stories is the idea of Chaos being the primordial state of the universe. Before anything was created, before there were any divisions made or limits imposed, there was Chaos. It was formless and shapeless and empty. In addition to the above tales, other myths exist in which Chaos was personified as the first god. In an unexplained feat of self-propagation, Chaos was said to have given birth to two children: Nyx (Night) and Erebus (variously translated as Darkness, Death, or the Abyss). Night later laid an egg in Erebus's bosom, out of which came Eros (Love). The appearance of love in the universe was followed by that of Light and of Uranus (Sky) and Gaea (Earth). The offspring of this last couple were the Hundred-Handed Ones, the Giants, and the Titans. After all these came the Olympians and mankind. By this time there was a very definite, recognizable order in the world.

In all these stories, the amorphous state of Chaos is contrasted with the orderly universe. The latter was called the Cosmos by the early Greeks. We have taken these two contrasting concepts from Greek mythology and applied them to the world around us. Today, we use the word *chaos* to describe total confusion and lack of organization. Any situation in which there is no prescribed order is dubbed *chaotic*. The antonym of chaos—*cosmos*—refers to harmony and order, or to any system characterized by these features.

See also: cosmos, erotic

chimera: an illusion or fabrication of the mind; in science, a hybrid

It is hard to imagine a more fantastic creature than the Chimera of Greek mythology. A fire-breathing she-monster with the head of a lion, the body of a goat, and the tail of a serpent, it was one of the offspring of the monstrous giant Typhon and Echidna, who was herself half woman and half serpent. The siblings of the Chimera were Cerberus, the three-headed hound of hell; the nine-headed water serpent called Hydra; and Orthrus, a two-headed dog who was father of the Sphinx and the Nemean lion through an incestuous liaison with Echidna.

Nowadays we call the products of an overactive imagination *chimeras:* flights of fancy or schemes that have no place in reality. The adjective *chimerical* means visionary, fantastic, or wildly improbable. Scientists, mindful of the lion/goat/serpent combination, have adopted the term *chimera* to denote a hybrid plant or animal.

Ironically, it was a mythological "flight of fancy" that put an end to the dreaded Chimera. The hero Bellerophon mounted the winged steed Pegasus and flew over the monster, wounding her with his arrows. When she was too weak to attack, he shoved a lump of lead into her fiery mouth. The molten metal ran down her throat, searing her insides, and the nightmare was over.

Cimmerian darkness: total darkness; gloom

"The fog-bound Cimmerians live in the City of Perpetual Mist. When the bright Sun climbs the sky and puts the stars to flight, no ray from him can penetrate to them, nor can he see them as he drops from heaven and sinks once more to earth. For dreadful Night has spread her mantle over the heads of that unhappy folk."

This is the description Homer gives, in the *Odyssey,* of a people he calls the Cimmerians. According to him, they lived at the edge of the earth, near the great river Ocean that circled the world of Greek mythology. Later writers assumed their county was called Cimmeria, although Homer never actually mentions it by name. The term *Cimmerian darkness* has long been used to describe darkness so complete, so dense, that absolutely no light penetrates it. An atmosphere that is Cimmerian is gray and gloomy, conducive to the same kind of unhappiness Homer attributed to the inhabitants of the City of Perpetual Mist.

The Cimmerians of Greek mythology should not be confused with the historical Cimmerians: a nomadic tribe that was driven from Asia by the Scythians and conquered Armenia and Phrygia around 700 B.C.

Circean/circean: dangerously bewitching

In Book 10 of the *Odyssey,* some of Odysseus's crew are lured into a castle by a beautiful voice they hear singing within. Once inside, they are fed a magic potion and turned into pigs. The woman responsible for their degradation is the enchantress Circe. Although she has the voice of a goddess, she is a cruel creature and herds her prisoners into a pigsty, where they wallow in the mud and root for the acorns and berries she throws to them. Adding to the horror of their plight is the fact that, although the men are trapped in the bodies of swine, their minds are unaffected, and they continually weep for their lost humanity.

Circe is the personification of evil masquerading as earthly delight. A woman who tempts men with her beauty is called a *Circe,* and the name has also given us the adjective *Circean,* to describe temptations that lure us to our downfall. Led on by the glamour of "life in the fast lane"—drinking, gambling, taking drugs—many of our contemporaries find themselves in the same predicament as Odysseus's crew. The latter were luckier than many of their twentieth-century counterparts, however. Aided by the god Hermes, Odysseus came to their rescue and forced Circe to turn them back into humans. Not only that, but the restored men looked younger, taller, and handsomer than before!

See also: Holy moly!

clue: a guide to a solution

In detective stories, the sleuth follows a trail of clues to find the solution to a mystery. The first recorded instance of someone using a clue to come up with the solution to a dilemma came long before Conan Doyle and Christie: it was in the Greek myth of Theseus and the Minotaur.

When Theseus arrived on Crete along with the other Athenian youths who were to be sacrificed to the monstrous Minotaur, his death seemed inevitable. But King Minos's daughter, Ariadne, saw him arrive and instantly fell in love with him. She begged Daedalus, the inventor of the labyrinth in which the monster was kept, to help Theseus escape. Moved by her pleas, Daedalus gave her a ball of yarn and told her that Theseus must tie one end of it to the door as he entered the labyrinth. Then, as he moved through the intricate passageways, he was to unravel the skein behind him, never letting it drop from his hands. Theseus followed Daedalus's instructions, slew the Minotaur, and made his escape by following the yarn back to the door of the labyrinth.

The Middle English word for a ball of yarn or thread was *clewe,* and, originally, it had only a literal meaning. When Chaucer and others popularized the story of Theseus and the Minotaur, Englishmen began using the word *clewe* in a figurative sense as well. In its new meaning—a hint or guide in solving a problem—it came to be spelled *clue* and is now essential to the vocabulary of both real-life and fictional detectives.

See also: Daedalian, labyrinth

CONSTELLATIONS

Many of the gods and heroes of ancient Greece come to life again each night, when the sun sets and the stars shine overhead. By international agreement, astronomers the world over currently recognize the existence of eighty-eight constellations; of these, forty-eight commemorate characters and events in Greek mythology.

The Greeks did not invent astronomy. As far back as 2000 B.C. the Sumerians had a system of constellations. The Egyptians seem to have gotten their knowledge of the stars from the Sumerians, and they passed it on to the Greeks, who superimposed their own myths and nomenclature onto the Sumerian system. The first real evidence we have for a Greek constellation system comes from the fourth century B.C., when first Eudoxus and later Aratus listed the names of, and told the stories behind, forty-seven star groups. In A.D. 150 Ptolemy listed forty-eight constellations in his Almagest. *With a few slight changes in the way they are grouped, and a couple of modern additions, we refer to these constellations by the same names today.*

In his excellent and comprehensive book Star Tales, *Ian Ridpath tells the full stories behind all eighty-eight constellations, as well as another two dozen or so that are now obsolete. For those who would like to delve deeper into this fascinating subject, I highly recommend Mr. Ridpath's work. With regard to the "mythological" constellations, here is how they got their names:*

Andromeda, Cassiopeia, Cepheus, Cetus, Pegasus, Perseus

These six proximate constellations were named for the principal characters in the well-known myth of Perseus and Andromeda. Andromeda was the beautiful daughter of Cepheus and Cassiopeia, king and queen of Ethiopia. A foolish and egotistical woman, Queen Cassiopeia boasted that she was more beautiful than the Nereids. To punish her, Poseidon sent a sea monster (Cetus) to ravage the coast of Ethiopia. Desperate to put an end to the monster's destruction, King Cepheus consulted an oracle. He was told that the only way to appease the creature was to sacrifice his daughter to it. Chained to a rock on the coast, Andromeda surely would have perished if the great hero Perseus had not flown overhead at that very moment. He had just slain the Gorgon Medusa and was mounted, some say, on Pegasus, the winged steed that had emerged from Medusa's dead body. Perseus slew the monster and returned the princess to her parents, who gave her to him in marriage.

It was said that the goddess Athena placed Andromeda in

the sky between Perseus and Cassiopeia. The latter, as punishment for her pride, was seated in Cassiopeia's Chair, which at certain times of the year appears to be upside-down. This undignified position, it was hoped, would serve as a reminder that the gods have their ways of getting even with mortals who dare to challenge their superiority.

Carina, Puppis, Vela

These three star groups have existed as independent constellations only since 1763. In that year, French astronomer Nicolas Louis de Lacaille published a catalog of the southern stars in which he broke the ancient constellation Argo Navis (the Ship *Argo*) into its component parts. He identified these as Carina (the Keel), Puppis (the Stern), and Vela (the Sails).

The original Argo Navis represented the ship in which Jason and his comrades sailed in quest of the Golden Fleece. Aratus explained the fact that not all of the *Argo* is visible in the sky by suggesting that its prow has passed into a fogbank. Other astronomers said the constellation represented the *Argo* as it was passing between the Clashing Rocks. Another explanation was that in his old age Jason was sitting beneath the *Argo,* which over the years had become a rotting hulk. When the prow fell off and killed him, Poseidon raised the rest of the ship up into the sky. Hyginus, however, says that Athena was the one who placed the *Argo* among the stars.

Aquarius

The constellation Aquarius represents a young man pouring water from a jar. It is possible that the Water Carrier originally represented the Egyptian god of the Nile, but the Greeks gave him another identity. To them he was Ganymede, cupbearer of the gods. When Zeus became infatuated with the handsome young Ganymede, he transformed himself into an eagle, swooped down, and carried the boy to Olympus to become his lover and cupbearer.

Other mythological figures with whom Aquarius has been identified are Deucalion (the only man to escape the Great

Flood) and Cecrops (a king who ruled Athens before man learned how to make wine and was, therefore, depicted making sacrifices to the gods with water).

Aquila

The Greeks had several explanations for the placement of the Eagle in the sky. One was that the constellation represented the eagle that carried Ganymede to Olympus. (Aquarius, generally supposed to represent Ganymede, is a neighboring constellation of Aquila.) Some believed, however, that the Eagle and the Swan (another proximate constellation) were placed in the sky simultaneously by Zeus. The god had fallen in love with Nemesis, who resisted his amorous advances. Enlisting the aid of the goddess of love, Zeus turned himself into a swan and had Aphrodite pursue him in the form of an eagle. Taking pity on the beleaguered swan, Nemesis took it in—and found herself face to face with Zeus. To celebrate his conquest and his cleverness, Zeus placed the images of Aquila and Cygnus in the sky.

Ara

Zeus and his fellow Olympian gods were not the first rulers of the world, according to Greek mythology. At one time the Titans, led by Cronus, were supreme over all. In an effort to thwart a prophecy that said he would be overthrown by one of his children, Cronus swallowed all of them, except Zeus, as soon as they were born. When Zeus reached manhood he forced Cronus to vomit up the other children, and all of them took an oath to overthrow their father.

After their victory, Zeus supposedly placed the altar on which the oath was taken in the sky, where it has since been known as Ara.

Aries

Only a very special ram could have earned a place in the heavens, and Aries was certainly very special. He was believed to be the ram of the Golden Fleece and is the subject of several myths. In the best known of these, he was sent by Zeus to save Phrixus, a young boy whose father had been tricked into sacrificing him. In gratitude for having been brought to safety by the ram, Phrixus sacrificed it to Zeus and gave its Golden Fleece to the king of Colchis. The fleece was later stolen by Jason and the Argonauts. On his return to Greece, Jason hung his prize in Zeus's temple. The Ram, however, lives on in the sky as the constellation Aries.

Auriga

The Charioteer has been identified with several different mythological characters. He may be Erichthonius, son of Hephaestus and king of Athens, whom the goddess Athena raised and taught to tame horses. Erichthonius supposedly earned his place among the stars by harnessing four horses to a chariot, a feat that until then had been accomplished only by the god of the sun.

Auriga might also be Myrtilus, the charioteer of King Oenomaus. When the king's daughter, Hippodamia, begged him to betray her father and help her lover win her hand, Myrtilus agreed, for he loved Hippodamia himself and could not refuse her anything she asked. Her lover, Pelops, rewarded Myrtilus by throwing him into the sea. Myrtilus's grieving father, the god Hermes, then placed his son's image in the sky as Auriga.

Another mythological character who was identified as the Charioteer was Hippolytus, whose stepmother, Phaedra, fell in love with him. She accused him of attempting to rape her, and her husband, Theseus, believed her. As a result, Theseus banished his son and called on the gods to destroy him. As Hippolytus drove away in his chariot, Poseidon caused it to crash; the innocent young man was killed, but he lives on in the stars.

Boötes

The constellation Boötes is directly behind Ursa Major in the heavens. In antiquity the latter was sometimes visualized as a cart being pulled by oxen, and Boötes was supposed to be the cart's driver. Because of its proximity to the Great Bear, Boötes was also called Arctophylax (the Bear Watcher or Bear Keeper) by the Greeks. The are many conflicting stories about the Herdsman or Bear Keeper. According to Eratosthenes, he represents Arcas, the son of Zeus and Callisto. For some reason, Arcas's father-in-law, Lycaon, cut the young man up in pieces and served him to Zeus. The angry god in turn killed Lycaon's sons, turned him into a wolf, and made Arcas whole again. He then placed him in the sky under the protection of Maia, one of the Pleiades.

Another version, which also identifies Boötes with Arcas, says that Zeus had turned Callisto into a bear to hide her from the jealous Hera. When Arcas encountered the animal in the woods, he gave chase, intending to hunt the bear down. Callisto took sanctuary in Zeus's temple, and the god turned her and Arcas into constellations in order to prevent the boy from committing matricide.

Another myth, related by Hyginus, identified Boötes as Icarius, the first man Dionysus taught to make wine. Icarius's fellow shepherds sampled his brew and, believing he was trying to poison them, killed him. His daughter, Erigone, hanged herself, and his dog, Maera, died of sorrow. Zeus reunited them all in the sky as Boötes, Virgo, and Canis Minor.

Cancer

The mythological figure of Cancer, the Crab, appears in one of Heracles' Labors. While fighting the many-headed Hydra in the swamp of Lerna, Heracles was bitten in the foot by a crab. Furious, the hero crushed it. The creature's attack was rewarded by Heracles' archenemy, Hera, who gave the crab immortality by placing it among the stars.

Canis Major

Canis Major is best known as Orion's guard dog, following behind him in the sky and holding the star Sirius in his jaws. Sirius is the most brilliant star in the heavens and is also known, aptly, as the Dog Star. Another, less well-known legend says that Canis Major is meant to represent Laelaps, the swiftest dog on earth, who was put in the heavens by Zeus to end his relentless, futile pursuit of an equally swift fox.

Canis Minor

At one time Canis Minor consisted of only one star, Procyon, whose name means "before the dog." It was given this name because it rose earlier than Canis Major. Both celestial canines were most often said to belong to the great hunter Orion. There is one later legend, however, that says the Little Dog was owned by Icarius (Boötes), and, when he died, the animal pined away. Zeus placed the Little Dog next to its master in the sky.

Capricornus

The Sumerians called this constellation "the goat-fish," and on many ancient star maps it is depicted as a creature with the horns and forelegs of a goat and the tail of a fish. Among the Greeks it was known as Aegoceros (the goat-horned) and said to be a heavenly portrait of the god Pan, but they really had to stretch their imaginations to account for his piscine attributes. They did so by inventing stories to connect Pan with the sea. One related that during the battle with the Titans he blew a conch shell or hurled shellfish at the enemy. Another said that he warned the gods of an attack by the monster Typhon and saved himself by leaping into the water and turning his lower body into that of a fish. In either case, Zeus was so grateful for Pan's help that he turned him into Capricornus.

Centaurus

This star figure is said to represent Chiron, the good Centaur. Like the others of his race, he was half man and half horse, but he was not wild and uncivilized the way they were. He was a skilled hunter, musician, and physician, who served as tutor to Asclepius, Jason, Achilles, and Heracles. When Heracles fought the other Centaurs, Chiron was accidentally hit by a poisoned arrow from his bow. Such a wound could not be healed, and rather than face an eternity of pain, Chiron asked Zeus to take away his immortality and allow him to die. Zeus did so, and placed him in the heavens. On star maps he is pictured preparing to sacrifice an animal (Lupus) on the altar of the gods (Ara).

Corona Australis

The Greeks thought of the Southern Crown as a wreath and did not count it as a separate constellation. They considered it a part of Sagittarius, the Archer. There were no specific legends associated with it, although Ian Ridpath believes that one of the myths about the Corona Borealis—that it represented the crown of myrtle leaves left behind by Dionysus after he brought his mother back from the Underworld—may originally have been associated with this group of stars.

Corona Borealis

The Corona Borealis is a semicircle of stars purported to be the crown of Ariadne—daughter of the legendary Cretan king, Minos. After she betrayed her father by helping Theseus to slay the Minotaur, she fled with the Athenian hero to the island of Naxos, where he promptly abandoned her. Looking down on the grief-stricken girl, the god Dionysus instantly fell in love with her. She consented to marry him, wearing the crown that had been crafted by Hephaestus and given to her by Aphrodite. (According to a variant myth, the crown was originally given to Theseus by Thetis, and the light from its dazzling jewels helped him to find his way through the labyrinth.) Whatever the crown's origin, after the ceremony the joyful bridegroom tossed it into the sky, where its jewels became the stars of the Northern Crown.

Corvus

Corvus (the Crow) and Crater (the Cup) were two related constellations, according to Greek astronomers. In Eratosthenes' account, Apollo was preparing to make a sacrifice to

Zeus and sent the crow to get some water for his purification rites. The bird was supposed to fill Apollo's cup at a nearby spring but got sidetracked when he saw a fig tree full of almost-ripe fruit. He waited several days for the figs to ripen, then gorged himself before returning with the water. To add insult to injury, he then tried to trick Apollo by claiming he hadn't been able to reach the spring right away because the water serpent (Hydra) had been blocking it. The angry god punished the crow by placing him in the sky, with the water serpent between him and the cup. There he remains, his thirst forever unquenched. Crater is now considered part of Corvus, rather than a separate constellation.

Cygnus

The Swan that is seen in the night sky was usually said to be the god Zeus on his way to his tryst with Leda. She was the wife of King Tyndareus of Sparta, and the god took the form of a swan to seduce her. The result of this unusual coupling was the egg out of which Helen and her brother, Polydeuces, were hatched. Leda slept with Tyndareus the same night and produced a second egg, which contained Castor and Clytemnestra. The Trojan War was fought for Helen; Clytemnestra married—and murdered—Agamemnon; Castor and Polydeuces (Pollux) became the well-known constellation Gemini.

Delphinus

Two different stories were told to explain the presence of the Dolphin in the sky. One version, told by Eratosthenes, is that he symbolizes the messenger of Poseidon, sent by the god to win Amphitrite over to his cause. The gentle dolphin convinced the Nereid to accept Poseidon's proposal and was given a place in the heavens as his reward.

Another myth revolves around a dolphin that was believed to have saved the musician Arion in the seventh century B.C. During a sea voyage, a group of sailors were about to rob and kill Arion, when he pleaded to be allowed to sing one last song. His beautiful music attracted a school of dolphins, and, as they passed alongside the ship, he jumped overboard onto the back of one of them. The dolphin carried him to safety, and Apollo, the god of music, put it in the sky with Arion's lyre (Lyra) to commemorate the rescue.

Draco

According to Greek legend, Draco represents the dragon that guarded the Golden Apples of the Hesperides. His name was Ladon, and he was generally said to be the offspring of two monsters, Typhon and Echidna. Heracles shot him with poisoned arrows, the Hesperides mourned him, and Hera placed him in the sky. Although some myths say Ladon had one hundred heads, on ancient sky maps he is depicted with only one, on which the hero (and neighboring constellation) Heracles is standing.

Equuleus

The Little Horse was first mentioned in Ptolemy's list of constellations, which dates from the second century A.D. Early mythologists do not mention it at all, and it seems to have been unknown even to Aratus, who lived some four hundred years before Ptolemy. Ian Ridpath suggests that Ptolemy himself may have invented this constellation. The story he gave for it was sometimes told in relation to Pegasus, but Mr. Ridpath believes it is more appropriate for Equuleus. Hippe, the daughter of Chiron, was seduced by Aeolus and became pregnant. Fearing her father's wrath, she hid in the mountains. When he came looking for her, she begged the gods to save her, and they did. They changed her into a mare, which Artemis placed among the stars. Equuleus still hides from her father, Centaurus, and only the head of the Little Horse is visible to him or to us.

Eridanus

The constellation Eridanus represents a river. Early mythologers told of a river of that name, which flowed into the great Ocean that encircled the world. In the myth of Phaëthon, the child of the sun god begged to be allowed to drive his father's chariot across the sky, but he lost control of the vehicle and plunged to his death in the Eridanus. The Argonauts were said to have found his body, still smoldering, when they journeyed up the river on their way to find the Golden Fleece. However, Eratosthenes and Hyginus believed the Eridanus was, in fact, the Nile. Later writers equated it with the river Po.

Gemini

The famous "twins" of Greek mythology were not really twins at all: according to most mythologers, they were only half-brothers. Castor and Polydeuces (Pollux in Latin) were both sons of Leda, but they had different fathers. Zeus sired Polydeuces and his sister, Helen, making both children immortal. Castor and his sister Clytemnestra, on the other hand, were the mortal offspring of Leda and her husband, King Tyndareus of Sparta. The two boys were inseparable, however, and could not have been closer even if they had been identical twins. They shared many adventures, including the quest for the Golden Fleece. Although accounts of Castor's death vary, all agree that Polydeuces was heartbroken at the loss of his brother. He could not bear to continue living without him, so he begged his father Zeus to allow him to share his immortality with Castor. Zeus agreed, and while one myth has the two spending alternate days in Hades and on Olympus, others say they were placed in the sky as Gemini, a celestial memorial to their brotherly devotion.

It seems that at one time this constellation represented not Castor and Polydeuces, but Apollo and Heracles. Ptolemy called the stars we know as Castor and Pollux "the star of Apollo" and "the star of Heracles," respectively. In keeping with this tradition, some makers of star maps placed a lyre in the hand we identify as Castor's and a club in that of Polydeuces.

See also: (by) Jiminy!

Hercules

Hercules is Latin for Heracles, the greatest of the Greek heroes and the one who appears in more myths than any other. For centuries we have regarded this constellation as the image of Heracles on his knees, his club raised as if to strike one of his foes. Perhaps, as Eratosthenes suggested, he is about to slay Draco, the dragon of the Hesperides. Or, as Aeschylus believed, the son of Zeus may be kneeling, tired and wounded, during his battle with the Ligurians. Given the number and fame of Heracles' exploits, the possibilities are endless.

Oddly enough, the early Greeks did not identify this constellation with Heracles at all. It was known to them simply as "the kneeling one." Aratus, writing in the third century B.C., said of this imaginary figure: "No one knows his name, nor what he labours at."

Hydra

Hydra is the largest of today's constellations, "snaking" one quarter of the way around the sky. It represents the Water Snake or Serpent killed by Heracles. Like Draco, the Hydra was one of the offspring of Typhon and Echidna. Although on star maps the Hydra is shown with only one head, ancient storytellers claimed it had nine. The creature's center head was the seat of its mortality, but the other heads could not be destroyed; each time one was cut off, two more grew back in its place. Heracles enlisted the aid of his charioteer, who, as the hero severed each head, seared the flesh at its base so it could not regenerate. Heracles then lopped off the center head, putting an end to the hideous creature, who now lives only in the sky.

In a less well-known legend, the Hydra was said to be a water snake put in the sky by Apollo to prevent the crow (Corvus) from drinking out of the celestial cup (Crater).

See also: hydra (under "Animals"), hydra-headed

Leo

Leo, the king of the beasts that now stalks the night sky, is the Nemean Lion that once terrorized the region around Corinth, in Greece. Because its pelt was impervious to all weapons, no man could kill this creature, and it destroyed all who tried. Only Heracles, the son of Zeus, was able to put an end to its reign of terror. Realizing that his arrows could not pierce the lion's hide, Heracles trapped the beast in its own lair and, barehanded, choked it to death. He skinned it with its own claws and, from that day on, wore its pelt as a trophy. Like that of Draco and Hydra, its presence in the sky is a lasting memorial to the strength and ingenuity of the great Greek hero.

Lepus

Eratosthenes says that Hermes placed Lepus, the Hare, in the sky in tribute to its swiftness. It is also associated with Orion and his dogs, who, according to Aratus, are in hot pursuit of the animal. Another myth, told by Hyginus, takes place on the island of Leros. At one time there were no hares at all on Leros. Then one man brought a pregnant female onto the island. In no time at all, the place was overrun by the creatures, and they had to be driven out. The inhabitants, Hyginus says, then placed the image of the hare in the sky to remind themselves that too much of anything is not a good thing.

Libra

The Greeks called this constellation Chelae (Claws) and visualized it as the claws of nearby Scorpius (the Scorpion). The Romans, however, were calling it Libra (the Balance) in the first century A.D., if not earlier. It is now known that the Sumerians referred to this area of the sky as "the balance of heaven" as early as 2000 B.C.—so the Romans seem to have preferred the earlier Babylonian interpretation to that of the Greeks.

Once the Balance was disassociated from the Scorpion, it was tied into the figure of Virgo: She was sometimes said to represent Dike or Astraeia—the goddess of justice—and Libra to be the scales of justice that she held aloft.

Lupus

Lupus, or the Wolf, was once known to the Greeks as Therium and to the Romans as Bestia and seems to have represented a wild animal of unknown species. The Babylonians knew it as a wild dog, UR-IDIM. The Greeks depicted it impaled on a long stick that was held by the neighboring Centaur and said it was an animal he was sacrificing on the altar of the gods (Ara). Otherwise, there are no myths relating to it, which is probably due to the fact that it was an "imported" constellation. It was not associated with a wolf until the Renaissance.

Lyra

This first lyre was invented by Hermes from a tortoise's shell, according to Greek myth. Its strings were made of cow gut, and it was played with a plectrum, also invented by the god. When Hermes angered Apollo by stealing some of his cattle, he placated the god by presenting him with the musical instrument. Eratosthenes says that Apollo later gave the lyre to Orpheus, whose playing became so skillful that it moved Hades himself to tears, and as a result the god of the Underworld consented to allow Orpheus's wife to leave his realm. Unfortunately, Orpheus turned back to look at her while they were still underground, and she was lost to him forever. After his death the Muses, one of whom was his mother, asked Zeus for permission to put Lyra into the sky in Orpheus's memory.

Star maps often represent the Lyre with an eagle behind it. The Arabs visualized the constellation as a bird of prey, and the name of its brightest star, Vega, comes from the Arabic *al-nasr al-waqi,* which means "the swooping eagle" or "the vulture."

Monoceros

Monoceros is one of two constellations that represent mythical creatures of non-Greek origin. Its name is Greek for "one horn," and many peoples have believed in the existence of one-horned animals that possessed magical powers. Monoceros was first delineated in 1613, on a globe crafted by Dutch theologian and cartographer Petrus Plancius.

See also: unicorn

Ophiucus

The Serpent Holder is a man with a snake (the constellation Serpus) coiled around him. He is holding the creature's head and tail in his hands. To the Greeks, the man was the great physician Asclepius, and the snake was the symbol of healing. (The caduceus, symbol of the medical profession, consists of a staff with two serpents entwined around it.)

Asclepius was the son of Apollo and was raised by Chiron, the good Centaur. Chiron taught him the art of healing, and he soon became so adept at it that he was raising people from the dead. Hades, god of the Underworld, was furious and demanded that Zeus put a stop to Asclepius's activities. Zeus struck the physician down with his thunderbolt but, to placate the angry Apollo, gave Asclepius immortality among the stars.

See also: Caduceus

Orion

This is one of the oldest constellations, called URU AN-NA (Light of Heaven) by the Babylonians. They thought its stars depicted their hero Gilgamesh fighting the neighboring constellation of GUD AN-NA (the Bull of Heaven). The Greeks called it Orion, the Hunter. None of the known Greek myths about Orion involve the constellation Taurus (GUD AN-NA). Instead, the Hunter is said to be pursuing the Hare (Lepus), accompanied by his dogs (Canis Major and Canis Minor).

Homer says Orion was a giant, and other myths make Poseidon his father. The Greeks told many stories about him. According to one, Orion's relentless pursuit of the Pleiades—daughters of Atlas represented by a cluster of stars within Taurus—caused Zeus to place them in the sky, where they would be safe from his amorous advances. In another, Orion boasted that no creature on earth could outfight him, and Earth punished him by sending a scorpion (Scorpius) to kill him. A third tale says that Artemis loved Orion, but Apollo tricked her into killing him, so she placed him among the stars where he would always be visible to her.

Because Orion is the most brilliant constellation, and the Hunter is often depicted with a club and a lion's pelt, Ian Ridpath speculates that at one time this constellation may have represented Heracles, the greatest Greek hero, whose attributes included these two objects. Strength is added to his case by the fact that the constellation we call Hercules was known to the early Greeks only as "the kneeling one," and it wasn't until quite late that it was associated with Heracles.

Phoenix

The Egyptians believed in the existence of a bird called the Bennu. Only one of this mythical creature lived at a time, and when it died it was buried in the temple of the sun. Herodotus brought tales of the Bennu back to Greece, translating its name as "Phoenix." Later Greek writers maintained that the Phoenix was not buried after its death but was ignited by the sun's rays which burned it to ashes. From these ashes arose the new Phoenix which carried its parent's remains to the temple of the sun. The constellation Phoenix was invented at the end of the sixteenth century by Dutch navigators Pieter Dirkszoon Keyser and Frederick de Hontman.

See also: (rise from the ashes like a) phoenix

Pisces

The events that led to the placing of the Fish in the sky are said to have occurred near the Euphrates River, which indicates that the Greeks were relating a Babylonian myth when they explained the origins of this constellation. After the Olympians defeated the Titans and imprisoned the Giants, their mother, Earth, sent another of her children, the monster Typhon, to avenge them. Pan saw him coming and, with his famous panic-inspiring cry, had time to warn the other gods before jumping into the river, where he turned himself into the goat-fish Capricornus. Aphrodite and her son, Eros, were saved when the river nymphs sent two fish to carry them to safety (or when they themselves were changed into fish). These are generally believed to be the two fish represented by Pisces.

Hyginus, however, identifies Pisces with the fish that assisted at Aphrodite's birth. An egg fell into the river and was rolled to shore by two fish. Doves sat on the egg until it hatched, and out came Aphrodite. In gratitude, she placed the fish in the sky as the constellation Pisces.

Piscis Austrinus

Eratosthenes called this constellation "the Great Fish," parent of the two smaller ones in Pisces. Its story is also Babylonian in origin. The Syrian fertility goddess Atargatis (called Derceto by the Greeks) fell into a lake near the Euphrates River. She was saved from drowning by a large fish, which is why, according to Hyginus, Syrians do not eat fish, but worship them as gods.

Sagitta

The Greeks and Romans told at least three stories about the placement of the Arrow in the sky. Eratosthenes said it was the weapon with which Apollo killed the Cyclopes after Zeus used a thunderbolt, forged by them, to strike down Apollo's son, Asclepius. Hyginus claimed it was one of the arrows Heracles used to kill the vulture that gnawed on Prometheus's liver. Germanicus Caesar identified Sagitta with the arrow of Eros, which the god of love fired at Zeus in order to make him fall in love with Ganymede (Aquarius). The lust-inspiring arrow is now guarded by Zeus's eagle (Aquila), which is next to it in the sky.

Sagittarius

From his place in the sky, the heavenly Archer is often said to be firing his arrows at the scorpion responsible for Orion's death. He is generally depicted as a Centaur, but he is not Chiron, the good Centaur, who is represented by Centaurus. Ian Ridpath says that the Greeks adopted Sagittarius from the Sumerians, and that is why there are so many conflicting stories about his identity. Eratosthenes did not believe the figure was that of a Centaur, but described it as a two-footed creature with the tail of a satyr, whom he said was Crotus, son of the Muses' nursemaid, Eupheme. Hyginus says Crotus's father was Pan, which accounts for the goatlike characteristics attributed to him. Crotus was raised with the Muses on Mount Helicon, and they loved to entertain him with their singing and dancing. He invented archery, and the Muses asked Zeus to place him in the sky, where he demonstrates his skill to all below.

Scorpius

The ancient Greek constellation of Scorpius was much larger than the one delineated by modern astronomers, and included the stars now designated as Libra. It was supposed to represent the scorpion that stung Orion to death. There were two popular versions of Orion's encounter with the creature. According to the first, Orion tried to rape the goddess Artemis, and she sent the scorpion to sting him. An alternate myth blames Orion for boasting that no creature could get the better of him; Mother Earth punished him by sending the scorpion to prove him wrong. Scorpius did not originate with the Greeks; the Sumerians had christened it GIR-TAB (the Scorpion) centuries earlier.

Serpens

Serpens is the large snake held in the hands of Ophiucus, the Serpent Holder. It is divided by astronomers into Serpens Caput (the head) and Serpens Cauda (the tail). The Serpent Holder is Asclepius, the famed physician of Greek mythology. The snake was a symbol of healing and rebirth to the Greeks, because each year it shed its old skin and replaced it with a new one. Asclepius saw one snake bring another back to life by placing a particular herb on its body. He began using the herb to restore dead people to life, with great success, until the angry

Hades convinced Zeus to halt his activities by hurling a thunderbolt at him.

Taurus

Taurus was known to the Sumerians as the Bull of Heaven, which was fought by the hero Gilgamesh. Greek astronomers alternated between two identities for the Bull: Zeus in disguise on his way to carry off Europa; or Io, the maiden Zeus loved and turned into a heifer. In the sky, only the front half of the bull is shown. Its face is made up of the Hyades, a V-shaped group of stars that is sometimes referred to, informally, as a constellation. Ovid says their name is related to the Greek word for rain, and that they were so called because they appeared during the rainy season. In mythology the Hyades were daughters of Atlas and Aethra and, thus, half-sisters of the Pleiades. When their brother, Hyas, was killed by a lioness, they wept unconsolably and were placed in the sky. Another story about them says that when his son Dionysus was born, Zeus gave the child to the Hyades to care for and rewarded the sisters by placing them among the stars.

The other famous group of stars in Taurus is the Pleiades, or Seven Sisters. The Greeks considered them a separate constellation that represented the seven daughters of Atlas and Pleione. The maidens were pursued by the hunter Orion, until Zeus arranged their escape from Orion's lustful advances by setting them among the stars. Since only six stars are visible and there were seven Pleiades, two different stories were told to explain the absence of the seventh sister. The first says that the missing Pleiad is Electra, whose son Dardanus founded Troy. Unable to bear looking down on the destruction of her son's home, she fled from the heavens as the Greeks set fire to Troy. The other tale is that the missing sister is Merope, who fell in love with Sisyphus and gave up her immortality to rule with him over Corinth.

Ursa Major

We see in this constellation several shapes, including the Great Bear, the Plough, and the Big Dipper. The Greeks most often visualized it as a bear, which they identified with two separate characters from mythology. The first was Callisto, one of Zeus's lovers and the mother, by him, of Arcas. The best-known story about her, known to us through Ovid, is that Zeus turned her into a bear to protect her from Hera's rage. Henceforth she roamed the woods, fleeing from huntsmen. One of these was her son; as he prepared to kill the bear before the temple of Zeus, the god spirited Callisto and Arcas up to heaven, where he set them among the stars. Eratosthenes, however, says that Callisto was turned into a bear by Artemis, because she broke her vow of chastity when she lay with Zeus. Another version says Callisto was killed when Hera urged Artemis to shoot the bear, and the grieving Zeus placed her in the sky.

There were also Greek legends that related the Great Bear to Adrasteia, one of the nymphs who cared for the infant Zeus. When the god grew up, he rewarded Adrasteia and Ida, his other nursemaid, by turning them into the constellations Ursa Major and Ursa Minor, respectively.

Ursa Minor

The Little Bear was given its name, according to Greek sources, by Thales of Miletus, an astronomer who lived from 625 to 545 B.C. Homer, who lived two centuries before Thales, mentioned only the Great Bear in his works. Thales was supposedly of Phoenician origin, so he may have introduced the constellation from that country's astronomy. According to Aratus, who called the constellation Cynosura (dog's tail), it represents one of the nymphs to whom Zeus's mother entrusted him at his birth. (Ursa Minor is usually identified with the nymph Ida, while Ursa Major is supposed to be Adastreia.) We also refer to the Little Bear as the Little Dipper.

Virgo

The Greeks called this constellation Parthenos and said it immortalized Dike (Astraeia), the goddess of justice. She was the daughter of Zeus and Themis, or of Astraeus and Eos. She is depicted with wings, holding an ear of wheat and a palm frond or, on some maps, the scales of justice (Libra). The best-known myth about Dike relates how, when the Golden Age ended and men became evil and immoral, Dike could not bear to live with them anymore, so she flew up to heaven, where she judges their deeds.

Some traditions held that Virgo was really Demeter, the goddess of agriculture whose daughter was abducted by Hades, and Eratosthenes suggests that she might represent Atargatis, the Syrian goddess of fertility. Hyginus said she was Erigone, daughter of Icarius (Boötes), who hanged herself after her father's murder and was placed in the heavens with him and his dog (Canis Minor).

cornucopia (horn of plenty): a symbol of nature's bounty; abundance

This popular symbol of bountifulness, which we tend to associate with Thanksgiving, originated long before the Pilgrims—in Greek mythology. The story was told that the great god Zeus was nursed in infancy by a goat named Amalthea, or a goat belonging to a nymph named Amalthea. In gratitude, he broke off one of the goat's horns and gave it to his surrogate mother. From that time on, the horn was constantly full of whatever food or drink its owner wished for.

Although the symbol originated with the Greeks, the English word *cornucopia* came from the Latin *cornu copiae*. The Romans associated their "horn of plenty" with another Greek myth, that of Heracles (whom they called Hercules) and Achelous. After the completion of his Labors, the great hero Hercules understandably longed to settle down and take it easy. He had fallen in love with a princess named Deianira, but the river god Achelous also loved her. Hercules was determined to fight the god for her and goaded him into combat. Achelous took the form of a bull, attacking Hercules head on. Hercules bested him, broke off one of his horns, and won the hand of the princess. Magically, the broken horn was always full of fruits and flowers; it became the symbol of nature's bounty to the Romans and, from them, to us.

cosmetic: *See cosmos*

cosmos: the orderly universe; harmony and order

The Greeks believed that the world started out in a state of Chaos. Little by little, order was imposed upon the universe: Uranus (Sky) and Gaea (Earth) were formed; the sun, moon, and planets were put into the sky; the earth was populated with plants, animals, and men. The orderly universe—the Cosmos—took the place of Chaos and was ruled over by the gods.

We still call our known universe the *cosmos,* and anything that affects a large part of it, that has far-reaching consequences, is dubbed *cosmic.* The prefix *cosmo-* refers to the entire world: a *cosmopolitan* person is one who is not limited by artificial boundaries, but who is at home anywhere in the world; many idealists have dreamed of *cosmocracy,* a system of worldwide government.

The Greeks equated order with beauty, and the Greek word *kosmetikos* meant skilled in decorating or making beautiful. When a woman applies *cosmetics* to her face or a person has cosmetic surgery, the result is a more pleasing, harmonious appearance. Chaos is replaced by Cosmos—and the results are readily seen in the mirror.

See also: chaos

(struck by) Cupid's arrow: lovestruck; impassioned

The Greek goddess of love, Aphrodite, was worshiped by the Romans as Venus; her son, Eros, was called Cupid by them. Cupid was most often represented as a baby or small boy with wings, who amused himself by flying through the sky shooting arrows into the hearts of gods and men for sport. He was sometimes portrayed as blind, or blindfolded, to stress the unpredictable nature of love, which can strike anyone, anytime, anywhere. Today, when a person falls madly, passionately in love, we still use this metaphor, saying he or she has been "struck by Cupid's arrow."

The characteristic shape of Cupid's bow, with its double curves (⌒‿⌒), has given us the expression "a Cupid's-bow mouth" for curved, sensuous lips on a man or woman.

The bow-and-arrow-armed cherubs that are often drawn on Valentine's Day cards are the modern representation of this mythological figure, as are the Kewpie dolls seen in amusement parks and arcades. The latter are fashioned after the Rose O'Neill drawing of a fat, winged baby with a topknot of hair, which she modeled on the Cupid of Roman mythology.

Finally, in a strange twist of language, the name of the Roman god of love is also the root of a very unlovely word: *cupidity.* The Romans called the intense passion and desire provoked by Cupid *cupiditas.* Over time, this word for sexual longing came to be applied to other intense desires, such as the yearning for material goods, as well. In modern usage, cupidity most often means avarice or greed—a perverse form of love, in which the object of one's desire is a thing rather than a person.

See also: erotic, Venus

Cyclopean/cyclopean: huge, massive; a type of construction using huge blocks of stone without mortar

The Greek word for circle is *kyklos;* the word for eye is *ops.* A giant with a circular eye was called by the ancient Greeks a Cyclops. Some of the Greek creation myths tell of the mating of Uranus (Sky) and Gaea (Earth), which produced the Titans, the Giants, and the three Cyclopes. The names of the latter— Brontes (Thunder), Steropes (Lightning), and Arges (Bright-ness)—were added to the original tales by later generations of storytellers. Imprisoned below the earth (first by Uranus and then by Cronus), the Cyclopes were master smiths whose fiery forges were located, some say, deep in the earth below Mount Etna. When Zeus decided to rebel against his father, Cronus, he released the Cyclopes. In gratitude, they forged him a magnificent thunderbolt. They also made Poseidon's trident and a helmet that rendered Hades (Death) invisible, so he could creep up on his victims and take them by surprise. With the help of these weapons Zeus and his brothers triumphed over Cronus, and the Cyclopes remained free.

Homer also placed their home in the region of Sicily, but the Cyclopes of the *Odyssey* are no longer the three master smiths who forged implements for the Olympians. Instead, they are fierce cannibals. There are many of them, living alone in caves, having no society to speak of, and terrorizing all who land on their shores. Possessing superhuman strength, they are able to lift massive rocks, which they use to block the entrances to their lairs. One of them, Polyphemus (whose name is the root of the word *polypheme,* a synonym for *giant*), tells Odysseus, "We Cyclopes care not a jot for Zeus with his aegis, nor for the rest of the blessed gods, since we are much stronger than they." Polyphemus kills and eats several of Odysseus's men before Homer's hero drives a red-hot pole into his single eye. As he continues to hurl boulders at their ship, the adventurers finally make their escape, leaving him praying for vengeance to the gods he disdained.

Homer's portrait is unique, however, and most of the tales of the Cyclopes portray them as allies of the Greek heroes. Callimachus, Pausanias, and other storytellers credit the Cyclopes with building the fortified walls around the ancient cities of Tiryns, Midea, and Mycenae. To this day, the style of building found by the excavators of those sites—massive, irregular blocks of stone piled on each other without cement—is labeled *Cyclopean*. The same adjective, by extension, may be applied to any object of huge proportions that is rough and ungraceful to the eye.

D

Daedalian/Daedalean: ingenious; intricate

While the Greek storytellers differ in their versions of Daedalus's parentage, they all agree on one point: He was a brilliant inventor. He was purported to be a master smith who had learned his trade under the watchful eye of the goddess Athena. His name, in fact, means "cunningly wrought," and among the many devices Daedalus was credited with inventing were the ax, the awl, and the level. Unfortunately, his sense of right and wrong was not nearly as well developed as his technical skills.

His young nephew, Talos, began to show signs of surpassing him in ingenuity, so he threw the boy off the Acropolis, eliminating the competition once and for all. When his crime was detected, Daedalus fled to the island of Crete, where he was welcomed by King Minos. Some say that he betrayed the king almost immediately, when he constructed an artificial cow for Queen Pasiphaë to hide in while she coupled with the great white bull of Poseidon; other stories say that Daedalus arrived on Crete after Pasiphaë had given birth to the Minotaur. All agree, though, that Daedalus conceived the idea of a labyrinth to contain the monster and prevent the youths that were brought to it for sacrifice from escaping.

The brilliant but morally bereft Daedalus came up with another ingenious scheme when Minos's daughter, Ariadne, begged him to help her save Theseus from the Minotaur. He told her to give Theseus a ball of yarn, which he could unwind behind him as he went deeper into the labyrinth; once he killed the Minotaur he would be able to retrace his steps by following the yarn back to the entrance. Theseus did just that and, afterward, fled with Ariadne. Faced with Minos's fury, Daedalus next conceived the idea of flying away to safety. The wings he made of feathers and wax brought him to Sicily, where he sought refuge and where his vanity almost cost him his life.

Knowing that Daedalus could not resist an intellectual challenge, King Minos set out after him, bringing along a puzzle only the great inventor could solve. Minos promised a reward to anyone who could pass a thread through a spiral seashell. Daedalus gave himself away when he bored a hole at the point of the shell and smeared the edges of the hole with honey. He then tied a thread around an ant, placing the insect at the shell's opening. The ant, of course, threaded the shell as it made for the honey. When the king of Sicily presented this solution, Minos knew he was harboring the fugitive and demanded that he surrender him. The king refused, Minos was killed, and Daedalus lived many more years.

Some tales say Daedalus went from Sicily to Sardinia, where he continued his career as an inventor, his works being called *Daedalia*. Speakers of English pay tribute to his creative genius whenever they use the adjective *Daedalian*, which means ingenious or intricate, like Daedalus's ideas.

See also: clue, Icarian, labyrinth

Daphnean/daphnean: *See: (be covered with) laurels*

DAYS OF THE WEEK

When the Germanic tribes (Anglo-Saxons) invaded the British isles, they brought with them their language and their gods. The latter were the same deities worshiped by the Scandinavians, who called them, collectively, the Aesir. While Christianity eventually triumphed over the Aesir as the predominant faith of the English-speaking peoples, these ancient deities are still remembered linguistically.

Old Norse and Anglo-Saxon were closely related, both offshoots of Teutonic. The Old Norse word for "day" was "dagr"; in Anglo-Saxon it was "daeg." "Sunnan daeg" and "Monan daeg" were consecrated to the sun and moon, respectively, and became our

Sunday and Monday. Each of the other days was believed to be sacred to one of the gods and bore his or her name:

Tuesday: Once *Tiwes daeg,* this day was named for the Norse god of war, Tyr. The son of Odin and Frigga, he was called Tiw by the Anglo-Saxons.

Wednesday: This began as *Wodnes daeg,* dedicated to the chief god of the Aesir, Odin. His wisdom entitled him to rule over the other gods in Valhalla, and he was known as Woden to the people of the British Isles.

Thursday: In Old Norse, this was *Thorsdagr,* which became *Thu(n)res daeg* in Anglo-Saxon. Thor was the son of Odin and Frigga. He was the god of thunder, the bravest and strongest god.

See also: thunder

Friday: Frigga gave her name to *Frige daeg,* now Friday. Also called Frig(g), she was the wife of Odin and the chief goddess of the Aesir. She was sometimes confused with Freyja, the Norse goddess of love. Some say that Friday was named for Freyja, not Frigga, just as the Romans named their sixth day *Veneris dies*—the day of their own goddess of love, Venus.

Saturday: This is the one day of the English week whose name is not derived from Norse mythology. It was called in Old English *Saeter daeg* or *Saeternes daeg,* in tribute to Saturn, the Roman god of agriculture.

Delphic: ambiguous; obscure

When the ancient Greeks went to consult the oracle of Apollo at Delphi, they communicated with the god through his priestess, the Pythia. If she felt inspired, she sat on her tripod and went into a trance. (The theory advanced by several Hellenistic authors—that she was intoxicated by vapors issuing out of a cleft in the earth—has been disproved geologically and architecturally. It seems more likely that the priestess was adept at self-hypnosis and was able to put herself into a trance at will.) Sometimes the pronouncements of the Pythia were intelligible, sometimes not. In any case, the questioner never received his answer directly from the priestess; an interpreter wrote down, in verse, what she was supposed to have said, and presented the written document to the questioner. This, of course, gave the earthly representatives of the god ample opportunity to stack the deck in his favor.

One of the most effective ways of doing this was to make the written response as ambiguous as possible so that, no matter what transpired, it would be the right answer. Perhaps the most famous example of this is the response given to King Croesus of Phrygia. Already the richest and most powerful monarch in Asia Minor, he was considering extending his territory by attacking the Persian Empire. When the oracle told him that if he went to war he would destroy a mighty empire, he was encouraged, and he attacked. The empire he destroyed was not that of Cyrus the Great, however; it was his own.

Answers like this caused the literal meaning of the word *Delphic*—of Delphi—to be overshadowed by its figurative sense—cryptic or ambiguous. Today, when we say someone has given a Delphic reply to a question, we mean that they have crouched their answer in such generalities, or phrased it so obscurely, that it can be interpreted any number of ways. It stands to reason, therefore, that Delphic answers are particularly prevalent among politicians in an election year.

See also: oracle

demon: an evil spirit; a person with great drive

For most of us, the word *demon* conjures up visions of a terrifying, malevolent spirit. When we "face our demons," we confront the things that frighten us most and try to overcome them. Demons weren't always associated with evil, however. The Greek word *daimon,* from which the English word is derived, was used to refer to a variety of different spirits, some of which were friendly to man and some of which were to be feared.

Daimon was a general term for a supernatural being. Homer uses the term interchangeably with *theos* (god). The spirits of the dead were also referred to by the ancient Greeks as daimones. They were considered to be lower than the gods but higher than man in the hierarchy of beings. Those daimones who had come by death tragically were believed to seek vengeance, and men were advised to pass by their tombs quietly so as not to attract their attention. Another type of daimon was the spirit that Zeus assigned to each human being at his birth. Like the tutelary spirit the Romans called a *genius,* a personal daimon stayed with a human throughout his life, acting as his guide and protector. The now obsolete English word *daemon,* which was once commonly used to mean inspiration from within or creative energy, was derived from the Greek concept of the personal daimon as a man's driving force.

Christianity, however, viewed all pagan gods as manifestations of the Devil. To the early Christians, therefore, demons had to be completely evil spirits, sent by Satan to corrupt men and alienate them from God. That is why demons, today, are things to be feared and shunned; the demonic is equivalent to the Satanic. Some Christians even impart the characteristics of evil spirits to inanimate objects that they believe the Devil uses to tempt men—for example, "the demon rum."

In one sense, however, the English word has retained its original mythological meaning. When we say someone is a "demon at work" or "works like a demon," we are paying tribute to their greater-than-human—almost supernatural— strength and energy, equating them with the gods of Homer and Hesiod.

The association of the Devil with demons led John Milton, in his *Paradise Lost,* to coin the word *Pandemonium* to refer to the place where Satan and his peers ("all the demons") gathered. Such a place would, of course, be totally lawless, filled with wild rioting and disorder. In the mid-nineteenth century,

Milton's linguistic creation became a synonym for great noise and confusion, a place where "all hell has broken loose."
See also: genius

(cut a) dido: play a trick or prank

Dido was the mythical queen of Carthage, also known as Elissa. In Virgil's *Aeneid* she falls in love with the Trojan hero Aeneas, and when, on Jupiter's orders, he leaves her, she stabs herself to death on a funeral pyre. However, the Dido who appears in earlier stories about the founding of Carthage was a much less romantic and far shrewder figure.

Her father was king of Tyre, and she was married to a man named Sychaeus or Acherbas. When her husband was killed by her brother, she feared for her own life and fled to North Africa. There she struck a bargain with the inhabitants: For a set price, they would allow her to purchase as much land as could be enclosed in a bull's hide. The crafty Dido got the best of them when she cut the hide into one continuous, hair-thin strip. Cut this way, it stretched around a huge section of land, on which she founded the city of Carthage.

The expression "cut a dido" or "cut didoes" comes from this story, and means to play a trick or prank on someone. Its first recorded use in English was in the early nineteenth century, and from it may have arisen the common phrases "cutting up" and "to be a cut-up."

Dionysian: unrestrained; immoderate; disorderly (opposite of Apollonian)

Dionysus is best known as the Greek god of wine, but he was also worshiped as a god of fertility and vegetation, of woodlands and wilderness. His alternate name, Bacchus, is of Thracian origin, and he was worshiped in Asia Minor before his cult spread to Greece and Rome. In Asia Minor he was said to be the son of the earth goddess, Zemelo, which accounts for his association with crops and the endless cycle of death and rebirth of vegetation. As the worship of Dionysus spread through Greece, he was given a place in the Greek pantheon as the youngest son of Zeus. A mortal woman, Semele, was invented to be his mother. The story was told that Hera, learning of Zeus's seduction and impregnation of Semele, obtained her revenge by convincing the young woman to ask Zeus to appear to her in all his splendor. Of course no mortal could survive such an awesome sight, and Semele was instantly annihilated by Zeus's thunderbolt. Fortunately for Dionysus, his divine father had the presence of mind to rip him from his mother's womb at the moment of her death, and to sew the unborn child up in his own thigh until he was ready to come into the world.

The boy grew up under the tutelage of the satyrs and Pan's son, Silenus, who taught him the uses of wine; he also learned how to induce self-intoxication by chewing on ivy leaves. If constant indulgence in these pastimes didn't rob him of his senses altogether, the jealous Hera did. She drove the young man mad and sent him wandering throughout the world in a state of frenzy. He soon picked up a train of female devotees known as Bacchantes (from his Thracian name) or as Maenads (from the same root as the word *maniac*). In order to commune with their god, the Bacchantes imbibed the same intoxicants he did. Drunk and uninhibited, they roamed through the wilderness cavorting with the satyrs whenever the opportunity presented itself. If they came upon a wild animal, especially a goat, they considered it to be the incarnation of their god and tore it to pieces, consuming the raw flesh in a sort of unholy communion.

There are indications that the cult of Dionysus included the sacrifice and consumption of human victims as well. Euripides' play *The Bacchae* describes the murder of King Pentheus by a band of Bacchantes that included his mother and sisters. Pentheus had opposed the worship of Dionysus, so the god produced a delusional state in the women, convincing them that the king was a dangerous wild boar that they had to kill.

The Greeks were aware that the consumption of alcohol can lead human beings in either of two directions: It can make us carefree and happy, or angry and violent. Stripping us of our inhibitions, it also takes away our intellectual powers, our sense of right and wrong, and the veneer of civilization that separates us from the beasts. Apollo was the Greek god who brought light, order, and rational thinking to men. Those who worshiped the god of wine risked losing their Apollonian attributes, to be left only with the Dionysian: the irrational, the disorderly, the dark.

See also: Apollonian, bacchanal, nymph

doubleganger: a living person's double

Even today, many people believe in the psychic phenomenon known as the *doubleganger.* Somewhere in the world, they say, there is an exact double of every living person, who exists independently from that individual. People's chance meetings with their doublegangers have been a popular theme in literature.

The word doubleganger comes from the German *doppel* (double) and *gänger* (walker). In German folklore and legend there are many stories of Doppelgängers, but the Germans were not alone in theorizing the existence of a person's double. In many mythologies, including the Finno-Ugrian, Siberian, and North American, it was believed that people possessed more than one soul. Their life-soul animated their body and died with it; their free-soul, on the other hand, existed independently outside their body. While a person lived, his free-soul walked the earth as his Doppelgänger; when he died, it continued to walk as his ghost.

(sow) dragon's teeth: sow seeds of strife; set the stage for trouble to come

Cadmus was the legendary founder of the Greek city of Thebes. According to the myths, he was a Phoenician prince whose sister, Europa, was abducted by Zeus. In an attempt to recover her, he went to Greece, but an oracle told him to give up his search for Europa and instead found a city. He was led to the site of the future Thebes, where his men were killed by a dragon, which he in turn slew. The goddess Athena then appeared to him, instructing him to sow the teeth of the dragon in a field. From these strange seeds an entire army sprang up. On Athena's instructions, Cadmus flung a stone into their midst, and the warriors proceeded to fight each other to the death until only five remained. These five "Sown Men" pledged their fealty to Cadmus and helped him found Thebes.

The fierce fighting that resulted from Cadmus's seemingly harmless act of "sowing dragon's teeth" became a metaphor for taking an action that sets the stage for trouble in the future, even though we may not intend that to be the outcome of our deed.

Another expression that drew its inspiration from this myth is *Cadmean victory*—a victory that is won at a terrible cost—in reference to the near elimination of Cadmus's huge army, so that only five men remained out of thousands. This phrase has the same sense as *Pyrrhic victory,* which stems from the historical battle of 279 B.C. in which Greek King Pyrrhus defeated the Romans but lost so many men he was quoted as saying, "One more such victory and we are lost."

dwarf: a small person; a smaller-than-normal variety of plant or animal

Everyone knows the story of Snow White and the Seven Dwarfs. The little men in that tale were utterly charming, as kind and helpful as could be to the damsel in distress. It's hard to believe they were descended from maggots, but in a roundabout way, they were.

The ancestors of the cute and cuddly dwarfs of our fairy tales were the dwarfs of Scandinavian mythology. The Old Norse word for dwarf was *dvergr,* which may have come from the Sanskrit word for demon: *dhvaras.* The Norse myths were first written down between A.D. 800 and 1200 in the *Eddas*. The *Eddas* tell us that the world was made out of the body of the slain giant Ymir. As Odin stood over the rotting hulk of flesh, he saw that it was covered with maggots—evil feeding upon evil. He condemned the creatures to eternal darkness, saying, "Dwarfs they will become . . . and live in unlighted caverns below the rocks. . . . They will take men's shapes, though not men's size."

Like the dark elves, with whom they were often confused, the dwarfs lived in their own underground realm. It was called Nidavellir, and it was there that they had their great forges. The dwarfs were master smiths, creating magical tools and weapons for the gods and for man. Thor's magic hammer was made by the dwarf Brokkr, as was Odin's magic ring, from which new rings of equal value were created each day.

The dwarfs appear as the Nibelungs in the *Völsunga saga,* which inspired the Germanic epic *Nibelungenleid* (the basis of Wagner's *Ring* cycle). It is chiefly through Teutonic folktales that the dwarfs of our children's stories evolved. Today we use the word *dwarf* for a smaller-than-average person, or for certain species of plants and animals that do not reach full size. In its literal sense, the verb *to dwarf* means to stunt growth, but it is also used figuratively, meaning to make something appear small and insignificant by contrast. Hence, the Allegheny Mountains are dwarfed by the Rockies; Shakespeare dwarfs other playwrights.

See also: elf, pygmy

E

echo: the repetition of a sound

Many myths originated from early man's attempts to explain natural phenomena that he found mysterious or perplexing. One such physical phenomenon is an echo, which is frequently heard in the mountains. Greece is a mountainous country, and, without any knowledge of physics, ancient inhabitants of the high country must have been amazed and puzzled when the words they shouted came back to them. We now know that echoes are produced when sound waves strike a solid object and bounce back through the air, but thousands of years ago man's imagination supplied other, more fanciful explanations.

The best-known tale invented to explain the repetition of sound was that of a mountain nymph, or Oread, named Echo. She was a confidante of Hera, but on several occasions her incessant chattering distracted the goddess and gave Hera's philandering husband, Zeus, the time he needed to spirit away his paramours before his wife could catch them *in flagrante delicto*. Furious, Hera punished the nymph by taking away her power to initiate speech. Henceforth, all she could do was repeat, or *echo,* the words of others.

As if this weren't misfortune enough, the unlucky Echo then fell in love with the handsome, self-centered Narcissus. She tried to express her feelings but could only repeat his words, including those that told her he would rather be dead than in her arms. Brokenhearted, Echo hid in the mountains, the forests, and the caves, refusing to eat or sleep. Finally, her body wasted away completely, and all that remains of her is her voice—endlessly repeating the words of those who venture into her lonely haunts.

See also: narcissistic

Electra complex: excessive attachment of a female child to her father and hostility to her mother

On the day he returned home from the Trojan War, the Greek king, Agamemnon, was killed by his wife. Either because he had sacrificed their daughter, Iphigenia, in order to procure a favorable wind for the Greek fleet, or because she had taken a lover in his absence and wanted to continue her illicit affair, Clytemnestra murdered him and showed no remorse.

Agamemnon's daughter, Electra, believed the killing to be unjustified. In the years that followed, her hatred of her mother grew, and she lived only for the day when her father's death would be avenged. Her brother, Orestes, had been exiled when Clytemnestra's lover moved into Agamemnon's palace. At last Orestes reached manhood and returned home. Electra urged him to kill Clytemnestra, which he did, and for this crime against nature he was pursued by the Furies until the gods absolved him of his crime.

Sigmund Freud, who believed healthy psychological development depends on our ability to resolve the early conflicts we feel about our parents, saw in this myth the archetype of a human dilemma. According to Freud, at about age two or three the female child, who until this time has identified with her mother, realizes that neither she nor her female parent has a penis. Her desire to possess a male organ (penis envy) leads to a strong attachment to her father. She also begins to resent her mother, whom she now perceives as a rival for her father's penis and love. Although not spurred on by the same fear of castration that makes a boy sublimate his similar illicit feelings, girls normally outgrow this phase and come to identify once again with their mother. If, however, a girl continues to be excessively attached to her male parent and hostile toward her female parent, Freud called this an Electra complex and suggested regressive psychotherapy so these subconscious conflicts can be resolved.

See also: Oedipus complex

ELEMENTS

Seventeen of the chemical elements are named for mythological figures:

Cerium: The asteroid Ceres was discovered at the beginning of the nineteenth century. A few years later, in a second tribute to the Roman goddess of grain and agriculture, this element received her name as well. Cerium resembles iron in color and luster but is soft and malleable.

Cobalt: A silver-gray magnetic element, cobalt's name comes from the German *kobold*—an underground spirit—which also gave us the English word *goblin*. Kobolds often played tricks on men, just as this element did when its lustrous sheen deceived miners into believing they had discovered a more precious metal.

Helium: Discovered in the nineteenth century, this element was first found in the gaseous atmosphere surrounding the sun, hence its association with the Greek god of the sun, Helios.

Iridium: Iridium was discovered in 1804. The iridescence of some of its solutions and the various colors of its compounds led to its identification with Iris, Greek goddess of the rainbow.

See also: iridescent

Mercury: Mercury is the only common metal that is liquid at ordinary temperatures. It was originally called quicksilver because of its mobile form and color. For centuries alchemists had used the symbol for the planet Mercury to represent it. Around the sixth century A.D. they began to refer to the element as *mercurius,* and it certainly has much in common with the fleet-footed messenger of the Roman gods.

See also: mercurial

Neptunium: This element was named after the planet Neptune, which itself had been given the Roman name of the god of the sea.

Nickel: Like cobalt, nickel is a shiny, silvery element, and its name is also rooted in Germanic mythology. Nickel's appearance to miners made it seem that it contained copper, but it yielded none. Therefore, they dubbed it *kupfernickel* (copper demon), *kupfer* meaning "copper" and *nickel* coming from the word *nix,* a water sprite akin to a goblin. The shortened form entered the English language as the name for this tricky element.

See also: Old Scratch

Niobium: In Greek mythology, Niobe was the daughter of Tantalus. The close relationship between this element and tantalum, which it closely resembles and which is almost always found with it in ores, led to its being named for Tantalus's child.

Palladium: Palladium was discovered in 1803. Since this event came right after the identification of the asteroid Pallas, the element was given the same name, also in honor of the Greek goddess Pallas Athena.

Plutonium: Plutonium, a radioactive element formed by bombarding uranium, was named after the planet Pluto. Both share the name of the Roman god of the Underworld.

Promethium: This element was named after one of the second generation of Greek Titans, Prometheus, who gave fire to mankind. Isolated in 1947 from atomic fission products, it bears an appropriate name, since it comes out of the fierce fires of an atomic furnace.

Selenium: This element closely resembles tellurium, the name of which comes from *tellus*—Latin for "earth." The close relationship between the planet Earth and its moon suggested to this element's discoverer that it be named for the Greek goddess of the moon, Selene.

Tantalum: Tantalus was a Greek hero who angered the gods and was punished by forever being tantalized by cool water and delicious food, which were always just out of his reach. The scientists who discovered this element had great difficulty dissolving its oxide in acids and, therefore, found it easy to identify with Tantalus.

Tellurium: *Tellus* is a Latin word for "earth" and was also the name the Romans gave to the great Earth Goddess. The name of this element was suggested by the German chemist Klaproth in 1798. He had previously named an element for Uranus, the Greek god of the sky, and thought it fitting that Tellus, the mythological wife of the sky, be honored as well.

Thorium: This heavy, gray, radioactive element takes its name from Thor, the Norse god of thunder. It was discovered and named in 1828.

Titanium: Discovered in the eighteenth century, this element was named for the mighty Greek Titans, first sons of the earth—a reference to the incarnation of natural strength in the metal.

Uranium: Herschel discovered the planet Uranus in 1781 and named it for the Greek god of the sky. Eight years later Martin Klaproth discovered this radioactive element and christened it in honor of Herschel and his "new" planet.

Vanadium: The name of this element comes from Old Norse. Vanadis was one of the names given to the Scandinavian goddess of beauty and love, Freyja, and the beautiful colors of vanadium's compounds in solution led scientists to pay homage to her when christening it.

elf: a small, lively creature; a diminutive person

Most of us associate elves with Santa Claus: we tell young children that elves are cute little people who help Santa in his workshop. They bustle about in pointed hats and shoes, filling all the orders for toys at Christmastime. But long before modern-day mythology relocated the elves to the North Pole, these tiny folk lived in their own realm.

In Norse mythology there were two kinds of elves: the dark

elves and the bright elves. The dark elves lived underground, in Svartalfaheim; the bright creatures lived in a kingdom between heaven and earth, called Alfheim. The *Eddas* say that the inhabitants of Svartalfaheim were "enemies of the Gods, thieves and mischief-makers, well versed in minor magic, but their power was unseen and their ways were devious." The bright elves, on the other hand, were friends of the Aesir, ruled by the sun god Freyr. Odin's messenger, Hermod, passed through their realm on his way to the land of the dead and saw "hundreds of tiny, glittering little elves, darting and winking like jewels in the rocks." He knew he had nothing to fear from them; they ran and hid only because they were afraid of burning him with their brightness.

Because of their diminutive size, and because the dark elves lived underground, elves were often confused with dwarfs in later folklore. Some of the dwarfs' malicious characteristics were attributed to them, and the elves of German legends, in particular, are often rather malignant creatures. During the Middle Ages it was believed that elves could harm people by firing "elf-arrows" at them and that they caused children to be born with deformities, "elf-marking" them.

The contemporary notion of elves is a lot closer to the residents of Alfheim, a modern-day elf being a sprightly, charming person—particularly a child. Such a person might be a little naughty but would not be considered harmful or demonic. Someone who is *elfin* is full of the mischievous, magical qualities known to be possessed by these little creatures.

See also: dwarf

Elysian Fields/Elysium: paradise; any place of peace and bliss

In early Greek mythology the Elysian Fields were located on earth. In Book IV of the *Odyssey*, Homer says that the Elysian plain lies at the world's end and that those who are favored by the gods are sent there after death. It is the land "where living is made easiest for mankind, where no snow falls, no strong winds blow and there is never any rain, but day after day the West Wind's tuneful breeze comes in from Ocean to refresh its folk." There is no mention in the early myths of virtue or high moral standards being a condition for entrance into the Elysian Fields.

In later myths, however, the Elysian Fields were described as part of the Underworld and were reserved for those who had led a righteous life on earth. In the *Aeneid,* Anchises, the father of Aeneas, appears to his son in a dream and tells him, "I am confined in no cruel Hell and in no shades of gloom, but instead I dwell in Elysium among the happy gatherings of the True." Led down into the Underworld by the Cumaean Sibyl, Aeneas is shown two paths: one leads to Tartarus, where evildoers are punished for their sins; the other goes to Elysium, "the Land of Joy, the pleasant green places in the Fortunate Woods, where are the Homes of the Blest." He sees spirits romping on a playing field of grass, while others are wrestling on yellow sand. Still others are dancing and singing or feasting. The company includes "a band who sustained wounds while fighting for their homelands, others who while life was theirs were priests without sin, or faithful seers whose speech never brought Apollo shame; some who had given life an added graciousness by inventions of skill, and some who had made others remember them by being kind." Only the good get to enjoy the comforts of Elysium.

The descriptions of this heavenly place have fired the imaginations of men for centuries and made the terms *Elysian Fields* and *Elysium* metaphors for places of extreme beauty and bliss. A real-life paradise for shoppers and art lovers is the grandest of Paris's grand boulevards, the Champs Elysées. This mile-long avenue, often called the most elegant in the world, is filled with palaces, parks, theaters, and boutiques. Strolling its length on a beautiful spring day, you could easily believe you'd died and gone to heaven!

erotic: having to do with physical love; arousing desire

In some of the early Greek creation myths, particularly in Hesiod's *Theogony,* Eros (Love) was said to be the first god. Born of Chaos, Earth, or Night—there are many different versions of his parentage—Eros was the force that brought order to the universe. Out of love came first light and then life. Without Eros, the world might have remained in its original state of dark, empty confusion. This very lofty, idealistic view of love and its powers is not, however, the one most associated with Eros, nor is it reflected in the way we use the word *erotic.*

The god Eros with whom we are most familiar is the son of Aphrodite. In most of the Greek myths he is portrayed as a vain, spoiled youth who flies through the air shooting arrows at gods and men, causing them to fall hopelessly in love. While he fires some of his arrows at the request of his mother, for the most part Eros uses his bow for sport, targeting anyone who comes his way. Those who are hit by his arrows are seized with uncontrollable passion, and Eros is thought of as the god of sensual love, arousing lust in his victims. Hence the use of the adjective *erotic* to describe something that arouses feelings of sexual desire in us.

Erotica are literary or artistic works that have a sensual theme, and *Eros* is a term sometimes used for sexual instinct or libido.

See also: aphrodisiac, chaos, (struck by) Cupid's arrow

F

(a) face that could launch a thousand ships: a great beauty

Helen of Troy was hatched from a swan's egg, but she was no ugly duckling! In fact, she was undisputedly acknowledged by the ancient Greeks to be the most beautiful woman in the world. There are many stories about her conception, the most widespread being that Zeus took the form of a swan and seduced the princess Leda, who soon afterward laid an egg containing Helen and her brother, Polydeuces (Pollux). Helen's beauty was so legendary that every noble Greek sought her hand in marriage. Her mother's husband, King Tyndareus of Sparta, was afraid to give her to any one of her suitors, fearing the wrath of the others. Before announcing his choice, therefore, he made all the princes take an oath that they would defend the honor of Helen's future husband against any who might wrong him. Then he gave her in marriage to Menelaus, brother of Agamemnon.

Several years later, when Prince Paris of Troy abducted Helen from Menelaus's house, the Greek princes, bound by their oath, rallied to Menelaus's side. In his *Agamemnon*, Aeschylus says they "launched a thousand ships from the Argive land" to bring Helen back. Homer is more specific. In Book II of the *Iliad* he recites the names of the Greek chieftains and the number of ships each contributed to the fleet. They total 1,206—but we still refer to a woman of unsurpassed beauty as one whose "face could launch a thousand ships."

See also: throw the apple of discord

fairyland: a beautiful or charming place

At Christmastime, when decorations and strings of colored lights are everywhere, people can often be heard to say the streets look "just like fairyland." We use this word when speaking of any very beautiful or charming place that seems removed from the often dreary, everyday world of reality.

Our modern-day concept of fairies and the world they inhabit comes from both Germanic and Celtic mythology. German folklore embroidered on the Norse myths about dwarfs and elves—small, often malicious creatures who lived underground. The kobold and the nix, both mischievous spirits, are Teutonic inventions. Countless types of fairies proliferated in Celtic lands: The Irish believed firmly in the existence of the *side* (the people of the hills), and in leprechauns. In England and Scotland pixies, brownies, kelpies, undines, and many other spirits were believed to share the earth with mankind. Some of these were entirely benevolent; others played tricks or brought harm to people if they weren't properly treated.

Most of the legends about these little people say that they were active at night, when most humans were sleeping peacefully in their beds. They loved to sing and dance in the moonlight, often holding hands and making a ring. (The fairy ring, a circle in which many types of fungi grow, received its name from this idea.) While some fairies took up residence in human households, there was also a kingdom of the fairies, the exact location of which was never specified in the tales. A king and queen ruled over the fairies, and in their kingdom there was no sickness, old age, or death. The inhabitants of this wonderland lived in houses filled with gold and spent their time feasting and dancing.

In the British Isles, much of the folklore about fairies was influenced by the French romance *Huon de Bordeaux* and by the Arthurian legends. The connection is apparent in the name of one of the major characters in the latter: Morgan le Fay. *Fay* was the Middle English form of *fairy* and came from the Latin *fata,* meaning "one of the Fates." (The Fates were the Roman equivalent of the Greek Morae, three supernatural beings who determined the length of a person's life. The idea that fairies possess magical powers may be traceable to the power the Fates held over mankind.)

See also: Brownie, leprechaun, pixie-led

Flying Dutchman: a type of dive; an express train

A common theme in many mythologies is that of the phantom ship. The most famous phantom ship is the *Flying Dutchman*. First appearing in a late medieval legend, the ship was named after its captain, a Dutchman condemned by God to wander the seas until the Last Judgment. There are several versions of his story, all of which take place around the Cape of Good Hope. Some accounts say the stubborn captain persisted in trying to round the Cape in a violent storm, in spite of the protests of his crew. When a heavenly form appeared to warn him, he fired on it and cursed it. He was then condemned to sail the seas around the Cape of Good Hope and lure other vessels to their doom. Other tales attribute his punishment to the fact that he was guilty of cruelty to his crew, or say that he was damned because he made a pact with the Devil.

Many people have claimed to see the ship, manned by a crew of dead men, off the Cape of Good Hope in stormy weather. Mariners live in fear of such a sighting and what it portends. Wagner immortalized the phantom ship in his 1843 opera *Der Fliegende Hollander*. In competitive diving, *flying Dutchman* is the name given to a half gainer: a back dive in which one flies through the air, heels over head. An express train from London to Bristol has also been named the Flying Dutchman after the ghostly ship.

fury: an angry, violent person, especially a woman

The Furies of Greek mythology existed to avenge violations of the natural order, such as the murder of one family member by another. It was only fitting that this role be assigned to them, since they came into the world as a result of a violent, unnatural act: the castration of Uranus by his son, Cronus.

Gaea and Uranus were the parents of the Titans and the Hundred-Handed Ones. When Uranus imprisoned the latter, Gaea became enraged and persuaded the Titan Cronus to castrate his father. The blood that flowed from Uranus's wounds fell upon Gaea, and she gave birth to the Erinyes.

In the earliest myths the number of Erinyes is not given, but later on there were said to be three of them: Alecto (the Unresting), Tisiphone (the Avenger), and Megaera (the Jealous). They were depicted as hideous, coal-black old women with bat wings, whose hair was made up of snakes and whose eyes dripped blood. They barked like dogs and brandished metal-studded whips as they pursued criminals. The sight of them was enough to drive a guilty person mad, knowing that, once aroused to their righteous fury, they would be implacable. They would pursue a guilty party to his death, accepting no excuses and making no allowance for individual circumstances, basing their judgment only on the deed that had been done.

The most famous appearance of the Erinyes in mythology is in Aeschylus's *Oresteia*. When Agamemnon returned from the Trojan War, he was murdered by his wife, Clytemnestra. When their son, Orestes, came of age, he avenged his father's death by killing his mother. Even though Orestes had acted on the command of Apollo, the Erinyes tormented him relentlessly, pursuing him through many lands, until Apollo sent him to Athens to plead his case before Athena. The goddess of wisdom deemed that Orestes had suffered enough and had made atonement for his sin of matricide. She ordered the Erinyes to cease their punishment of the young man. When they did so, according to Aeschylus, their name was changed to the Eumenides—the gracious ones—and they became the protectors of suppliants. According to other myths, however, the name Eumenides was a euphemism used to propitiate the Erinyes: It was considered bad luck to use their real name, and people tried to win them over by referring to them as "the gracious ones," hoping they would be flattered and leave one alone.

Neither Greek name—Erinyes or Eumenides—has taken on a figurative meaning in our language, but the Latin name for these avenging spirits—the Furiae—has given us another term for a violent, angry person. A fury is someone who has a horrible temper, who rages with anger at the slightest provocation. Because the Furies were female, the term is most often applied to women, but it is also used when speaking about an ill-tempered man.

G

(Sir) Galahad: a perfect gentleman

It is ironic that Sir Galahad's name is now used to describe a man who is extremely solicitous of the opposite sex, for, of all the knights of the Round Table, he was the one who had the least to do with women. In fact, it was his total purity and unworldliness that led to his fame.

Celtic legends tell us that when the Round Table was founded, one seat was deliberately left empty. This was the Siege Perilous—*siège* being the Old French word for "chair"—and it was left for the knight who would one day find the Holy Grail. Such a man would have to be of unequaled purity and, to prove his worthiness, would have to pull a certain sword out of the stone in which it was embedded. Several of King Arthur's retinue, including Gawain and Perceval, tried unsuccessfully to draw out the sword. Lancelot, knowing his adulterous relations with Queen Guinevere had made him unworthy, declined to attempt it.

Then Galahad, the son of Lancelot and Elaine, arrived in Camelot. An unknown old man led him into the dining hall and to the Siege Perilous. Before he could take the seat, however, he had to prove himself, and he did so when he easily drew out the sword and put it into his own scabbard. After this, the knights of the Round Table set off in quest of the Holy Grail, and, as had been prophesied, Galahad was the first to see it. Afterward, he could not bear to return to the world of men and prayed to be taken from this life. His soul was carried to heaven by the angels, and a hand came out of the clouds to take the Grail into the sky. No one has seen it since.

Somehow, over the centuries, the image of Sir Galahad as a Christian ascetic was supplanted by that of a courtly gentleman. Perhaps, as Bergen Evans suggests, this was due to the fact that his name bore a close resemblance to the world *gallant*. Whatever the reasons, *Sir Galahad* lives on in the English language as a term describing a paragon of chivalry and courtesy toward the opposite sex: a perfect gentleman.

See also: (to search for the) Holy Grail

Ganymede: *See: catamite*

genie: *See: genius*

genius: a great inspiration or driving force; a brilliant person

In its earliest form, the Roman genius seems to have represented the male reproductive power. Along with its female counterpart, the juno, the genius had a place of honor in every Roman home. When a couple entered into marriage, a bed (the *lectus genialis*) was made for the male and female spirits that assured the continuance of the family line. Each home also had its altar, where the genius of the head of the house was worshiped. At this stage in the evolution of Roman religion, the genius of other family members does not seem to have received any attention.

Later, under the influence of Greek thought, the concept of the genius changed. The Greeks had long believed that Zeus assigned a daimon, or guardian spirit, to each human being at his or her birth. The genius eventually became the equivalent of the daimon, guiding and protecting a person and shaping his character as well. Romans began to worship their personal genius, especially on their birthday. Things, groups of people, and even places were believed to possess a genius: the *genius loci* determined the general atmosphere of a place; the *genius populi Romani* protected the Roman people; military units and trade guilds each had their own genius.

The English word *genius,* when used to denote the unique

character of a historical period, a nation, etc., can be traced back to these Roman beliefs. So can its meaning of a person who exerts a strong influence over another, e.g., "an evil genius." Its most common use in modern English, as a synonym for extraordinary intellectual or creative ability or a person who possesses such ability, is relatively recent, dating only from the seventeenth or eighteenth century.

The Latin genius became *génie* in French. When French translators of Arabic literature encountered the word *(d)jinni*—a nature spirit that can take on the shape of any human or animal—they used the same term for it. The word *génie* was borrowed from French by the English, which is why a genie comes out of Aladdin's lamp in English translations of the *Arabian Nights*.

See also: demon

ghoul: a grave robber; someone who performs horrible acts or enjoys loathsome things

When the newspapers carry stories about vandals who desecrate cemeteries, opening up and robbing graves, they often refer to the culprits as *ghouls*. This very appropriate appellation came into English from Arabic, where it was the name of a demonic grave robber.

In Arabic folklore there were male ghuls and female ghulahs. Both varieties were evil spirits that robbed tombs, especially those of young children, and fed on the flesh of the stolen corpses. According to popular belief, if a ghul could not find a graveyard it would prey upon the living.

Besides applying the term to those who literally rob graves, we now use it figuratively as well, when referring to a person who takes pleasure in performing or witnessing gruesome acts. Sadists, necrophiliacs, cannibals, and other twisted personalities are dubbed ghouls, particularly in the popular press, which capitalizes on the sense of horror the word evokes in most readers.

giant: an extremely large being; larger than normal

Some of the Greek creation myths say that Mother Earth (Gaea) and Father Sky (Uranus) peopled the world with several sets of beings before mankind appeared. First came the Hundred-Handed Ones; next to be born were the Cyclopes; then the Titans appeared; and fourth in succession came the Giants (Gigantes). The latter were sometimes said to be the children of Gaea and Tartarus (Hell) or to have sprung from the blood of Uranus when he was wounded by his son, the Titan Cronus. Cronus then unseated his father and ruled the earth until his own son, Zeus, rebelled against him and took over the world.

But Zeus's rule did not go unchallenged for long. Angered because he had banished their brothers, the Titans, to Tartarus, the Giants rose up against him in what became known as the Gigantomachia or Gigantomachy. The most complete description of this mythological rebellion is given by Apollodorus, who says there were twenty-four Giants. The huge, hairy monsters had serpent tails for feet, and they hurled massive boulders and firebrands at the Olympians. Hera prophesied that no god could kill the Giants, but that a "lion-skinned mortal" would be able to do so. Zeus realized that she meant his son Heracles—who went about garbed in the skin of the Thespian Lion he had killed as a youth—and sent for the hero. During the fighting that ensued, it was Heracles who dealt the fatal blow to each Giant after the Olympians had disabled them one by one.

From the Greek name of these mythological monsters English got its word for a larger-than-life being. The adjectives *giant* and *gigantic* are now used to describe anything or anyone of extraordinary size. In plant and animal names, *giant* refers to a species that is huge in comparison to related or similar species.

The medical terms *giantism* and *gigantism* are given to a condition in which an overactive pituitary gland causes excessive growth of the long bones, resulting in unusually large size.

golden age: a period of great prosperity

To students of history, Greece's golden age occurred in the fifth century B.C. It was then that Periclean democracy flourished in Athens, the leader of the Greek city-states. The plays of Aeschylus, Sophocles, and Aristophanes were being performed in the open-air theaters, and the magnificent temple we know as the Parthenon was rising on the Acropolis. The groundwork on which all Western civilization is built was being laid.

But according to the Greek myths, the world experienced a Golden Age long before Pericles. Hesiod says that in Cronus's time, when he was the king of heaven, there lived on earth "a golden generation of mortal people." These fortunate men lived much like the gods: They knew no sorrow, hard work, or pain; they never grew old. Death was nothing to fear, either; when the time came, they simply went to sleep.

The Golden Age was followed by the Silver and the Bronze Ages, the Age of Heroes, and, finally, the Iron Age. The hero-men performed valiant deeds, but their age was marred by war and violence. It was the Golden Age on which Hesiod and the other storytellers looked back with nostalgia and longing. From their depiction of this glorious time, we have adopted the term *golden age* to refer to a period when a nation, civilization, or institution is at its peak. When there is peace and prosperity, when culture and the arts flourish—it is then that we remember the long-lost generation whose virtues were extolled by the storytellers of old.

(cut the) Gordian knot: solve a perplexing problem by taking decisive action

Gordius was a legendary king of Phrygia, in Asia Minor, and the adoptive father of King Midas. A popular tale explained how, although born a peasant, he became a rich and powerful ruler.

When the king of Phrygia died suddenly, without an heir, an

oracle prophesied that the new king would approach his palace in an oxcart. One day while Gordius was out driving, an eagle—the sacred bird of Zeus—perched on the pole of his oxcart. The young man realized this was an omen but had no idea what it meant, so he turned the cart toward the city of Telmissus, where there was an oracle who might be able to explain it. As he approached the town, the people remembered the prophecy and acclaimed the stranger their new king. In gratitude, Gordius dedicated the cart to Zeus, and he tied its yoke to its pole with a knot so intricate no one else could undo it. It was said that the man who succeeded in unraveling the knot would rule all of Asia. Legend has it that for centuries the Gordian knot stumped all those who tried to undo it, until Alexander the Great tackled the job. With one slash of his sword he cut through the knot; he then proceeded to extend his empire from Macedonia all the way to India.

Like Heracles, who realized he could never clean the Augean stables using traditional methods and, therefore, came up with the idea of letting two rivers do the job for him, Alexander opted for an unorthodox, but effective, solution to his dilemma. The legend of Alexander's ingenuity spread, and "cutting the Gordian knot" remains, to this day, a popular metaphor for solving an intricate problem with quick, decisive action.

gorgon: *See: (a) look that could turn you to stone*

(beware of) Greeks bearing gifts: watch out for people with hidden motives

In Book II of the *Aeneid* Virgil relates how the priest Laocoön importuned his fellow Trojans to be wary of the huge wooden horse left behind by the Greek forces in their apparent retreat. "I fear the Greeks even when they bear gifts," he exclaimed, but his warnings were ignored. When two giant serpents came up out of the sea and devoured him and his small sons, the

Trojans were even more disposed to believe the lies of the carefully coached Sinon. The only Greek soldier who remained behind after the Greeks' withdrawal, Sinon convinced the Trojans that the last thing the Greeks wanted them to do was take the horse into their citadel. In a fine example of the power of reverse psychology, the Trojans opened their gates and rolled it in. By the time they realized Laocoön had been right, it was too late, as armed Greeks, freed from the confines of the horse's belly, rushed through the sleeping city delivering their real gifts: death and destruction.

Ever since, "Beware of Greeks bearing gifts" has been a way of saying that there are often strings attached to people's seemingly generous gestures, and we shouldn't always take them at face value.

See also: Trojan, Trojan horse

H

(hot as) Hades: unbearably hot; sweltering

The ancient Greeks would have been totally mystified by our common expression "hot as Hades." The Hades they believed in was anything but hot: It was a cold, dark place that was never penetrated by the brightness and warmth of the sun. It was usually described as a subterranean region and, in fact, was most often called the Underworld.

The Norse myths also depicted a cold, dark afterworld, ruled by the goddess Hel. Her name became synonymous with her realm and is the root of the English word *hell*. The association of both Hades and hell with heat comes from Christian theology, rather than from these early "pagan" myths.

In the Bible the Hebrew words *Sheol* and *Gehenna* are used to refer to the afterworld. English translators used the Greek Hades and the English-from-Norse hell interchangeably wherever these words appeared in the text. The idea that sinners will be punished by fire appears in the New Testament. In the Book of Matthew (25:41) Christ describes the Last Judgment, saying: "Then shall he also say unto them on the left hand, 'Depart from me, ye cursed, into everlasting fire, prepared for the devil and his angels.' " Most of the early Christian writers accepted the words of the Bible literally and interpreted Christ's words to mean that damnation consisted of burning for eternity. The Koran (xi) also speaks of "Hell-fire" and "the flames of Hell."

Most English speakers, therefore, automatically associate Hades and hell with eternal conflagration rather than icy darkness. And so, when we say it is "hot as Hades," we mean it is sweltering!

See also: hell, inferno

halcyon days: days of perfect peace to be recalled with nostalgia

The Greek word for "kingfisher" is *halkyon,* and at one time the Greeks believed the kingfisher made its nest and brooded its eggs at sea. The name of the bird and its departure from traditional nesting habits were explained by the touching myth of Alcyone and her husband, Ceyx.

Alcyone was the daughter of Aeolus, keeper of the winds. On the occasions when her father released these fierce powers, Alcyone saw firsthand the damage they could do, especially at sea. She greatly feared them, and when her husband told her he was planning to make a sea journey to consult an oracle, she begged him not to go. Although he loved her passionately, Ceyx felt compelled to make the trip. Filled with foreboding, the weeping Alcyone stood on the shore and watched her beloved sail into the unknown. According to some storytellers, Alcyone had committed the sin of comparing herself and her husband to Zeus and Hera, and the angry gods sent a storm to punish her audacity. Other writers simply tell us that a fierce storm arose the first night Ceyx was at sea, and he drowned with the name of his wife on his lips.

Unaware that her husband was dead, Alcyone continued to pray to Hera for his safe return, until the goddess sent Morpheus to her in a dream. Taking the form of her husband, Morpheus told her he was dead and would never return to her. Waking, Alcyone rushed down to the water's edge, where she saw the body of her husband floating a little way from shore. As she plunged into the water to reach him, the gods took pity on her. They changed her into a kingfisher and she flew to her mate, who had also been restored to life as a bird. Reunited, the two continue to fly over the waters, and each winter they make their nest and raise their young on top of the waves. During this time—seven days before and seven days after the winter solstice—Aeolus forbids the winds to blow. No clouds cover the sky; no rain falls; and Alcyone and Ceyx raise their young in perfect peace and tranquility.

These calm and clear days, which actually do occur in the Mediterranean region in winter, were named for Alcyone. We still use the expression *halcyon days* to refer to times of peace and contentment, especially those gone by, never to return again.

harpy: a shrewish or grasping person, especially a woman

Today, when we call someone a *harpy* we are delivering a terrible insult, comparing him or her to the hideous, vulturelike creatures of Greek mythology whose appearance was accompanied by a horrific stench. The term is most commonly used to mean an ill-tempered, shrewish woman, but it can also refer to any grasping person, male or female. It originated in the physical descriptions of Harpies left to us by Apollonius of Rhodes and, later, Virgil.

In the third century B.C., Apollonius wrote the *Argonautica,* chronicling the mythical quest for the Golden Fleece. In this work, the Harpies are depicted as flying monsters with the heads of women and the bodies of birds of prey. Jason and his men meet up with them as they are slowly starving the seer Phineus to death. Because Phineus angered Zeus, the Harpies were sent to swoop down on his food just as he was beginning to eat. Their name is related to the Greek verb meaning "to snatch," and that is what they did: They snatched most of Phineus's food and befouled the rest, so that he was unable to obtain any nourishment and was slowly wasting away. Calais and Zetes—the sons of the North Wind—pursue the Harpies and are about to kill them when Zeus's messenger, Iris, intercedes and promises they will no longer plague Phineus.

The *Aeneid,* written in the first century A.D., perpetuated this image of the Harpies as loathsome, stinking monsters, describing them as "birds with girls' countenances, and a disgusting outflow from their bellies." Before Apollonius and Virgil, however, the Harpies had none of these revolting characteristics. Generally numbered at two or three, they were said to be the daughters of the sea deities Thaumus and Electra, who were also the parents of Iris, goddess of the rainbow. In Homer, their connection with the forces of nature is very evident; Homer's Harpies are actually personifications of winds and storms, particularly at sea. In the *Iliad* one of them, Podarge (Swift-Foot), is said to have mated with the West Wind, Zephyrus, and given birth to Achilles' famous steeds. In the *Odyssey* they are believed to snatch people away and take them to the Underworld. E. V. Rieu translates their name as "Storm-Fiends" and "Demons of the Storm." Telemachus tells Athena that he believes they have spirited his father away (i.e., driven his ship off course and caused his death). Although not exactly benign in these early representations, the Harpies are a far cry from the disgusting creatures of Apollonius and Virgil, whose name has become synonymous with grasping, predatory behavior.

See also: argonaut

hector: bully; brag

As a verb, *hector* means to bully or to brag. When used as a noun, it refers to a bully or a swaggering, boastful person. Most scholars believe both forms come from the name of Hector, the Trojan prince who, King Priam says in the *Iliad,* "walked among us like a god and looked more like a god's son than a man's." Hector was, in fact, the bravest and noblest hero who fought for Troy. How, then, did his name take on such a negative connotation?

As in the case of another Trojan, Pandarus, whose name gave us the equally pejorative word *pander,* the metamorphosis seems to have been the work of authors who wrote long after Homer. Evidently, medieval dramatists portrayed Hector as a domineering, blustering figure—although no one knows exactly why—and the characterization stuck.

Another theory is that the noun and verb both come from the name of a gang of youths who terrorized London at the end of the seventeenth century. Considering themselves paragons of courage, they called themselves Hectors, after Hector of Troy, and proceeded to run rampant through the city, destroying property and bullying innocent bystanders. Their ignominious deeds, and not the heroic actions of the Trojan hero, are remembered in our modern-day use of the word *hector*.

hell: the place where sinners are punished after death; extreme misery

Jews, Christians, and Moslems all believe in hell—a place where sinners are punished after death. But the word *hell* is totally unrelated to Judeo-Christian theology or to Islam. It is derived from the name of the Norse goddess of death and, by extension, her realm.

The Norsemen believed that only those who died in battle went to dwell with the gods in Valhalla. The old, the infirm, cowards, and evildoers went to Niflheim, which was said to be located somewhere to the north of Midgard, the abode of the living. Like the Greek Underworld, Niflheim was a cold, gray, misty region, totally devoid of sunlight and cheer. It too was below ground, consisting of nine levels, with the lowermost reserved for those sinners who were doomed to suffer the worst torment.

The ruler of Niflheim was the goddess Hel, daughter of the evil god Loki and the giantess Angurboda. Odin gave her the land of the dead as her domain in order to keep her away from gods and men. She was a true hag, shrunken and pallid, covered with black-and-blue bruises. She dined on the bones of men and sat on an icy throne surrounded by filth and the smell of rotting flesh. Just as the Greek Underworld came to be called Hades after its ruler, Hel's name was eventually used to designate her kingdom. English translators of the Bible used it, interchangeably with the Greek Hades, whenever the Hebrew words *Sheol* and *Gehenna* appeared. The Arabic *Jahannan* was likewise referred to as hell by translators of the Koran.

Figuratively speaking, hell is any event, condition, place, or experience that makes us miserable or tortures us. The adjective *hellish* is used to describe such an event or place and is synonymous with *infernal*.

The entrance to Hel's realm was guarded by a huge, bloody-breasted dog named Garm. Like Hades' watchdog, Cerberus, Hel's snarling beast prevented living beings from passing through the gates to the Underworld. With these Greek and Norse canines in mind, the unflattering term *hellhound* was devised to describe an overly tenacious person, one who never gives up his pursuit of a cause or who persecutes others unmercifully.

See also: (give a sop to) Cerberus, (hot as) Hades, inferno, Valhalla

Herculean/herculean: of extraordinary strength or size; requiring such strength

Heracles is probably the best known of the Greek heroes. There are probably more stories about him than any other figure in Greek mythology. He is the prototype for the circus strong man, who wears a lion skin and carries a club just as Heracles did. He was an extremely popular character among the Romans, and his name, in the Latin form of Hercules, has become synonymous with extraordinary strength.

Heracles' mother, Alcmene, was the wife of Amphitryon, but she slept with Zeus and became pregnant by him, believing him to be her husband. Later that night she slept with the true Amphitryon and conceived a second child. The two, Heracles and Iphicles, grew up as brothers, but Zeus's son already showed signs of his enormous strength while he was in the cradle. When two snakes were put into the crib he shared with his brother—either by Hera to avenge Zeus's infidelity, or by Amphitryon to discover which child was his—Heracles immediately seized them and strangled them to death. He soon grew to be far bigger and stronger than most men—almost a giant—and throughout his life he continued to astound everyone with his physical prowess.

Amphitryon accepted the young giant and raised him as his

own, but Hera continued to take out her anger at Zeus on his illegitimate son. First she caused him to go mad and kill his wife and children. When he came to his senses, he was horrified by what he had done and sought some way to atone for his terrible deeds. Hera then arranged for him to be given the penance of performing twelve tasks for King Eurystheus. Each of these Labors of Hercules appeared, at first glance, to be impossible. Although the order in which the tasks were set out varies, they included: 1) slaying the Nemean Lion; 2) killing the many-headed Hydra; 3) capturing the Erymantian Boar; 4) capturing the Cerynean Hind; 5) driving off the Stymphalian Birds; 6) cleaning the Augean stables; 7) capturing the Cretan Bull; 8) killing the mares of Diomedes; 9) obtaining the girdle of Hippolyta; 10) fetching the cattle of Geryon; 11) gathering the Apples of the Hesperides; and 12) bringing Cerberus up from the Underworld.

Brute force was not enough to accomplish these seemingly impossible tasks, and Heracles had to utilize his ingenuity and cunning as well as his strength. The son of Zeus had plenty of both, and he succeeded in spite of Hera's ill will. In the end even she was forced to accept him on Mount Olympus, where his father rewarded him with immortality. The Labors to which he was so unfairly sentenced gave rise to the phrase *Herculean task* to denote a chore or project that requires all our resources. Although at the outset our chances of accomplishing such a task may seem slight, by following Heracles' example and giving our all, we just may be as successful as he was.

See also: Amphitryon, (clean the) Augean stables

hermaphrodite: one that has characteristics of both sexes

In ancient Greece the god Hermes was associated with virility and was often represented by a stone pillar with a phallus attached to it. Aphrodite, the goddess of love, was the epitome of feminine charm, inspiring sexual desire in all who beheld her. The fruit of their union, Hermaphroditus, was given both their names and their seductive powers as well. In one version of the myth, Hermaphroditus literally inherited both parents' physical attributes and was a double-sexed being. The more common tale, however, is that Hermaphroditus was born male. He possessed Hermes' virility and Aphrodite's beauty, and the combination was irresistible. One day he went swimming in a fountain that belonged to the nymph Salmacis. She immediately fell in love with him, and when he rejected her advances, she appealed to the gods. She prayed to be united with Hermaphroditus forever, and her prayers were answered: Their two bodies grew together, forming the first hermaphrodite.

Today, the word *hermaphrodite* is a biological term used to describe an individual who possesses both male and female reproductive organs. Hermaphroditism is common among invertebrates and some lower vertebrates, such as fish. Human hermaphrodites are rare, and one or both sets of their reproductive organs are nearly always imperfectly developed.

The adjectives *hermaphroditic* and *hermaphroditical* are sometimes used figuratively to describe the joining of two things of contrary nature, or two discordant elements that we would not normally associate with one another.

hermeneutic: interpretive; explanatory

According to the *Random House Dictionary,* the Greek word *hermeneus,* meaning "interpreter," comes from the name of the god Hermes. This makes sense, since Hermes was the Olympian chosen by Zeus to deliver his messages to the other gods and to mortals. As a mediator or go-between, Hermes would have had to listen to and interpret messages from both sides.

An English word that is related to the Greek *hermeneus* is *hermeneutics.* Used mostly among philosophers, theologians, and literary critics, it once meant strictly the interpretation of the Bible. Over the centuries, however, it has taken on a broader meaning and is now used to refer to the science or methodology of interpretation in general. By extension, the adjective *hermeneutic* has come to mean interpretive or explanatory.

hermetic: magical; occult; airtight

Ibis-headed Thoth was revered by the Egyptians as the god of knowledge. Often represented as a scribe, he was believed to have given man numbers and hieroglyphs. At the ceremony of the weighing of the heart after death, it was Thoth who recorded the verdict that sent the deceased to his proper place in the afterlife. In Greek mythology, Hermes was the god who conducted souls to the judges of the Underworld, which may be why the Greeks identified him with Thoth. In later classical times, Hermes Trimegistus (thrice greatest) was the name the Greeks gave to the Egyptian Thoth. They too credited him with giving mankind arithmetic and writing, and with being the first magician.

There was a cult of Hermes Trimegistus that flourished well into the Middle Ages. Various Hermetic Writings—treatises on magic and the occult—were attributed to him and passed down through the centuries, particularly by alchemists. The adjective *hermetic* came to mean "pertaining to magic or the occult sciences." It was also used to describe the airtight seals alchemists put on the jars that contained their mysterious concoctions. Such seals were formed by fusing the glass together under high heat and could be undone only by breaking the jar. Today, when we say something is *hermetically* sealed we mean it is impervious to all outside contaminants.

hero: a person of great courage who performs noble deeds; a protagonist

Our word *hero* comes from the Greek *heros*. The heroes of the *Iliad* and *Odyssey* were men of superhuman strength, courage, or ability who were favored by the gods. Many were, in fact, demigods: beings born of the union between a god and a mortal, a separate race that figured somewhere between men and the gods in the hierarchy of beings.

According to Hesiod's *Works and Days,* there was actually a time when all men were heroes. After the vicious and stupid men of the Bronze Age brought about their own extinction, a new, superior race came into being. They were the men of the Heroic Age, and they lived in complete harmony with nature and the gods. Their offspring, however, fell from grace. Hesiod believed that the men of his own time—the Iron Age—were doomed to lives of toil and sorrow because they no longer possessed the bravery and integrity of the earlier heroes.

Among the legendary heroes of Greece were Achilles, Perseus, and—greatest of all—Heracles. These three were demigods, possessed of great strength and cunning, and many Greek myths deal with their superhuman exploits. Also considered heroes in the more modern sense were Jason and Odysseus, protagonists of the *Argonautica* and the *Odyssey,* respectively. They were mortals who undertook great adventures and exhibited extraordinary courage in the face of danger.

With the exploits of these legendary figures in mind, we use the term *hero* for someone who performs acts of great courage. The adjective *heroic* is also applied to such people and their deeds. In a looser sense, the protagonist of a literary work or the central character in a drama, with whom we are meant to identify or sympathize, is referred to as its hero.

(search for the) Holy Grail: go after an unattainable goal; be on an idealistic quest

If ever there was, in the words of Winston Churchill, "a riddle wrapped in a mystery inside an enigma," it is the origin of the Holy Grail. Entire volumes have been written on the subject, tracing the symbol of the Grail back to ancient Babylonian and Greek fertility rites, to early Christian theology, or to the magical vessels of Bran and other Celtic gods and heroes. Whatever its origins, the Holy Grail has become a symbol for an unattainable goal, and when one "searches for the Holy Grail" one is likely to be unsuccessful, as were most of the knights of King Arthur's Round Table.

Although the legendary King Arthur and his retinue appear

in poems going back as far as the tenth century, the first mention of the Holy Grail in Arthurian legend dates back only to 1180, when French author Chrétien de Troyes composed *Le Conte del Graal.* The hero of his tale is Perceval, a young Welshman who, on his way home from Arthur's court, meets up with a fisherman. Invited to dine at the man's castle, Perceval watches as a squire enters the room carrying a lance that drips blood. Later, a beautiful maiden enters carrying the Grail, a golden cup set with brilliant jewels. Although the Grail passes before him several times and arouses his curiosity, Perceval does not ask any questions about it and leaves the next morning, his curiosity unsatisfied. He meets another maiden who tells him he has just left the castle of the wounded Fisher King, and if he had asked about the lance and the Grail, the king's wounds would have been healed. Stricken with guilt over his failure to help the Fisher King, Perceval vows to go in search of the Grail and discover the answers to the questions he failed to ask the first time. The rest of the story, which Chrétien never finished, relates Perceval's adventures over the next five years. Perceval never finds the Grail, but he eventually meets a hermit who tells him it contained the sacred Host. He receives communion and is welcomed back into Christ's fold.

Later stories about the Grail contain even more Christian iconography and place strong emphasis on Christian values. In the sequels to Chrétien's story it is explained that the bleeding lance is the sword that pierced the side of Christ as he hung on the cross. The Grail is the chalice out of which Christ and his Apostles drank at the Last Supper, and which Joseph of Arimathea later held up to catch Christ's blood. Tales of the Holy Grail proliferated in England and France, and in them several knights of the Round Table undertook the quest for the Holy Grail. Most of the stories recount that Lancelot, because of his adultery with Queen Guinevere, was unsuccessful in his search. In the *Queste del Saint Graal,* however, when Lancelot repents his sin and promises to renounce Guinevere, he finds the Grail castle and is allowed one glimpse of the holy vessel. Arthur's nephew, Gawain, is another knight who goes after the Grail but fails in his quest; although he is a noble warrior and a model of chivalry, he is far too worldly to win this spiritual prize. Only Galahad, the son of Lancelot and the daughter of the keeper of the Grail castle, is sufficiently pure to find the Grail. After his mystical experience he no longer wishes to live and is taken up to heaven with the Holy Grail. No man has seen the Holy Grail since, although many have sought it and many others continue to do so—even if only in a figure of speech.

See also: (Sir) Galahad

Holy moly!: an exclamation of surprise

The exclamation *Holy moly!* is often used to express surprise and shock. But what is moly, and why is it holy?

Some of the answers can be found in Book 10 of Homer's *Odyssey*. After Odysseus's men are fed a magic potion and turned into swine by the enchantress Circe, he is determined to rescue them. With no idea how he will accomplish his task, he sets out alone for Circe's castle. Just before reaching his destination he is greeted by the god Hermes, who offers him a magical plant that will render Circe's potions harmless. Called moly by the gods, it has a black root and a milk-white flower. Homer adds that it is difficult for a mere mortal to dig up, but the gods—who can do anything—pluck it with ease. Protected by this gift from the Olympians, Odysseus is able to dine with Circe and not fall under her spell. He makes her turn his companions back into men, and they are able to resume their long journey home.

Over the centuries scholars have attempted to identify Homer's moly with many real-life plants, but none has been able to make a definitive case for one over another. At some point, however, the association of this mythical herb with the holy gods inspired a clever speaker of English to make up the wonderful rhyming phrase *Holy moly!* to express his incredulity.

See also: Circean

hurricane: a tropical storm accompanied by high winds; a large social event

The Quiché were a Mayan tribe who inhabited southern Guatemala, and the *Popol Vuh,* written in the Quiché language, preserves their history and legends. Among the gods worshiped by the Maya was Hurakán, who was instrumental in the creation of the universe. The *Popol Vuh* relates how the world began as a watery waste, over which Hurakán passed in the form of a mighty wind. He whispered the word for "earth," and a solid mass rose out of the waters.

Although he took part in the Creation, Hurakán was also a destructive god. Because the first inhabitants of the earth were imperfect, he sent a flood to wipe them out and then replaced them with four perfect men. As the god of thunder and lightning, Hurakán was greatly feared. The now-extinct aborigines of the West Indies and Bahamas, the Taínos, called the evil spirit that brought tropical storms a *hurricán.* To the Galibi or Carib Indians the word *hyorocan* meant "devil."

The Spanish borrowed these names of West Indian gods to create the word *huracán,* which they used to describe the storms they encountered in the New World. Our English word *hurricane* comes from the Spanish and designates a cyclone that is accompanied by rain, thunder, lightning, and gale-force winds. In a figurative sense, the word is occasionally used to describe a large, crowded social event: a veritable whirlwind of human activity.

hydra-headed: hard to eliminate; multifarious

Sometimes we find that no matter how hard we try, we can't get our problems under control. No sooner do we resolve one concern than a new problem presents itself. We solve that, and another crops up. And so it continues, *ad infinitum.* Such a situation is aptly called *hydra-headed,* after the Hydra of Greek mythology.

The Hydra was one of the monstrous offspring of Typhon and Echidna. As its name indicates, it made its home in the water, haunting the lake or swamp of Lerna. Its blood was poison; even its breath and the scent it left in its tracks were fatal to any who came in contact with them. It had a doglike body and, by most accounts, nine heads. As one of his Labors, Heracles was sent to slay the ferocious beast. Ovid says he tried to cut off its heads; other storytellers say he tried to crush them with his club. All his efforts were futile, however, for each time a head was destroyed two more grew back in its place. Finally, the hero used the ingenuity for which he was famous to come up with a novel solution to his dilemma: He had his charioteer, Iolaus, sear the flesh at the base of each head as he cut it off. The burned flesh could not regenerate, and Heracles had only to cut off the Hydra's center head, which was the seat of its mortality, to end its reign of terror. While the head was still hissing he buried it under a heavy rock and proceeded to disembowel the creature.

Besides referring to something that continues to plague us in spite of all our efforts to eliminate it, the expression *hydra-headed* is also used, nonjudgmentally, to mean diverse or multifarious, having many parts or elements.

See also: hydra (under "Animals"), Hydra (under "Constellations")

hygiene: *See: panacea*

hymeneal: relating to marriage

The refrain of the song sung at weddings in ancient Greece was "Hymen, O Hymenaeus." The Greek god of marriage and protector of virgins was Hymen, who was also known as Hymenaeus. All the myths about him seem to be attempts to explain how his name came to be invoked during the marriage ceremony.

Some legends say that Hymen was the son of Apollo and one of the Muses, but in other tales Dionysus and Aphrodite are named as his parents. Hymen had the misfortune to fall in love with a young girl whose parents opposed the match. In order to be with her, he disguised himself as a female and followed her to Eleusis, where the rites of Demeter were celebrated. His disguise must have been very convincing: When a group of ruffians kidnapped his beloved and several other young women, they abducted Hymen as well. But before they could harm the maidens, Hymen revealed himself and slew the culprits. His beloved's parents were so grateful they gave her to him in marriage. From that day on, in honor of Hymen's championship of the young ladies and his happy marriage, all wedding songs were dedicated to him. The term *hymeneal rites* is now a synonym for the marriage ceremony.

The story of Hymen is really an allegory. The Greek word *hymen* means "skin" or "membrane" and is still the term we use for the virginal membrane. Before a young woman's marriage, Hymen protected her from men who tried to force themselves on her. When she married, her virginity—her hymen—was dedicated to the god of the same name, who was invoked to watch over and bless the event that marked a turning point in her life.

hyperborean: very far north; frigid

Our use of the adjective *hyperborean* to describe a frigid northerly climate is a good example of how, over time, a word can lose its original meaning and, as in this case, even come to mean the exact opposite.

Hyperborean means "beyond Boreas." Boreas was the Greek god of the north wind, whose icy breath was believed to bring frigid weather to northerly countries. But even when he blew with all his might, Boreas couldn't bring winter to those lands that lay on the other side of Oceanus. According to the Greeks, Oceanus was the river that encircled the known world, and on its far banks were found the gloomy home of the Cimmerians, the island home of the Muses, and the entrance to the Underworld. The land of the Hyperboreans was also on the other side of Oceanus. Its inhabitants lived to be one thousand years old and were never troubled by sickness or old age; when they were ready to die they simply decked themselves with garlands and threw themselves into the sea. Because it was beyond the reach of the bitter-cold north wind, the climate of the Hyperboreans' home was one of eternal summer. It was so warm and sunny that Apollo chose to winter there, leaving chilly Mount Parnassus to take up residence in this tropical paradise.

Through the centuries, however, these delightful stories about the land of the Hyperboreans were forgotten, and all that was remembered was that it was located in the far north. To those unfamiliar with the Greek myths, that could only mean one thing: It was cold. The adjective *hyperborean* came to be applied to places that are very far north and, therefore, have an arctic climate.

Hyperion to a satyr: so superior that there is no comparison

Hamlet, comparing his dead father to his uncle Claudius, says the former was "so excellent a king; that was, to this, Hyperion to a satyr. . . ." In these lines, as in so much of his work, Shakespeare's reference is to classical mythology.

Hyperion was one of the Greek Titans who ruled heaven and earth before the Olympians overthrew them. His name meant "dweller on high," and he was father of the sun, the moon, and the dawn. Because he ruled over the sun (his child, Helios), the two were sometimes confused, and the myths impart to both father and son great splendor and majesty.

A satyr, by contrast, was a repugnant creature who hid in the sunless woods by day and caroused there at night. Like Pan, whom they worshiped, the satyrs were half man and half goat, and they were known for their debauchery. No creature could be farther removed from the sublime ruler of the sun!

Hence Shakespeare's—and our—use of these contrasting images to underscore the difference between two people, one of whom is so superior there really are no grounds for comparison.

See also: satyr

I

Icarian: overly daring; foolhardy; rash

Icarus was the son of the mythical Greek inventor Daedalus. The two were living on Crete, at the court of King Minos, when Daedalus fell out of favor with the monarch. They managed to escape from the labyrinth in which Minos had imprisoned them, but they were hunted men on a small island. All ships putting out to sea were searched, so that avenue of escape was closed to them. Their capture seemed inevitable when a brilliant idea came to Daedalus: If they could fly, they could escape by air, and no one would be able to catch them. He set about constructing two sets of wings, made of feathers held in place by wax. Before taking off, Daedalus warned his son not to fly too close to the sun, lest its heat melt the wax.

Then they took off together, soaring to the northeast, and all who gazed up at them believed they were gods. Giddy with the sensation of flight and the newfound feeling of power, Icarus flapped his wings harder and harder and flew higher and higher. Daedalus lost sight of him for a while and then, looking down, saw the feathers floating on the sea. . . .

The ancient Greeks called the part of the Aegean that lies to the northeast of Crete the Icarian Sea, and the small island where Daedalus was said to have buried his son's remains still bears the name Icaria. The English adjective *Icarian* was also coined in memory of Icarus's one and only flight. It means foolhardy or rash—too daring—as Icarus was when he allowed himself to be carried away by his sense of power and flew to his doom.

See also: Daedalian

incubus: a handicapping burden; a nightmare

The people of medieval Europe greatly feared night demons. They believed such spirits visited humans while they slept, with evil intentions. A female night demon was called a succubus, meaning "one who lies underneath," and these lascivious fiends found sexual satisfaction with sleeping men. (The Latin word for a whore or strumpet was *succuba,* so evidently human women of the night were not thought to be very different from their demonic counterparts.)

The name given to a male demon of the night was incubus, from the Latin verb *incubare* (to lie upon). Incubi, it was said, came to the beds of sleeping women and had intercourse with them. If a female was impregnated by an incubus, she gave birth to a witch. The Anglo-Saxons also believed in the *mara incubus,* a spirit that sat on people's chests, causing them to have bad dreams. *Mara* evolved into *mare,* the second syllable of our modern English word *nightmare,* which means literally "night demon."

The idea that an incubus lay on top of people gave rise to the figurative use of the word in English. Today, a person or situation that is a burden on us, weighing us down, is referred to as an *incubus.* It's just another, more erudite way of saying we've got a monkey on our back!

inferno: a hellish place; a place of intense heat

To the Romans, a Towering Inferno would have been a contradiction in terms. The Latin noun *infernus* meant "that which is lower or beneath," not that which rises up. And what was beneath, in Roman mythology, was the Underworld or abode of the dead.

Like the Greeks before them, the Romans believed that the souls of the dead went to an afterworld. The location of this place was generally believed to be deep within the earth, and consequently it was a cold, shadowy realm. All souls, good or bad, passed into the Underworld after death. While some sinners were punished in the Greek and Roman Underworld, it was Christianity that introduced the concept of two clearly separated abodes of the dead: heaven and hell. In Christian theology, those who had led virtuous lives went up to heaven, where they spent eternity in the presence of their maker. Evildoers, on the other hand, were cast down into hell, where they were punished for their misdeeds. The Italians used the word *inferno,* which they had derived from the Latin *infernus,* for this latter place.

With Christianity came another idea: that the damned were punished by fire. The infernal regions, therefore, came to be thought of as a place of intense heat, where sinners burned for eternity. That is why we refer to a blazing fire or any place of intense heat as an *inferno.*

We also use the adjective *infernal* to describe something hellish, which brings to mind the torments of the damned in the world below.

See also: (hot as) Hades, hell

iridescent: shining; reflecting many colors

An iridescent object shines with all the colors of the rainbow. Its hues change constantly and rapidly, as light moves over it or as we look at it from different angles. In these respects it resembles Iris, the swift-moving goddess who personified the rainbow in Greek mythology and whose name is the root of the word *iridescent.*

Like Aurora, who rode across the sky bringing light to the world, Iris often traveled through the heavens, taking an arched path as she went. Perhaps the most beautiful description we have of her is that written by Ovid, who says, "She slipped on her cloak / And in that thin embrace of shining colours / She was a rainbow fleeting through the skies."

In the *Iliad,* Iris serves as Zeus's messenger and is variously called "Wind-swift Iris of the Fleet Foot," "Iris of the Whirlwind Feet," and "Iris of the Golden Wings." Greek artists portrayed her as a young woman with wings who, like Hermes, carried a messenger's wand. In the *Odyssey* she and Hermes share courier duties, and in later myths she becomes Hera's principal emissary.

The colored portion of the eye, which catches and reflects light, is also named for the shimmering goddess of the Greeks.

See also: iridium (under "Elements"), iris (under "Plants")

J

Janus-faced: deceitful; duplicitous

A person—or a god—would need to have eyes in the back of his head to be able to stand in a doorway and see what was going on inside and outside at the same time. That, literally, is what the Romans believed the god Janus had—and could do.

Janus was thought to live in and watch over every door, gate, and passageway in the land. He was able to accomplish this seemingly impossible task because he not only had eyes in the back of his head, but actually had two heads! Janus *bifrons* (two-faced) is represented on many Roman coins, his heads facing in opposite directions. Latin texts also occasionally mention Janus *quadrifons* (four-faced)—the same deity with four faces, who was able to guard gateways located at intersections, where traffic came from four directions.

The Latin word for a ceremonial arch *(janus)* derives from the god's name, as does the word for a door *(janua)*. Our English word *janitor,* originally a doorkeeper, comes from the latter. The most famous temple of Janus was located in Rome, on the north side of the Forum. The temple was aligned east and west, where the day begins and ends, since Janus was also the god of beginnings and endings. It was a simple rectangular building with double doors at each end. The doors were closed only in times of peace. When Rome was at war—which was almost always—they were kept open, possibly so Janus could keep his vigil.

Janus had no reputation for double dealing or being anything less than noble, and originally the expression *Janus-faced* may have meant "vigilant." Nowadays, however, like *two-faced,* it is used strictly in a pejorative fashion, implying that a person is hiding his true nature, showing us one side of himself while concealing the other.

See also: January (under "Months")

(by) Jiminy!: an expression of surprise; a mild, euphemistic oath

The most famous pair of twins in Greek mythology were not really twins at all. According to most of the myths, they were half-brothers, the sons of Leda by different fathers. Zeus was the father of Polydeuces, and Leda's husband, King Tyndareus of Sparta sired Castor. The two boys were, however, as close as real twins and were inseparable in life and in death. The Romans called them Castor and Pollux, or simply *Gemini*—the Latin word meaning "twins."

In ancient Rome one swore by the gods, and the Romans took many oaths "by Gemini." In a corrupted form, the oath "by Jiminy" is still used in the English language. Nowadays it is used mostly as an exclamation or an expression of surprise.

See also: Gemini (under "Constellations")

jovial: merry; jolly

In prehistoric times, Indo-European practitioners of the Vedic religions worshiped Mother Earth and Father Sky. In Sanskrit the latter was called *Dyaus-pitr*, "light" or "sky" plus "father." Those Indo-European peoples who migrated to the Italian penins brought the worship of this ancient god with them. There, the first syllable of his name evolved into Jove and his full name became Jupiter. Jupiter/Jove was the supreme god in the Roman pantheon. When the Greek gods were introduced into the Roman Empire, he became associated with Zeus, whose name and origins also go back to their common Indo-European ancestor. (Dyaus-pitr became *Zeus pater,* then simply Zeus to the peoples who migrated to what is now Greece. This same god traveled to the Scandinavian and Germanic lands, where he was called Tiw and Tyr.)

Dyaus-pitr, under all these names, was a god of the sky and that which emanated from it: light, rain, thunder, lightning, etc. In Italy, Jupiter was believed to bring rain. In times of drought, offerings were made to him in the temple of Jupiter Pluvius, so that he would bless Rome with his life-giving water. He was also Jupiter Fulgur, god of lightning, and Jupiter To-nans, god of thunder. Both these natural phenomena were interpreted as signs of his will. As Jupiter Lucetius he was the bringer of light, and the expression *sub Jove* meant "under the open sky." Jupiter was also the protecting deity of Rome and the god of oaths and treaties. In the latter aspect he repre-sented man's solemn vows and conscience.

All in all, Jupiter/Jove was a stern figure, not much given to merriment. Why, then, has his name given us the adjective *jovial,* meaning merry and cheerful? The answer is that the Latin adjective *Jovialis,* which meant "of or relating to Jupiter," referred to Jupiter the planet rather than Jupiter the god. Jupiter was the largest of the planets known to ancient man, and Roman astronomers named it after the great god of the sky. Astrologers then, as now, believed that the planets exer-cised great influence over men's characters and the events in their lives. They calculated that those born under the planet Jupiter were destined to be happy and cheerful, hence the use of the word *Jovialis* to describe such people. Jovialis became *jovial* in English and retained this astrological association.

The name of the ancient Italian god of the sky also shows up in a couple of mild expletives that have pretty much gone out of fashion nowadays but were once quite common. "By Jupi-ter!" and "By Jove!" were popular euphemisms for "By God!" in Victorian times. Using the Lord's name was considered blasphemy, but the taboo obviously didn't extend to the names of pagan gods. So Jupiter/Jove became a convenient substitute, just as saying "Egad!" was permissible while "Oh, God!" was not.

See also: Jupiter (under "Planets")

judgment of Paris: *See: throw the apple of discord*

juggernaut: an inexorable force; something that enslaves us

The Hindus view Vishnu as a benevolent deity and were shocked when the name of his image entered the English language as a synonym for an inexorable force that crushes everything in its path.

To us, a juggernaut is any institution or practice to which we are blindly enslaved and which we allow to take over our lives. The word is an Anglicization of the Hindustani *Jagannath,* which, in turn, comes from the Sanskrit *Jagannatha,* meaning "lord of the world." The Jagannath is a large wooden image of Vishnu that is kept in the temple at Puri in northeastern India. The statue is tended with great ceremony and is bathed, clothed, and "fed" by special servants. There are various legends surrounding the origin of the wooden image: that it was discovered and secretly worshiped by a Savara hillsman; that King Indrayumna was told to have it fashioned and to place the bones of Krishna inside it; that the same king was told that the wood for the statue would rise out of the sea and take a certain form, which he was then to place in the temple and worship; etc.

Each year, in June or July, the huge statue is hoisted onto a wheeled cart and dragged through the streets of Puri to the god's "summer home." As early as the fourteenth century, European onlookers at this procession claimed to have seen worshipers of the Jagannath purposely throw themselves under the wheels of the cart in a frenzy of devotion. In the erroneous belief that this martyrdom was sanctioned by the Hindu faith, the Europeans came to view the Jagannath as a cruel, inexorable god and to use its name as a metaphor for a destructive force that people follow blindly.

We now know that the deliberate shedding of blood in the name of Vishnu is viewed by the Hindus as a sacrilege and was never an accepted part of his cult. The deaths that occurred must, therefore, have been accidental or the acts of a few unbalanced individuals. Unfortunately, by the time this knowledge reached Europe, the term *juggernaut* was firmly entrenched in our language, carrying with it implications of cruelty and inhumanity totally absent in Hinduism.

Junoesque: statuesque and regal

Juno was the Roman queen of the heavens and the wife of the supreme god, Jupiter. Although she occupied the same place in the Roman pantheon as Hera did in the Greek, the two goddesses could not have been more different in character. The Greek myths are full of stories in which the jealous Hera takes revenge on Zeus's paramours and their innocent offspring. The Greeks said that Hera and Athena caused the Trojan War because Paris did not judge them to be as beautiful as Aphrodite. Virgil and other Romans who retold the Greek myths continued to portray the goddess as petty, vengeful, jealous, and conceited. But the Juno who was worshiped by the indigenous Italians long before the Hellenization of Rome was a totally different goddess; she was truly Juno Regina—Juno the Queen.

A very ancient goddess, originally associated with the moon and fertility, Juno remained the protectress of women in labor. In this aspect she was called Juno Lucina or Juno Sospita and was said to be present at every birth. As Juno Pronuba, she presided over betrothal ceremonies and was the patroness of married women. The Matronalia, or festival of married women, was celebrated in her temple. She was also the goddess of the home (Juno Domiduea), and newlyweds were led to their domicile by her priests.

In all of these roles, Juno had a dignity and queenliness never possessed by the Greek Hera. Out of reverence for her, a statuesque, regal woman was called *Junoesque,* and the epithet remains in use in our language today.

See also: money

(by) Jupiter!, (by) Jove!: *See: jovial*

K

karma: fate, destiny; the vibrations a person gives off

Both Hindus and Buddhists believe in reincarnation. They contend that living things are born and reborn, time after time, until they reach enlightenment (Nirvana) and are freed from the cycle of rebirth. They carry their deeds and experiences from each incarnation with them through their many lives. This is called karma, from the Sanskrit *karman,* meaning "deed" or "action." Since one's acts determine what one will be in the next life, karma is essentially a concept of causality. One's destiny depends on one's karma.

In the 1960s, with the growth of interest in Eastern religion and philosophy, the word *karma* was popularized in American English. Confusing the deeds one does with their results, people began using the word as a general term for fate or destiny. They also said someone had good karma or bad karma, meaning the impression he or she gave was positive or negative. At a time when many were interested in the concept of auras—different-colored lights that emanated from a person's body and reflected their inner state of mind or soul—*karma* was often used interchangeably with *aura* to denote the effect we have on other people: the "vibes" we give off.

See also: nirvana

L

labyrinth: a maze; a complicated, perplexing arrangement

The original labyrinth was the creation of the mythical Greek inventor Daedalus. Built to contain the Minotaur—a monster that was half man and half bull—it was a masterpiece of confusion. So twisted and convoluted were its intricate passageways that, once inside, it was impossible to retrace one's steps to the entrance. This ingenious prison proved to be equally escape-proof for the man-eating Minotaur and the young Athenians whom Minos sacrificed to it. Trapped in the maze, these innocent victims ran up and down its passageways, searching in vain for the way out, until they inevitably encountered the hungry beast and were devoured.

This was the state of affairs on Crete when the great hero Theseus arrived. When he and other young Athenians were left inside the labyrinth, their deaths seemed assured. Theseus, however, had received a ball of thread from Minos's daughter, and by attaching it to the door and unraveling the skein as he penetrated the maze, he was able to sneak up on and slay the monster, then retrace his steps to freedom.

Thereafter, the term *labyrinth* began to be applied to anything of great intricacy or complexity—literally in such structures as the inner ear (in which we sometimes develop the disease *labyrinthitis*) and figuratively, as in the "labyrinth of human thought." The adjective *labyrinthine* is also applied to anything of great intricacy and complexity, in which it is easy to become lost.

See also: clue, Daedalian

lares and penates: personal or household effects

In many societies it is the norm for several generations to live together under one roof in an extended family, but the Romans went one step further: Their extended families included the dead. For centuries the dead were buried in their own homes, until this practice was forbidden by law. But even if their loved ones' bodies were not present, the Romans believed the spirits of their departed relations remained in the home, watching over the living and taking part in their activities. These spirits were called Lares, and each family had an ancestral Lar, which was represented by one or two small statues that were dressed and displayed on the household altar. Offerings of food and drink were made to the Lar at every meal, and it was regularly consulted on matters of importance to the family.

Roman religion also included the worship of Penates—gods of the food cupboard. They were believed to guard the household stores and, hence, insure the family's prosperity.

From this devotion of the Romans to their household gods we have adopted the term *lares and penates* to denote our most treasured possessions. No Roman would ever have moved and left behind his Lares—the ancestors who made him what he was—and today we hire huge moving vans to transport the objects with which we create a sense of self in *our* domiciles. And, while we may be quick to scoff at the Romans' "naive" belief that the Penates brought prosperity to a home, how many of us keep good-luck charms on the shelves and in the closets of our abodes?

(be covered with) laurels: receive honors or recognition

In ancient Greece and Rome, military heroes and the winners of competitions—in poetry, singing, athletics, etc.—were all crowned with wreaths made of laurel leaves. In time, a myth was made up to account for the origin of this custom. Although its characters are Greek, the tale has come down to us through the Roman poet Ovid, who tells it beautifully.

It seems that the river god Peneus had a beautiful daughter named Daphne. She was a mountain nymph and was dedicated to Artemis, the virgin goddess. When her beauty aroused the young Apollo, causing him to fall in love for the first time, her vows of chastity meant nothing to him. He had to possess her. He pursued the girl through the woods, and as he closed in, she prayed to her father to save her from his sacrilegious assault. Peneus did so, transforming her into a laurel tree. A sad Apollo embraced its trunk and declared that henceforth it would be his favorite tree and its leaves would stay forever green. He then made the laurel's leaves into a crown that he wore in memory of his unrequited first love.

Although trophies and medals have replaced laurel wreaths as prizes nowadays, we still say that someone is "covered with laurels" or "wears laurels" when he or she is recognized or honored by others for outstanding achievements.

This popular tale also brought about the creation of the adjective *Daphnean,* which means bashful or shy. This meaning isn't exactly in keeping with the original myth. In fact, Daphne ran from Apollo not because she was shy, but because she had dedicated her life—and her virginity—to Artemis.

leprechaun/leprecaun: a small male fairy, symbol of treasure and trickery

In Irish legend, a leprechaun was a fairylike being ranging in size from a few inches tall to the height of a small child. The origin of the word *leprechaun* is uncertain. In 1850 Thomas Keighley, in *The Fairy Mythology,* said it came from the English *lubberkin,* an Elizabethan name for a fairy, but the fifteenth-century tale of Iubdan already tells of the "king of the Lupracan." Later etymologists, including Funk and Wagnalls, trace the word back to the Old Irish *lu-chorpan,* meaning "little body."

However they got their name, leprechauns were solitary creatures, who spent their time making shoes. They were usually depicted wearing cobbler's aprons and carrying hammers.

In fact, it was usually the sound of their hammering that gave away their whereabouts to the greedy humans who were constantly on the lookout for them.

It wasn't their shoes people were after, however; it was their gold. Each leprechaun was believed to possess a pot of gold, which he kept carefully hidden. If a person could capture one, he could be forced to tell where he kept his treasure, but one had to be craftier than he. The little man would try all kinds of tricks to distract his captor, such as telling him his bees were swarming and going off or his cows were getting into the oats. If the gullible human took his eyes off the leprechaun for a second, the latter would vanish, along with the knowledge of his treasure's whereabouts.

While the name of this creature hasn't taken on any figurative or metaphoric meaning in English, we include it because the leprechaun has become one of the popular symbols of Irish culture and is so often represented in popular art and decoration, especially around St. Patrick's Day.

See also: Brownie, fairyland, pixie-led

lethargy: the state of being lazy, sluggish, or indifferent

The ancient Greeks believed in the reincarnation of souls, and they had an interesting way of explaining why, when we are reborn, we have no memory of our past lives.

In Greek mythology the Underworld, or abode of the dead, was separated from the world of the living by five rivers. One of these was Lethe, the river of forgetfulness. Before a soul could go back to the upper regions and be born again, it had to drink the waters of Lethe, which wiped out all recollection of past events. The Greek myths give very few details about the Underworld, and it was the Roman poet Virgil who painted the most vivid picture of Lethe's banks, teeming with countless souls waiting their turn to drink and be reborn. Virgil's imagery gave rise to the Latin word *lethargia,* meaning morbid drowsiness and forgetfulness. This was transformed, through Old

French, into the English word *lethargy,* which now also has the broader meaning of indifference or apathy. The adjective *lethargic* describes someone who cannot rouse himself to action—whose brain has been emptied, as if by drinking from the river Lethe.

Another, less common adjective that comes from the name of the underground river is *Lethean:* causing or inducing forgetfulness.

See also: lotus-eater

(a) look that could turn you to stone: an angry, discomforting stare

Have you ever made someone so angry that they gave you "a look that could turn you to stone"? Such a look disturbs us and makes us feel very uncomfortable but, being only a figure of speech, usually isn't fatal. It would be, though, if it were the glare of one of the Gorgons of Greek mythology.

The Gorgons were three sisters: Stheno, Euryale, and Medusa. They had once been beautiful women, but Medusa incurred the wrath of Athena when she lay with Poseidon in one of the goddess's temples. Athena took revenge by turning all three Gorgons into terrifying monsters. She covered their skin with scales; gave them long, tusklike teeth; made their hands into brass; and filled their hair with writhing snakes. Not only were they hideous, but they were dangerous as well: Anyone whose eyes met theirs was instantly, irreversibly turned into cold, lifeless stone. Stheno and Euryale were immortal, but Medusa was not, and the hero Perseus, with the help of Athena and Hermes, finally succeeded in beheading her. Afterward, Athena placed Medusa's veiled head on Zeus's aegis. When she went into battle she unveiled it, allowing its still-powerful glance to permanently immobilize her enemies.

Today, the word *gorgon* is used as a synonym for a very ugly or frightening person—especially a woman—in much the same way that we use the names of those other female Greek monsters, the Furies and the Harpies.

See also: medusa (under "Animals")

Lorelei: *See: siren*

lotus-eater/lotos-eater: an indolent person; a daydreamer

The lotus of Greek mythology was a plant that wiped out all memories in those who consumed it. Their minds emptied of the past, they lived only for the present—a present they were content to while away in carefree indolence. The Lotus-eaters first appeared in Homer's *Odyssey,* when three of Odysseus's crew tasted the "honeyed fruit" and promptly "forgot that they had a home to return to." Odysseus had to drag them away and set sail as fast as he could, for fear more of his men would taste the fruit and fall under its spell.

As has occurred so often in the evolution of myths, later storytellers embellished greatly on the little that Homer had to say about the Lotus-eaters. Because one or two edible plants known to the Greeks as *lotos* grew in northern Africa, Scylax, Herodotus, and other writers claimed that was the home of the Lotus-eaters. Very specific locations, such as "a promontory in western Libya," were given for this mythical land. Homer's simple lotos was described in great detail as a "stoneless, saf-fron-colored fruit about the size of a bean, growing in sweet and wholesome clusters" or "a kind of apple from which a heavy cider is brewed." Pliny maintained that the fruit in question was the *Cordia myxa,* or sour plum, which grows in northern Africa.

While all these embellishments are entertaining and intrigu-ing, it is from Homer's original, brief description of the Lotus-eaters that we have adopted the metaphoric use of their name. A *lotus-eater,* in modern parlance, is someone who has no ambition and wants only to daydream his life away. Likewise, *lotusland* is a metaphor for a state of indolence or dreamy inactivity, such as the one experienced by Odysseus's three men after tasting the fabled fruit.

lunatic: a deranged person

Nowadays, when people around us are behaving strangely, we say jokingly that "there must be a full moon." Ancient civilizations, however, took the power of the moon very seriously. The moon was personified as a goddess by both the Greeks and the Romans, among others. Her Latin name was Luna, and it was believed that she induced spells of madness in those who angered or offended her. Hence, a *lunaticus* was a person who was being punished by the goddess.

This concept of divine retribution is behind the English words *lunatic* and *lunacy* and the expression *moonstruck*— smitten by the goddess of the moon.

lycanthropy: *See: werewolf*

M

magic wand: a stick or cane waved in magic acts

A magic wand is an important part of every magician's act: He waves it over a hat and pulls out a rabbit; he passes it over a plain piece of cloth and the cloth is transformed into a bouquet of colorful flowers. The magician's prop is, however, only the most recent of a long line of rods and staffs to which people have attributed supernatural power.

The Book of Exodus relates how Moses waved his staff over the Red Sea, parting its waters so the Israelites could come out of Egypt. Mesopotamian priests, magicians, and healers all carried staffs, and it is very likely that Moses' rod was modeled on these. The Egyptian gods and pharaohs were nearly always portrayed carrying some kind of stick or stave: papyrus scepters, the royal crook-scepter, the uas. According to some Greek myths, the god Hermes possessed two extraordinary wands. The first was his herald's staff, given to him by Zeus so all men and gods would recognize him as the great god's messenger. (Confused with the serpent-entwined staff of the healer Asclepius, it became the caduceus that now symbolizes the medical profession.) The second was the golden rod Apollo gave to him in exchange for one of the musical instruments he invented. Apollo had used it to herd his cattle, and in the hands of Hermes it was reputed to calm human passions and make men more rational. Another magic wand of Greek mythology was that of Circe, the enchantress of the *Odyssey,* who struck Odysseus's men with it as she turned them into swine.

Another type of magic stick, the divining rod, has been used for centuries. The ancient Medes, Persians, Greeks, and Romans used such a device to search for underground water and minerals. Marco Polo reported seeing it used in Asia. In northern Europe divining rods, like other magic wands, were generally made of hazel wood. The hazel bush was believed to have magical properties, was sacred to Thor in Scandinavian mythology, and was a symbol of immortality to the Germans. St. Patrick was said to have held a rod of hazel as he cast Ireland's snakes into the sea. Hazel also symbolized fertility in England and Germany, and a hazel rod was carried in wedding processions to insure that the couple would have many children.

See also: caduceus

martial: having to do with war or fighting

Karate and judo are martial arts: ways to fight off an adversary who is threatening us. A court-martial is a judicial proceeding held by our military. Martial music often accompanies a parade of troops and inspires us to support our fighting forces. Through these and other uses of the word *martial,* the Roman god of war lives on in our language and our society.

The Latin adjective *Martialis* meant "of or belonging to Mars." Although the Romans later identified him with the Greek god Ares, Mars was an ancient Italian deity, originally associated with agriculture and the coming of spring. Prior to 153 B.C., when the Roman calendar was officially changed, the first month of the year was dedicated to this god of fertility and called, after him, Martius (March). Since Martius was also the month when warfare resumed after winter's hiatus, Mars was invoked at that time to protect the troops and assure them victory in the coming months. Priests of the god paraded through the countryside, chanting and carrying spears and shields. The purpose of their incantations was to call down Mars's blessing on renewed life in the fields and on renewed death on the battlegrounds.

Mars was a very important god to the Romans, second only to Jupiter in their pantheon. He was viewed as the protector of Rome, and as the empire grew, so did his cult. Our continued association of his name with all aspects of the military and warfare is just one of the many ways in which the

Roman Empire has left an indelible impression on Western civilization.

See also: March (under "Months"), Mars (under "Planets")

mentor: a teacher or counselor

A graduate student getting a Ph.D. works with a mentor, an older, established professor who acts as a guide through the academic world. A young athlete who aspires to the pinnacle of his sport puts himself in the hands of a coach, or mentor, who oversees his training. These acknowledged experts in their field, who have agreed to share their knowledge with less experienced individuals, might be surprised to learn that their title comes from the name of a character in Homer's *Odyssey*.

The original Mentor was the wise old friend of Odysseus who remained behind in Ithaca when the Greeks sailed off to fight in the Trojan War. Odysseus had so much faith in Mentor's ability and judgment that he entrusted his entire household, as well as the upbringing of his only son, Telemachus, to him. The goddess Athena knew that Telemachus was accustomed to receiving sage advice from his surrogate father, so she took Mentor's form when she wanted to encourage the young man to set off in search of the long-lost Odysseus.

So respected was Mentor by the Ithacans that, after Odysseus returned and slew his wife's suitors, the goddess again chose his form in which to establish peace. Coming between Odysseus and the revenge-seeking relatives of the dead men, Athena/Mentor ordered all to drop their arms and spare the city any further bloodshed. They listened to the wise counselor, and the *Odyssey* ends with the restoration of peace in Ithaca.

See also: (the) patience of Penelope

mercurial: swift; changeable

If you've sent flowers to someone recently, you've probably called on a Roman god—or at least his symbol—to do it. The insignia you see on the doors of florists who participate in FTD, a leading flower delivery service, is a representation of Mercury, the messenger of the gods.

Known to the Greeks as Hermes, this god was the son of Jupiter and Maia. Today he would no doubt be diagnosed as a hyperactive child. When he was less than a day old, he was already talking and walking—and running and flying. He slipped away from his mother when her back was turned and stole Apollo's cattle, angering the older god. Fortunately for Mercury, in his first twenty-four hours of life he had invented the lyre, and he was able to bargain his way out of his predicament. The child gave the instrument to Apollo as a peace offering, and all was forgiven. It was due to these early escapades that Mercury became the patron of tradesmen, bargainers *par excellence*—his temple was presided over by a merchants' guild, the Mercuriales—and of thieves.

Mercury was as fleet of foot as he was quick of mind. Depicted by the Greeks and Romans as a vigorous young man wearing wings on his sandals and on his hat, he spent his time flying through the heavens, carrying messages from the gods to each other and to mortals. Although many of his errands were of a rather frivolous nature, he was also charged by Jupiter with the solemn duty of conducting the souls of the departed to the Underworld.

The name of Mercury was given to the fastest-moving planet and to the liquid metal originally called quicksilver. And, just as the element mercury changes shape and form in an instant, *mercurial* people constantly change their minds and undergo rapid mood changes. They are as "flighty" as the god who sped through the heavens so long ago.

See also: Mercury (under "Elements"), Mercury (under "Planets")

mermaid: a creature who is half woman, half fish

Many ancient peoples believed in the existence of beings who were half human and half fish. In the oldest legends, these creatures were gods: The Chaldeans believed in the sea god Ea, Lord of the Waters, who had a fish's body and a man's head and feet; the Greeks worshiped a host of divine and semidivine sea creatures including Poseidon's son Triton, who was half man and half fish. In later Greek myths, Tritons were a class of minor sea deities, men from the waist up and fish below.

In later European folklore, mermaids and mermen were considered to be spirits, somewhat like fairies. Although they were not immortal, they lived a very long time and possessed many supernatural powers. Under certain conditions, they could assume human form and live on land. A popular theme in legends about these creatures—particularly those of Northern Europe and the British Isles—is that of a marriage between a man and a mermaid. If the man steals an object belonging to the mermaid, such as her comb or mirror, he gains power over her and she must marry him. As long as he possesses the object she remains with him, but if she finds it she leaves him and returns to the sea.

Both mermaids and mermen could be evil, causing storms and shipwrecks if angered, but the female of the species was especially dangerous. Mermaids often lured sailors with their singing and caused them to wreck their ships. (The Sirens of Greek mythology, whose songs were also fatal to seamen, originally had birds' bodies but were later thought of as mermaids, as tales of the latter became more popular.)

During the Renaissance the word *mermaid* was a euphemism for a courtesan or a prostitute. Although this usage is now obsolete, and the word has no figurative meaning in modern English, we have included it here because of the popularity of the image. Sightings of mermaids, like those of unicorns and leprechauns, continued well into modern times, an indication of the power of man's imagination and the endurance of the ancient myths.

Midas touch: the ability to be successful at whatever one attempts

> Goldfinger.
> He's the man,
> The man with the Midas touch. . . .

James Bond fans will immediately recognize the above lyrics and the villain they describe. Ian Fleming's Goldfinger is the personification of evil. On the other hand, Midas, the king who served as Fleming's inspiration, was not really evil, just foolish—and greedy. He was King of Phrygia and possessed great lands and riches. However, he was not satisfied with all this. He thought he could never have enough gold. So, when in return for his hospitality to one of Dionysus's followers the god offered to grant him a wish, he didn't think twice: He wished that whatever he touched would turn to gold. At first, of course, the granting of his wish seemed to be a blessing without bounds, and he was able to add to his great stores of wealth every time he stretched out his hand. The *Midas touch,* therefore, is the ability to create wealth and success at every turn, and it is thus that we apply the phrase to individuals who seem to succeed at every enterprise they undertake.

But Midas's story didn't end there. The moment of reckoning came when he sat down to eat. As the food and drink he put to his mouth turned to lumps of gold, and his hunger and thirst could not be sated, he realized the folly of his wish. To save his life he had to find Dionysus and beg him to take back his gift. (By some accounts it was not until he turned his beloved daughter to gold that he was willing to give up the power.) Dionysus told Midas to wash himself in the river Pactolus; he did, losing the golden touch but gaining some wisdom.

See also: ass-eared

mint: *See: money*

Momus/momus: a critic; someone who finds fault incessantly

Momus was one of the sons of the Greek god of night. According to Hesiod's *Theogony,* he made his first mistake when he criticized Zeus for putting a bull's horns on its head rather than on its shoulders, which Momus felt were stronger and better suited to bear the weight. The final straw came when he ridiculed Aphrodite's shoes or feet; the Olympian gods threw him out of heaven.

Based on these anecdotes, the name Momus became an English synonym for someone who is always criticizing and finding fault. A person who delights in making fun of others may also be called a "son (or daughter) of Momus."

money: coin, currency

Modern money may carry the portraits of kings, queens, and presidents, but it owes its name to a goddess. Juno was foremost among the Roman goddesses, wife of Jupiter and queen of the heavens (Juno Regina). Among her many other epithets were Juno Lucine (goddess of childbirth), Juno Juga (she who yokes man and woman together in marriage), Juno Domiduea (goddess of the home), and Juno Moneta (she who warns or admonishes).

The origin of this last epithet is unclear; it has been suggested that Juno's worshipers looked to her for signs of approaching evil, so they might protect themselves against it. In gratitude for her warnings, a temple to Juno Moneta was built on the Capitoline Hill in Rome, and in it her priests made currency, which came to be called *moneta* after her. When Latin evolved into Old French, the coins became *moneie.* From there, the word entered English, becoming *money* to us.

The word *moneta* was also applied to the building in which Juno gave her warnings and where her coins were made. In the speech of the Anglo-Saxons it evolved into *mynet* and then became our modern word *mint:* the place where money is manufactured.

See also: Junoesque

MONTHS OF THE YEAR

The English names of the twelve months come from several different sources, but they all have Latin roots. In ancient Rome, the year began on March 1. That made September, October, November, and December the seventh through tenth months, which was reflected in their names. It was not until 153 B.C. that the Romans officially changed the beginning of their year from March 1 to January 1. September, October, November, and December then became the last four months of the year but retained the names they were given centuries before.

The next major change in the Roman calendar came during the reign of Julius Caesar, when the names of what were originally the fifth and sixth months—Quintilis and Sextilis—were changed to Julius (July) and Augustus (August), in honor of the two Caesarean emperors.

Through all these "modern" reforms in the calendar, six of the months retained the original names they had been given in honor of ancient gods and their rites:

January (Januarius): Named for Janus, the god of portals and of beginnings and endings. Although Januarius was not originally the first month of the year, two-faced Janus—able to see the past and future simultaneously—is the most fitting god to be called upon as one year ends and another begins.

See also: Janus-faced

February (Februarius): On what is now February 15, the Romans held a yearly festival of purification, the Februa. Dedicated either to Juno Februaria (goddess of fertility) or to Februa (god of purification), it lent its name to the month in which we now celebrate Groundhog Day, St. Valentine's Day, and the birthdays of important U.S. presidents.

March (Martius): Mars was the Roman god of war and also the fertilizing god of spring. The Romans dedicated Martius, which was originally the first month of the year, to him and his virile energy.

See also: martial

April (Aprilis): There are two theories as to the origin of this month's name. One is that it came from the Latin *aperire* (to open), referring to the budding of trees and flowers in the early spring. The other, more accepted etymology is that it came, through the Etruscan *Apru,* from the Greek *Aphro.* This was a shortened form of Aphrodite, the Greek goddess of love, and most scholars now believe the month was dedicated to her by the Romans.

May (Maius): Maia was one of the names of Cybele, the Mother goddess. The Romans identified her with several ancient Italian goddesses of spring, including Bona Dea and Maia Maiestas. May, the month in which crops are planted, was sacred to her.

June (Junius): There are also several theories as to the origin of this month's Latin name. Some say Junius honors the family name of the murderers of Julius Caesar; other scholars associate it with Lucius Junius Brutus, first consul of Rome, and believe it commemorates his ouster of the Tarquin kings. There are also those who say it was dedicated to Rome's young people, or *juniores.* The theory that ties it to mythology is that June was named for Juno, the wife of Jupiter and the patroness of women and marriage. Support is lent to this last theory by the fact that June, even going back to ancient times, has been the most popular month for weddings.

moonstruck: *See: lunatic*

morphine: a narcotic derived from opium

Morphine is a powerful narcotic that gives the pain-racked body relief and allows it to slip into a healing sleep. Because of its sleep-inducing properties and the euphoria it generates in those who ingest it, this drug was named after the Greek god Morpheus.

The Greek word for sleep is *hypnos,* which gave us the English words *hypnotize* and *hypnotic.* Hypnos was the mythological personification of sleep, and he was said to have three sons who often visited the human beings their father had lulled into oblivion. Icelus aroused in them dreams of birds and beasts; Phantasus conjured up inanimate objects; and Morpheus brought before them the shapes of other people.

The drug morphine was first isolated by the German chemist F. W. A. Serturner in 1806, and it was he who gave it its fanciful name.

Mother Earth/Mother Nature: the force that allows all living things on our planet to prosper and reproduce

"It's not nice to fool Mother Nature," Americans were advised in a television commercial of the 1970s. Oddly enough, that was exactly the belief of many ancient peoples who were aware of the tremendous power the Earth Mother wielded and were careful never to offend her.

Since it is from the woman's body that life emerges, nearly every civilization has personified the earth as a female. The Egyptians are the one notable exception, claiming that the sky was the goddess Nut and the earth was her brother, Geb. (Although not associated with the fertility of the earth, Nut was considered the mother of the celestial bodies. She was often depicted as a cow on whose teats the stars nursed nightly, and she was believed to give birth to the sun each day.) The Greeks personified the earth as Gaea and the sky as Uranus. Gaea, the female, gave birth to the Titans and was, therefore, the grandmother of the Olympian gods. Her name actually meant "earth" in Greek and is the root of our prefix *geo-,* which means "of the earth." In Norse mythology the primeval earth goddess was Jord, whose name became Erda in the Germanic countries and gave us the English word *earth.*

Besides personifying the earth as a female out of whom all life came, which is a rather primitive and basic concept, more sophisticated myths were told to account for the changing seasons, the yearly death and rebirth of vegetation, and such catastrophes as drought and famine. These myths also revolved around goddesses, rather than gods, except, again, in Egypt. There it was Osiris, the son of Nut, who was associated with the fertility of the land and with agriculture. His mythical death and rebirth symbolized the alternate recession and flooding of the Nile and the resulting periods of famine or feast. As powerful as Osiris was, it was up to a female—his sister/wife, Isis— to bring him back from the dead. To the Greeks it was the goddess Demeter who made the flowers bloom and the crops grow. The dying of vegetation each winter occurred when Demeter's daughter, Persephone, was forced to spend several months in the underground kingdom of Hades. In deep mourning for her child, Demeter stopped all things from growing until spring came and Persephone walked the earth again. The Latin names for Demeter and Persephone were Ceres and Prosperine, and they were worshiped by the Romans as well.

The Romans had another, indigenous Earth Mother. They also worshiped the ancient Italian goddess Terra or Tellus, whose name means "earth" and forms the root of such words as *terrestrial* and *terra-cotta*. One of her epithets, Alma Mater (nourishing mother), is now a common way of referring to the school from which one has graduated. Alma Mater was also an epithet for Ceres and for Cybele, a mother goddess whose cult came to the Italian peninsula from Asia Minor and who eventually came to be honored as the Great Mother of the gods. (Cybele was also identified with the Greek Rhea, wife of Cronus.)

The "pagan" goddess Ashtoreth, who is mentioned frequently in the Old Testament, was none other than Astarte, the Great Mother as she appeared in Near Eastern mythology. She was called Ishtar in Babylon and Inanna in Sumeria, but she had many of the same characteristics as Demeter and Terra. She caused the earth to grow green each spring; she insured the propagation of the species in man and the animals. Like Isis, she had a husband or brother who died each year; also like Isis, she descended to the nether world to bring him back so that spring would come once more.

See also: Adonis, cereal, sacred cow

mumbo jumbo: nonsense

The rhyme, and the resemblance to the words *mumble* and *jumble,* would lead one to believe this phrase—which means nonsense or meaningless talk—is just that. It does, however, have an etymology: In its original form, it was the name of an African god. Mama Dyambo was the spirit or god who protected the villages of the Khassonke, a Mandingo tribe that lived on the Senegal River. In their language the words mean "ancestor wearing a pom-pom." During Mama Dyambo's rites, one of the male villagers would dress up as the god, wearing a frightening mask and a tufted headdress, and make horrible noises designed to frighten away evil spirits. The men of the village often conspired with the actor playing Mama Dyambo to instill fear into their wives, who were terrorized, bound, and beaten by the "god."

Just as the ravings of the Mama Dyambo during these ceremonies bore no relationship to the everyday language of the villagers, confusing talk or technical jargon that doesn't make any sense to us is *mumbo jumbo,* as opposed to plain English.

muse: an inspiration; a creative spirit

"This is the tale I pray the divine Muse to unfold to us.
Begin it, goddess, at whatever point you will."

The Greek bards—including Homer, whose opening lines of the *Odyssey* appear above—began their recitals by calling on the Muses for inspiration. These goddesses were originally three in number and were generally said to be the daughters of Zeus and Mnemosyne (Memory). In early mythology they were not given individual names or distinguished from one another. Like the Graces, the Muses danced and sang at banquets on Olympus, to the accompaniment of Apollo's lyre. Their singing was reputed to be the most beautiful on heaven or earth, and they once competed with the Sirens, beating the latter hands down.

Hesiod was the first to give each Muse a name and to associate each with a specific area of knowledge or the arts. Although there is great variance among the storytellers as to the specialties of the Muses, they are generally said to be: Calliope, epic poetry; Clio, history; Erato, love poetry and marriage songs; Enterpe, Dionysiac music; Melpomene, tragedy; Polyhymnia, religious song and oratory; Terpsichore, dance; Thalia, comedy; and Urania, astronomy.

As a symbol for creative genius or inspiration we still use their collective name. Modern writers and artists depend on their muse to give them the impetus to go on with their work, especially in the middle of writer's block or another dry period.

Zeus's daughters' name is also the root of the English word *museum*. A Greek Mouseion was a place sacred to the Muses, a temple dedicated to them and their arts. The great library at Alexandria, built by Ptolemy Soter in the third century B.C., was also know as a Mouseion and was regarded as the center of culture and civilization of the ancient world.

Another common word that is derived from their name is *music*. At one time the Greek *mousikos* meant "belonging to the Muses" and was applied to any art over which they presided, but eventually it came to be applied more or less exclusively to lyric poetry that was set to a tune and sung (*mousikē*).

The Muses have also left their linguistic mark on the decorative arts. The ancient art of mosaic—setting small pieces of colored stone or glass into patterns—came to us from the Greek word *mouseious* (related to the Muses) through the Latin *musaicus*.

Interestingly, the English verb *to muse,* meaning to be absorbed in thought, is *not* related to the Greek goddesses of learning. It comes instead from the Old French *muser* (to loiter or reflect), which in turn came from the Latin *musus* (the muzzle of an animal).

While there are very few references in the myths to the Muses as individuals, two of their names are immortalized in English words. The adjective *terpsichorean* is often used when speaking about the dance, which was Terpsichore's special domain. And, although Calliope was the Muse of epic poetry, for some unknown reason the calliope (sometimes pronounced *kál-ē-ōp*)—a whistling organ used in circuses and sideshows—was named after her.

See also: (dressed to the) nines

myrmidon: a subordinate who executes orders without question

Ants live in a highly structured society and exist to serve their "queen." To maintain order in the anthill, each ant is genetically programmed to carry out certain functions and goes about its assigned duties instinctively and unerringly. The Greek word for ant is *myrmex*, and the Myrmidons of Greek mythology had much in common with the ants for whom they were named. In fact, legend has it they were originally ants, transformed into men by the great god Zeus.

According to the most widespread version of the myth, Zeus seduced a maiden named Aegina, and she gave birth to a son, Aeacus. The boy grew up and became king of the island of Aegina, which he named for his mother. Zeus's wife, Hera, however, continued to bear a grudge against Aegina and her son and eventually took revenge by sending a plague to wipe out the island's inhabitants. With almost no one left living in his realm, King Aeacus prayed to his divine father to replenish its population. He saw a trail of ants carrying grain up an oak—Zeus's sacred tree—and begged the god to give him as many subjects as there were ants on the oak. That night, he dreamed he saw the ants falling off the tree and becoming people. When he awoke, his dream had come true: A host of men, whose faces he recognized from his dream, approached his palace and offered homage to him as their ruler. Aeacus called the new race of people the Myrmidons, and they became renowned for their antlike thrift, industry, and devotion. Their descendants fought with Aeacus's grandson, Achilles, in the Trojan War, and it was Homer who compared them to "flesh-eating wolves in all their savagery."

Unfortunately, modern-day myrmidons are, indeed, more like fierce wolves than industrious ants. We now use the term pejoratively, to refer to a subordinate who carries out the orders of his superiors unquestioningly. Without regard for the morality of their acts, or their cruelty, myrmidons in the Gestapo, the KGB, and other similar organizations have committed atrocities the world over, under the guise of obedience to their leaders.

N

narcissistic: in love with oneself; conceited

A person who is narcissistic is so preoccupied with himself that he has no interest in anyone else. He often ends up alienating others and comes to a tragic, lonely end—which is just what happened to the original Narcissus, a character in Greek mythology.

According to Ovid and others, Narcissus was the son of the water nymph Liriope and the river god Cephisus. Shortly after his birth, his mother consulted the blind seer Tiresias and asked him how long her son would live. The prophet foretold that the boy would live to great old age, "if he never came to know himself." It was only when Narcissus reached the age of sixteen that Tiresias's words began to make sense. Narcissus was so handsome that countless young men and women made advances to him, yet he spurned them all. He was so taken with himself that he found no other man or woman worthy of his attention. When he rejected the nymph Echo, she was so devastated that she pined away until only her voice remained. Whether in punishment for his cruelty to her, or because a young man whom he had rejected put a curse on him, Narcissus suddenly found the tables turned on him. *He* fell in love with someone unattainable.

It happened when he saw his reflection—"knew himself"—for the first time. He had come upon a pool of water deep in the forest and had leaned over it to drink. When he saw the beautiful youth looking back out of the water at him, he instantly fell in love. But each time he reached into the water to touch the object of his desire, the image broke up and vanished; whenever he stepped back from the water's edge, he lost sight of the beautiful face, so he remained riveted to the bank. He could not bear to leave his love's side to eat or sleep.

Unaware that the figure in the water was himself, he begged it to come out and return his love, to no avail. Finally, overcome by despair, he lay down in the grass and died. Only Echo came to his side and repeated his words of farewell as his spirit slipped away. When her sister nymphs came to bury him, Narcissus's body had vanished, and in its place stood a flower of gold with white-rimmed petals.

We still call a conceited person a *Narcissus* or *narcissist*. Freud developed the clinical term *narcissism* to refer to what he considered a normal stage in our sexual development, when our own bodies arouse erotic feelings in us. According to Freud, most of us outgrow this, and it is only fixation at (or regression to) this stage that should be considered pathological.

See also: echo, nemesis, narcissus (under "Plants")

nectar and ambrosia: something extremely delicious

Most Americans think of ambrosia as a dessert made with oranges, coconut, cherries, marshmallows, and whipped cream. And to most people nectar is the liquid that bees gather from flowers and use to make honey. They may think of both as smelling and tasting good, but unless they speak Greek or have studied Greek mythology, they probably don't realize how closely connected these two common English words really are.

Both words can be traced back to classical Greek and have the same literal meaning. *Ambrosia* comes from the two Greek words *a* (not) and *brotos* (mortal). At the root of *nectar* is the combining form *nekro-* (relating to the dead) and the Sanskrit *tarati* (he overcomes). Nectar and ambrosia were, therefore, the sustenance of those who were not mortal, who had overcome death: the Olympian gods.

According to most Greek storytellers, including Homer, nectar was a sweet, fragrant beverage. In Book I of the *Iliad* Hephaestus pours it from a two-handled cup into the drinking vessels of Hera and the other gods. Hence, botanists' use of the term *nectar* for the liquid produced by plants, the odor and taste of which attract a great variety of birds and insects. The name of the sweet, juicy fruit we call a nectarine also derives from the Greek name for the drink of the immortals.

Ambrosia is generally referred to as the food of the gods, and Homer says that each day Zeus sent his doves out, past the Wandering Rocks, to bring the delicious concoction back to Olympus. He also tells us that the sea god Poseidon fed his horses on "ambrosial fodder." On occasion ambrosia was also used by the Greek gods as an unguent, to clean and anoint their bodies. Harkening back to these tales, we apply the adjective *ambrosial* to anything that delights our sense of taste or smell. And we use the phrase "nectar and ambrosia" to describe a culinary masterpiece that is so tasty, it is "fit for the gods."

nemesis: an unconquerable foe or stumbling block; an agent of retribution

The Greek verb *nemein* means "to distribute or deal out." Nemesis dealt out retribution or punishment, putting back into their place those whose arrogance and pride caused them to defy the gods or otherwise incur their displeasure. The concept of hubris—excessive pride or presumption—is very prominent in Greek mythology. "Pride goeth before a fall" is, in fact, the central message of Greek tragedy. Those mortals whose hubris leads them to believe they can outwit the gods, or escape the destiny that has been arranged for them, are always punished in the end. Nemesis was one of the agents of that punishment.

Retribution and other concepts, such as Deception, Discord, Fate, etc., were first conceived of as abstractions by the Greeks. In Hesiod's *Theogony* their birth, out of Night, is purely allegorical. Later, however, Nemesis and other such concepts were personified and worshiped as gods and goddesses. The goddess Nemesis was sent to punish Agamemnon for his pride in victory; it was she who made Narcissus fall in love with his own reflection, subjecting him to the pain of unrequited love just as he had caused it in others. As a deity, Nemesis was also associated with reversals of fortune. The goddess Tyche blessed certain people with great wealth or prosperity, but that didn't mean it couldn't be taken away. Nemesis kept a watchful eye over such individuals, and if they let their good luck go to their heads—forgetting to show their appreciation to the gods or neglecting to share their bounty with the less fortunate—she took it all away.

These Greek myths have given us the word *nemesis* to denote an agent of retribution. We also say someone has "met his nemesis" when he runs into someone or something he cannot conquer, an insurmountable obstacle: Muhammad Ali was the nemesis of many boxers hoping to gain the heavyweight championship of the world; taking tests is often the nemesis of otherwise "A" students; chocolate cake may be the nemesis the dieter just can't muster enough strength to pass up.

See also: narcissistic, wheel of fortune

nepenthe: anything that produces euphoria

In Book IV of the *Odyssey,* Odysseus's son, Telemachus, visits Menelaus to obtain information about his father's fate after the Trojan War. Menelaus has been reunited with the beautiful Helen, for whom the war was fought. As Helen listens to the reminiscences of the men and sees them on the verge of tears, she has an idea to lift their spirits. Into their wine she slips "a drug that had the power of robbing grief and anger of their sting and banishing all painful memories." Homer goes on to explain that the drug is one of many Helen received from an Egyptian lady, the Egyptians being the world leaders in medical knowledge.

The Greek word for this mythical antidepressant is *nepenthe,* from *ne* (not) and *penthos* (sorrow). We have adopted it into English, in a figurative sense, as a word for anything that produces euphoria or enables us to forget our pain and misery.

Thus, Karl Marx's famous quote might be paraphrased as "Religion is the nepenthe of the people" by someone who wanted to show off a knowledge of mythology!

(shirt of) Nessus: a fatal gift, one that brings about the recipient's downfall

When you present a bottle of liquor to someone who has a drinking problem, you are giving that person a *shirt of Nessus*: a gift that is likely to cause great problems, and may even be his or her undoing.

Nessus was one of the Greek Centaurs, creatures that were half man and half horse, and often lusted after human females. He lived near the river Evenus and acted as an equine ferryman, carrying travelers across the water on his back. When the great hero Heracles arrived at the river with his bride, Deianira, Nessus agreed to transport her while Heracles swam to the other side. But no sooner had Heracles plunged into the water then the Centaur galloped away with the terrified Deianira on his back. Taking her down the shore a little way, he threw her to the ground and attempted to violate her. Heracles grabbed one of the arrows he carried on his back and fired it at the beast, hitting him in the back. Nessus knew that he was doomed—after slaying the Hydra Heracles had dipped his arrows into her poisonous blood—and as he lay dying he plotted his revenge. The most common version of the myth says that he pulled the arrow from his wound, allowing his own now-poisonous blood to soak into his shirt. He then offered the shirt to Deianira, telling her it would serve as a talisman to win back Heracles if he should ever fall in love with another woman. The gullible young woman accepted the dying Centaur's gift and hid it away.

Years later, when she saw how smitten Heracles was with his latest mistress, the young and beautiful Iole, she feared she was losing his love forever. In desperation she took out the shirt of Nessus and sent it to Heracles to wear while he was making an offering to the gods. As soon as he put it on the poison from the Hydra's blood seeped into his pores. He felt as though his flesh were on fire, all the way down to the bone. When he tried to rip the shirt from his body, chunks of flesh came off with it, and the agony was unbearable. Driven mad by the excruciating pain, he killed the messenger who had presented him with Deianira's gift and wanted to kill her as well: But she had committed suicide as soon as she became aware of the Centaur's deception.

There was only one thing left to do. Heracles commanded his son to build him a funeral pyre. He then mounted it, lay down, and waited for the flames to engulf both him and the instrument of his destruction: the shirt of Nessus.

nestor: a wise old man; an elder statesman

As a young man, Nestor took part in the hunt for the Calydonian Boar, watched Theseus do battle with the Centaurs, was given the city of Messene by Heracles, and, some say, was one of the Argonauts who went with Jason on his quest for the Golden Fleece. Since all of these mythological events are said to have occurred long before the Trojan War, Nestor must have been an old man indeed when he sailed with Menelaus to lay siege to the walls of Troy.

As the oldest member of the Greek forces, Nestor was revered for the wisdom he had amassed throughout his long life. The *Iliad* contains numerous passages in which Nestor addresses his comrades, giving them sage advice and inspiring them to carry on the fight. It is Nestor who, with his good sense and eloquence, convinces Agamemnon that he was wrong to take Achilles' concubine and should apologize and make peace with the angry prince. Homer tells us, "This was not the only time his wisdom won the day."

Nestor survived the Trojan War and lived to a ripe old age—some say three hundred years. Today, we call a person of great age and wisdom—in particular an elder statesman—a *nestor,* in honor of the oldest Greek warrior and his attributes. Such a person may give us *Nestorian* advice, meaning advice that is, like Nestor, extremely sage.

nightmare: *See: incubus*

(dressed to the) nines: dressed in one's finest

We "dress to the nines" on special occasions and when attending events where it is important that we look our best. The implication is that the nines represent perfection, an ideal toward which we strive. Likewise, we say something is "up to the nines" when it is top-notch, the nines being the highest point on our scale of evaluation. But what, exactly, are these "nines" that we wish to emulate or attain?

They are the nine Muses of Greek mythology, the lovely daughters of Zeus and Mnemosyne (Memory) who ruled over the arts and inspired men to new heights of creativity. The Muses were the epitome of beauty and gentility. While in the early myths little distinction was made among them, Hesiod and later storytellers assigned each Muse a specific area of art or culture, over which she reigned supreme.

See also: muse

nirvana: bliss; oblivion to care or pain

One of the principal doctrines of Hinduism and Buddhism is the belief that living beings, after repeated incarnations, can eventually be released from the bondage of rebirth. Before this can happen, however, they must reach Nirvana. The word *nirvana* comes from the Sanskrit and literally means "blowing out." What must be blown out, or extinguished, is the "fire of life": a person's passions, desires, ego, attachment to the things of the world. Once this has been accomplished, the individual can become one with all things in the universe. In this state of nonfeeling and nonbeing lies ultimate bliss.

Among Hindus, the heretical Jainist sect visualizes Nirvana as the place "at the ceiling of the universe" where liberated souls live in eternal bliss. Orthodox Hindus and Buddhists, however, envision Nirvana not as a place but as a spiritual state. To them, Nirvana is not like Judeo-Christian heaven, where one goes after death if one has led a virtuous life. Nirvana, if one is fortunate, is reached while one is still alive, and death after Nirvana is called Pari-Nirvana (final Nirvana).

With the widespread interest in Oriental religion and philosophy that sprang up in the United States in the second half of the twentieth century, the word *nirvana* entered popular English and seems to be here to stay. In everyday usage, it has become a synonym for such expressions as "flying high" and "being on top of the world." When we are so happy that we are completely oblivious to the world around us, we are experiencing nirvana, American style.

See also: karma

nymph: a beautiful young woman

In Greek mythology, as in most primitive religions, there was a large element of animism. Early man thought that many inanimate objects were, in fact, inhabited by spirits. The ancient Greeks believed that female spirits, called nymphs, lived on earth in many such objects. The mountains were the home of the Oreads; the forest was inhabited by Dryads or Hamadryads; Naiads lived in fountains and rivers; and Nereids, daughters of Nereus, lived in the sea. All these resident nymphs were young and beautiful, although not immortal. While some were trapped inside their object—like the Hamadryads, who each lived in a tree and died when it died—many roamed the countryside at will.

The forest nymphs, in particular, were free spirits, both literally and figuratively. There was no double standard among the followers of Pan and Dionysus, and the nymphs frequently threw themselves into unrestrained revelry with their male counterparts, the satyrs. Their reputation for sexual promiscuity has followed them through the centuries, and while *nymph* has become a synonym for a beautiful young woman, the more common appellation, *nymphet,* indicates a sexually precocious girl. Also, in medical/psychiatric jargon, a woman who possesses an insatiable sexual drive is classified as a *nymphomaniac*, just as a male with a similar affliction is diagnosed as a *satyromaniac*.

See also: Dionysian, satyr

O

ocean: the body of salt water that covers two-thirds of the earth; an immense expanse or quantity

The ancient Greeks visualized the world as a flat circle, around which flowed the waters of the great river Oceanus. Far away, on the other side of Oceanus, lay the lands of the Cimmerians and the Hyperboreans, the island of the Muses, and the entrance to the Underworld.

Oceanus was the realm of the Titan of the same name and is, in many myths, personified by him. Like the other Titans, Oceanus was the child of Uranus (Sky) and Gaea (Earth), but he did not side with his siblings against Zeus and was not, therefore, exiled to Tartarus with them. He continued to rule over his great river, although Poseidon became king of the seas. By his sister, Tethys, Oceanus was the father of three thousand daughters—nymphs called the Oceanids—who inhabited his huge river. In addition, each of the rivers on earth was ruled over by one of his sons.

Today the word *ocean* refers specifically to the great body of salt water that covers two-thirds of the earth. Oceanographers generally break down this expanse of water into five geographical subdivisions: the Atlantic, Arctic, Antarctic, Indian, and Pacific Oceans. By extension, any expanse or quantity that is so huge it seems virtually limitless may be called an ocean, as in the expressions "an ocean of problems" and "the ocean of eternity."

odyssey: a long journey; a spiritual quest

An odyssey is a long journey, either real or symbolic. The word is often used to describe a person's spiritual quest or evolution. It is Greek in origin and means "Odysseus's tale."

Odysseus was a mythical king of Ithaca. Homer's *Odyssey* tells the story of his wanderings from the time he and his fellow Greeks destroy Troy until he arrives home ten years later. At the beginning of the epic, Odysseus is stranded on an island with the enchantress Calypso. His homeward journey has been interrupted time after time: by the Lotus-Eaters, the Cyclops Polyphemus, the winds of Aeolus, the cannibal Laestrygonians, and the wicked Circe. After spending a year with the latter, Odysseus makes the perilous journey to the Underworld to seek the guidance of the prophet Tiresias. He is told by the seer that he will eventually find his way home—if he keeps a tight rein on himself and his men. Odysseus then returns to earth and his adventures. He manages to escape from the Sirens, the Wandering Rocks, and Scylla and Charybdis. But, while he succeeds in mastering himself, he is unable to control his men; they slaughter the Cattle of the Sun and are, in turn, killed for their sacrilege.

When the gods finally decide it is time to end Odysseus's wanderings, they send Hermes to free him from Calypso's clutches. After a few more delays, the hero finally meets his son, Telemachus, who informs him that he still has challenges ahead of him: a bevy of local princes have settled in his house and are trying to persuade his wife, Penelope, to proclaim herself a widow and marry one of them. With the help of the goddess Athena, Odysseus returns home, kills the insolent suitors, and—his long odyssey finally ended—reestablishes his supremacy in Ithaca.

See also: (the) patience of Penelope

Oedipus complex: a male's excessive attachment to his mother and hostility to his father

At Oedipus's birth it was prophesied that he would kill his father and marry his mother. In an effort to thwart fate—which of course failed, as do all such efforts in Greek mythology—King Laius of Thebes gave the child to a shepherd who was told to expose it on a nearby mountain. Moved by pity, the shepherd could not bear to let the infant die and arranged for him to be adopted by the childless king and queen of Corinth, who raised him as their son.

When Oedipus reached adulthood, the oracle at Delphi repeated the same prophecy: Oedipus was going to kill his father and marry his mother. Horrified, he ran away from Corinth and the parents he believed to be his own. Fate directed him back to Thebes, and on the way he quarreled with a stranger and killed him. The stranger was none other than King Laius; in spite—or because—of Oedipus's efforts to avert it, the first part of the prophecy had come true.

When Oedipus proceeded to rid Thebes of the dreaded Sphinx, its grateful populace gave him the hand of King Laius's widow, Jocasta, in marriage. The second part of the prophecy was now fact, and Oedipus's mother bore him four children before they learned their relationship was incestuous. Jocasta hanged herself; Oedipus put out his own eyes and became a wanderer on the face of the earth. The tragedy was complete.

Freud viewed Oedipus's murder of his father and incestuous relationship with his mother as a representation of the unconscious wish of every young male child. He believed that between the ages of two and four a boy begins to experience severe conflicts because he is sexually attracted to his mother and jealous of his father's relationship with her. Because he is afraid these feelings will cause his father to stop loving him and, perhaps, to castrate him, the child learns to sublimate them. The healthy child eventually comes to identify, rather than compete, with his male parent. If, however, the child does not outgrow these infantile feelings, he will remain hostile to his father and excessively attached to his mother, suffering from an Oedipus complex. The only way, said Freud, for him to resolve these conflicts—to avert the tragedy, as it were—is to undergo regressive therapy to unlock the feelings he has repressed into his subconscious and deal with them as an adult.

See also: Electra complex

ogre: a cruel person; one to be dreaded

The word *ogre* first appeared in French in 1697, when Charles Perrault published his *Contes de ma mère l'oye*. These children's stories were soon translated into English as *Mother Goose Tales,* and Perrault's fictional giants who fed on human flesh became *ogres* in English as well. Generations of youngsters since have shuddered in fright at the thought of these dreadful creatures, similar to the bogeymen of later horror tales.

Perrault seems to have coined the word *ogre* himself, and while he never specified where it came from, the consensus among etymologists is that it is a French form of a word used in Italian dialect: *ogro.* This, in turn, comes from the standard Italian word *orco,* which means "fiend" or "demon." *Orco* can be traced to the Latin Orcus, one of the names the Romans gave to the god of the Underworld and his realm. Orcus was identified with the Greek Hades but was portrayed as taking a more active role in recruiting subjects for his kingdom. He was frequently depicted carrying a sickle—an image that has come down to us, through the Middle Ages, as the "grim reaper."

The word *ogre* is now used to refer to a cruel and oppressive person, someone we dread meeting as much as we would the god of death. To children, teachers are often perceived as ogres; with adults, it's usually the boss who gets the title. If the dreaded individual happens to be a woman, she can be called an ogress. The adjective *ogreish* or *ogrish* has been coined to describe the character traits of someone who is mean, overbearing, and threatening.

(An alternate etymology for the word *ogre* is given in *Webster's New International Dictionary* and by Isaac Asimov, among others. The ancestors of the present-day Hungarians came from Asia and began their raids on the Germanic people around A.D. 900. Until the invaders were defeated by King Otto I and his knights in the year 955, the Germans lived in terror of these Magyars, or Uigurs, as they were also called. It is suggested that the word *ogre* is a derivation of Uigur, and that its usage to describe a horrible, bloodthirsty villain stems from the memory of these invasions.)

Old Scratch: the Devil

Old Scratch is a colloquial name for the Devil, which comes from Norse mythology. In Old Norse, a *skratti* was a supernatural being, a sort of imp or goblin who possessed the powers of sorcery. In Middle English people used the word *scratte* for both a wizard and a monster, and it was only a short time before the word began to be applied to the worst monster of all: the Devil.

The origin of another name for the Devil—Old Nick—is less clear. Some scholars say it comes from the name Nicholas, for Saint Nicholas, but this really doesn't make much sense. That it comes from the Old German word *nix*—a goblin or malicious spirit—seems more likely. There's also a third explanation: that it is derived from the first name of Niccolò Machiavelli, the unscrupulous Italian statesman whose last name gave us the term *Machiavellian*.

See also: nickel (under "Elements")

Old Sol: the sun

We lightheartedly call people who enjoy basking in the sun "sun worshipers," but the sun has been a real object of religious reverence since the beginning of civilization. The star that provides us with life-giving warmth and light has been personified as a god by peoples all over our planet. Sun cults existed in Babylonia, Assyria, and Egypt. On the other side of the world, the Plains Indians of North America performed an elaborate Sun Dance in honor of Sun Old Man, while the Aztecs and Incas considered their rulers to be incarnations of the sun. Interestingly, almost all these solar deities were conceived of as males—father figures. One notable exception could be found in Japan, where the sun goddess Amaterasu was considered to be the supreme ruler of the world.

The Sanskrit word for "sun" was *surya,* and the Indo-Aryans who practiced the ancient Vedic religions gave that name to their sun god, who rode across the sky each day in a flaming chariot. As the Aryans migrated, their gods went with them and began to be worshiped by new names. Some younger solar gods, whose names can be traced back to the Sanskrit Surya, include Hvar in Iran, Helios in Greece, and Sol in both the Italian Peninsula and Northern Europe. Unlike the Aryan Dyaus-Piter, who became the great god Zeus to the Greeks and Jupiter to the Romans, none of Surya's descendants became supreme in their pantheon. Helios, for example, played a very minor role in Greek mythology, was never one of the Olympians, and was soon eclipsed by Apollo, who became identified with the sun at an early stage. (The exception to this was in Rhodes, where Helios was considered the chief god.)

In ancient Italy, it wasn't until fairly late in the Roman Empire that the indigenous god Sol enjoyed a resurgence of popularity and attempts were made to install him as the principal god of Rome. In the third century A.D., the emperor Aurelian erected a magnificent temple to Sol Invictus (the Unconquered), where he was worshiped as the special protector of the emperor and the Empire. The cult of Sol remained the chief imperial cult until Christianity finally triumphed over the "pagan" religions.

We use the name of the ancient Italian sun god in English when we refer to the sun as *Old Sol.* And old he is, being the same god who was worshiped by the first settlers in the Fertile Crescent of the Near East nearly ten thousand years ago.

Olympian: godlike; majestic

Mount Olympus is separated from the smaller Mount Ossa by the Vale of Tempe. Looking up at its peaks, which rise 9,570 feet in the air, the early Greeks must have been filled with awe. Long before Homer, they believed Mount Olympus was the abode of the gods. In the *Iliad* Homer also speaks of the dwelling place of the immortals as a mountain, saying that

Athena "sped down from the peaks of Olympus" and that she and Hera found Zeus "sitting aloof from the other gods on the topmost of Olympus's many peaks." But there were also Greek myths that said the gods lived in the sky—in a heavenly abode above the mountains of earth—and Homer sometimes reprises these, as in the *Odyssey,* when he tells the story of two young giants who tried to climb up to heaven and unseat Zeus. He says, "It was their ambition to pile Mount Ossa on Olympus, and wooded Pelion on Ossa, so as to make a stairway up to heaven."

Whether it lay on the slopes of an actual mountain or in the sky above it, Olympus was believed to be a delightful place. "Shaken by no wind, drenched by no showers, and invaded by no snows," says Homer in the *Odyssey,* "it is set in a cloudless sea of limpid air with a white radiance playing over all. There the happy gods spend their delightful days. . . ."

The Greek gods were called the Olympians after their home, and *Olympian* is now a synonym in our language for godlike or majestic. Many of the activities in which the Greek gods indulged—deceit, adultery, vengeance, petty jealousies—are anything but majestic to us. But to those who believed in them, this was of little consequence. Even if their actions didn't entitle them to the epithet, their power did.

See also: (pile) Pelion on Ossa

oracle: a person who speaks with authority and wisdom; a wise statement

The Latin word for an oracle was *oraculum,* from the verb *orare* (to speak). The Greeks and Romans both believed that the gods spoke to mortals through oracles, and there were many famous oracles in antiquity.

At Dodona in Greece, the rustling of the leaves on Zeus's sacred oak tree was interpreted by priestesses, and the resulting predictions were passed on to those who queried the god. At the shrine of Asclepius at Epidaurus, those who sought answers to their health problems slept on the hides of sacred animals, hoping to receive advice from the healer god in their dreams. Visitors to the cave of Trophonius at Lebadea were swept along by an underground river and either heard voices or saw visions giving them knowledge of the future. The most famous Greek oracle was, of course, that of Apollo at Delphi. There Apollo's priestess, the Pythia, went into a trance, and her ravings were recorded by priests. The priests then interpreted her words for the truth-seeker, often phrasing their predictions so ambiguously that they could not fail to come true.

The best-known oracle in ancient Italy was that of Fortuna at Praeneste (Palestrina). Aptly, divination at the shrine of the goddess of chance was by lot, with inscribed *sortes* (pieces of wood) being stirred and pulled out, in the same way we draw numbers or names from a hat. Greek and Roman writings also contain many legends about Sibyls, women who entered a trance and delivered messages from Apollo. The original Sibylla seems to have been a legendary prophetess of Asia Minor, whose name became a generic title for a female who foretold the future.

The oracles of the ancient world spoke with great authority, and the people had no doubt they conveyed messages from the gods. Today, a person who makes pronouncements with great authority, whom we trust as much as the Greeks and Romans trusted their prophets, is referred to as an *oracle*. The word may also be used to describe the statements made by such a person. The adjective *oracular* is applied to those who resemble the oracles of antiquity in their wisdom and authority—or in their ambiguity.

See also: Delphic, sibylline, (to have seen the cave of) Trophonius

Orphean/orphean: charming; bewitching

You might say that Orpheus came from a musical family. His mother was Calliope, one of the nine Muses from whose name the word *music* is derived. Some storytellers say his father was a king of Thrace, whose subjects were the most musical people in ancient Greece. By other accounts Apollo fathered him, and it was from the god that he inherited his lyre and his musical genius. Orpheus's playing enchanted not only men but animals, trees, and rocks, which moved from their places to follow the sound of his lyre. During the Argonauts' long journey in quest of the Golden Fleece, Orpheus stopped their squabbles and relieved their boredom with his music. Its magic gave them the impetus to row faster as they passed between the Clashing Rocks; it drowned out the voices of the Sirens, who would have lured them to certain death.

But all of that was nothing compared to the effect Orpheus's music had in the Underworld. Unable to accept the death of his wife, Eurydice, Orpheus was determined to bring her back to the world of the living. He descended to plead his case, accompanied only by the plaintive strains of his lyre. The usually impassive ferryman, Charon; the vicious hound Cerberus; the inflexible Judges of the Dead, all fell under the spell of Orpheus's playing. As he and his queen listened to the beautiful notes, Hades himself was moved to tears and consented to release Eurydice from his grasp. Orpheus was told he could lead her out of Hades' realm, but he must not look back at her until they reached the upper world. Before they emerged, however, Orpheus could not resist the temptation to turn toward his beloved, and she was once again lost to him—this time forever.

Fortunately, the stories of Orpheus's music were not lost to us, and from them we coined the adjective *Orphean* to describe something that enchants and casts a spell—like the sounds that, for one brief moment long ago, enabled love to triumph over death.

P

palladium: something on which the safety of an individual or a people depends

At the end of the *Iliad* the Trojan prince Hector is dead, but the city has not yet been taken by the Greeks. The most vivid account of the fall of Troy—and the role of its Palladium—was told several centuries after Homer, in Virgil's *Aeneid*.

For nearly ten years the Greeks had tried unsuccessfully to breach the walls of Troy. But the Trojans held out against their onslaughts, protected by the Palladium. This was a statue of Pallas Athena (Minerva to the Romans) that was believed to have been thrown down from heaven by Zeus when Troy was founded. It had been prophesied that as long as the statue remained inside the city's walls, Troy's enemies would never conquer her. When the Greeks learned of the Palladium's existence, they were determined to remove it from Troy. Diomedes, accompanied by Odysseus, stole into the city after dark and brought the sacred image back to the Greek camp. It was then that Odysseus came up with the idea of the Wooden Horse, which enabled the Greeks to infiltrate the citadel and take the Trojans by surprise, ending the war.

Virgil says that Aeneas brought the Palladium to Italy and that it was enshrined in the temple of Vesta in Rome. For centuries, many cities in Greece and Italy disputed this legend and claimed to possess the true Palladium of Troy.

Over time the term *palladium* came to mean a safeguard, something on which an individual or a nation depends for continued well-being. Thus, the Bill of Rights might be called the palladium of our civil liberties, and trial by jury is the palladium of an individual accused of a crime.

panacea: a cure-all

Asclepius was the Greek god of medicine, known to the Romans as Aesculapius. He was a son of Apollo, and he learned the art of healing from Chiron the Centaur. Unfortunately, Asclepius incurred the wrath of Zeus either by saving too many mortals from death or by bringing them back from the dead. In retaliation, the angry god struck him down with his thunderbolt, but Asclepius had at least four children to whom he passed on the secrets of his art before he died. His two sons, Machaon and Podalerius, are remembered only because, according to Homer, they tended the Greek wounded during the Trojan War. Two of Asclepius's daughters, on the other hand, have made lasting contributions to our language.

The first, Hygeia, was revered by the Greeks and Romans as the goddess who brought good health. Her name lives on in our modern English word *hygiene,* which makes sense since it is only by observing hygienic practices that we can maintain good health.

The second daughter was called Panakeia by the Greeks, Panacea by the Romans. Her name comes from the Greek words *pan* (all) and *akeisthai* (to heal). Hence, she was believed to be able to heal all mankind's illnesses and injuries. Today, the term *panacea* refers to a cure-all, something touted as the answer to all our problems, physical, mental, or spiritual. Because so many charlatans over the centuries have claimed to possess panaceas—which they were, of course, willing to share for the right price—the term is often applied derisively. So, while it seems the Greeks' faith in the goddess Panakeia was justified, we would do well to remain somewhat skeptical of modern-age panaceas.

pandemonium: *See: demon*

pander: cater to low tastes; act as a procurer

In the *Iliad* Homer speaks of "the famous son of Lycaon, Pandarus, who owed his skill with the bow to Apollo himself." Pandarus fought on the side of Troy and is variously called stalwart, admirable, and noble. Homer also has occasion to call him a fool, when Athena tricks him into shooting Menelaus and breaking the truce between the Trojans and the Greeks. He later acquits himself nobly, however, when he fights Diomedes. But again Athena takes the side of the Greeks, miraculously heals Diomedes' wounds, and allows him to kill Pandarus.

Our English verb *to pander,* meaning to cater to low tastes or to act as a sexual procurer, comes from the name of Pandarus. So do the nouns *pander* and *panderer,* which are alternative terms for a procurer or pimp. How, you might wonder, did this hero of Greek myth come to be associated with such base, despicable activities?

The transformation, it seems, began with Boccaccio. In 1344 he wrote a romance, *Filostrato,* which was set in Troy. In it, Pandarus became Pandaro, a friend of the Trojan prince Troilus, and it was this character who procured the Greek maiden Criseida for his comrade. Both Chaucer's *Troilus and Criseyda* and Shakespeare's *Troilus and Cressida* are variations of Boccaccio's tale. Shakespeare made Pandarus the uncle of Cressida, a rough fellow who urges his niece to give in to Troilus's advances, which she does, telling him, "What folly I commit, I dedicate to you." Thus Homer's admirable and stalwart Pandarus became a coarse, immoral panderer and left a lasting, if ignoble, mark on our language.

Pandora's box: a source of all kinds of troubles, best left alone

Wherever there's trouble, the French say, *cherchez la femme,* "look for the woman." This tendency to blame the ills of the world on women has existed in many patriarchal societies and religions throughout history. Judeo-Christian theology attributes the fall of mankind to woman: If it hadn't been for Eve's curiosity, we might still be living in the Garden of Eden. Likewise, the Greek myth of Pandora relates how the first woman, unable to master her inquisitiveness, unleashed evil upon the world.

The earliest known version of the story of Pandora is found in Hesiod's *Theogony* and *Works and Days.* In the opinion of Robert Graves, it is "not a genuine myth, but an anti-feminist fable, probably of his own invention, though based on the story of Demophon and Phyllis." (When Phyllis was abandoned by Demophon she gave him a casket, which she told him to open only when he was certain he would never return to her. Out of curiosity he lifted the lid, and the sight of the contents—never revealed to us by the storytellers—drove him mad.) Hesiod tells how the Titan Prometheus angered Zeus, first by trying to trick him into taking the inedible portions of sacrifices—leaving the best parts for man—and, later, by stealing fire from Olympus and giving it to mankind. Zeus punished Prometheus and also took his anger out on the human race.

At this time mankind consisted only of males, who were living in a Golden Age—free from worry, toil, and sickness, just as Adam and Eve lived in the Garden of Eden before their fall. Zeus decided that the best way to take revenge on men would be to create a "beautiful evil": the female of the species. He had Hephaestus fashion a woman out of clay and told each of the Olympians to give her a gift that would make her irresistible to the opposite sex and eventually bring about man's downfall. Zeus had his messenger Hermes present the woman to Prometheus's brother, Epimetheus, who was so taken with her beauty that he ignored Prometheus's warnings and married her.

Unfortunately, Pandora brought with her a dowry: a *pithos* (jar) that contained all the evils heretofore unknown to man. The only positive thing in the jar was Hope. Although Pandora had been instructed never to open the jar, she, like Eve, was unable to resist the temptation to sample "forbidden fruit." When she raised the lid of the jar all the ills that have since plagued mankind—Sickness, Vice, Old Age, Insanity, etc.—flew out. Only Hope remained behind, to bolster human beings in their continual struggle against the forces of evil.

When Erasmus translated the story of Pandora in the sixteenth century, he used the Latin word *pyxis* (box) for the Greek *pithos*. Since then, the phrase *Pandora's jar* has been replaced by *Pandora's box* as a metaphor for a situation that is best left alone, lest by disturbing it we bring upon ourselves more problems than we can handle. Countless generations of children have been told the story of Pandora's box as a warning against being too curious and, perhaps, as a reminder by men of the trouble women can cause if they aren't watched carefully!

See also: Promethean

panic: feel sudden, irrational fear

Imagine how you would feel if you were walking alone at night, in a dark wood, and you suddenly heard shouts and shrieks coming through the darkness. You'd probably panic, just as the ancient Greeks did when they heard the nocturnal revelry of Pan and his followers.

Pan's origins are obscure, but the belief that he was the son of Hermes and the she-goat Amalthea makes more sense than any other version of his parentage, given the fact that he was often portrayed as a horned man with the lower body of a goat. Pan did not reside on Olympus, although he maintained a close relationship with the gods. He is said to have assisted Zeus in his overthrow of the Titans, and in the final battle for supremacy it was supposedly a shout from Pan that startled the Titans into flight.

Whether he was making love or war, Pan's vocalizations were equally eerie. We still hear their echo, across the centuries, in our English noun and verb *panic*.

(climb) Parnassus: embark on a career in the arts

The most renowned oracle of ancient Greece was that of Apollo at Delphi. The god's messages were not actually delivered in the village of Delphi, but in a cave on nearby Mount Parnassus. The entire mountain was sacred to Apollo and was believed to be his home on earth; there the god of poetry, music, and dance played on his lyre, enchanting all who heard its strains. One of Apollo's popular epithets was Musagetes (leader of the Muses). Although these goddesses of the arts were originally said to live on Mount Helicon, their connection with Apollo led Roman poets to perpetuate the myth that they too made their home on Parnassus, singing and dancing to the music provided by their leader.

The neighborhood of Paris that has long been a mecca for artists and writers is called Montparnasse. Mount Parnassus's connection with the arts, particularly with poetry and music, also gave rise to the English expressions "climb Parnassus," "make the ascent to Parnassus," and "take the road to Parnassus." All have the same meaning: embark on a career in the arts, especially as a poet or musician.

In the late nineteenth century, a group of French poets, led by Leconte de Lisle, rebelled against the emotionalism of the Romantics, extolling the virtues of technical perfection and precise, impersonal description in poetry. They published an anthology of their work in 1866, calling it *Le Parnasse contemporain.* As a result, they became known as *les Parnassiens,* and a *Parnassian* has since become an English synonym for a poet.

(the) patience of Penelope: endless patience; patience under adversity

We say someone has "the patience of Penelope" when he or she is able to withstand all kinds of adversity and seemingly endless delays. The comparison makes a lot of sense when you hear the Greek myth of Penelope, the faithful wife of Odysseus.

Odysseus left Penelope behind in Ithaca when he went off to fight in the Trojan War. That war lasted ten years, and, during all that time, she waited at home, managing her husband's affairs and raising their young son, Telemachus. But when the war ended and other women's husbands returned home, Penelope was still left waiting. It took Odysseus ten more years to make his way home to Ithaca, and his adventures on the way are chronicled in the *Odyssey*. When he finally arrived, there was Penelope: still waiting, still faithful—and as cunning as "the wily Odysseus" himself.

When the other Greeks began to take it for granted that Odysseus was dead, they started paying court to his "widow." Ever loyal to her absent husband, Penelope steadfastly rebuffed their advances, putting them off for years. One of her ploys was to tell them that she could not consider marrying until she had finished weaving a shroud for Odysseus's aged father, Laertes. The suitors agreed to bide their time until the work was finished—but it never was. Unbeknownst to them, each night Penelope unraveled all she had woven during the day! For almost four years she deceived them, buying time for herself, until a servant betrayed her and she was forced to finish the work. Penelope's weaving, or "web," as it was translated into English, became a symbol for a project which, by design, will never be completed.

In the end, Penelope's patience was rewarded. Odysseus returned to find the suitors making themselves at home in his house, harassing his wife, and mocking his son. With the great bow that only he could string, he fired arrows into the band of insolent men until all lay dead. Then, after twenty years, he finally took back his rightful place as head of the household and husband of the patient Penelope.

See also: mentor, odyssey

(mount) Pegasus: soar to the heights; do inspired or creative work

When Perseus cut off the head of the Gorgon Medusa, a winged horse named Pegasus sprang forth from her body. Some myths say that Perseus mounted the steed, flew over Ethiopia, and saved Andromeda from the sea monster. Other sources claim that Pegasus flew off and became the pet of the Muses, living with them on Mount Helicon. One day he happened to stamp his hoof on the ground and a magical spring poured forth. It was called the Hippocrene (horse's fountain), and its waters filled anyone who drank them with poetic inspiration. Pegasus's connection with the Muses and poetry brought about the creation of the adjective *Pegasean* from his name. Although rarely used in modern English, it means poetic or pertaining to poetry.

Another English expression that comes from the winged horse's association with the Muses is "to mount Pegasus," meaning to do inspired or creative work. A second sense of the same phrase refers to Pegasus's adventures with the Greek hero Bellerophon. Bellerophon was unjustly accused of attempting to rape a married woman, Antaea. Antaea's father thought he could avenge the insult to his daughter by ordering Bellerophon to slay the dreaded Chimera, a fire-breathing monster that was part lion, part serpent, and part goat. But the gods were on the side of the innocent young man, and Athena helped Bellerophon to capture Pegasus, whom he mounted for the battle. From the back of the magical steed he was able to wound the Chimera with his arrows, until he could get close enough to the weakened monster to shove a lump of molten metal down her throat. Hence, "to mount Pegasus" is also a figure of speech for achieving great success: soaring to the heights of fame or success in one's chosen profession.

See also: chimera

(pile) Pelion on Ossa: heap difficulty upon difficulty

There were two boy Giants in Greek mythology who caused the gods a great deal of trouble—and paid for it with their lives.

Otus and Ephialtes were the twin sons of Poseidon by Iphimedia. According to Homer, they did not resemble the monstrous, hirsute Giants of old but were handsome beings, "the tallest men Earth ever nourished on her bread." Each year they grew one cubit in breadth and one fathom in height, and when they were nine years old and nine fathoms tall they decided to climb up to heaven and unseat the Olympian gods. Since it had been prophesied that no other man or god could kill these twin Giants, they fully believed their endeavor would succeed.

They began their revolt by imprisoning Ares in a brass jar, thus depriving Zeus of his best fighter. They then piled Mount Ossa on top of Mount Olympus, and Mount Pelion atop Mount Ossa, in an attempt to reach the abode of the gods. One version of their defeat is that Zeus was about to strike them down with his thunderbolt, but Poseidon intervened and promised him that the unruly boys would give him no more trouble if he spared their lives. Another is that Apollo told Artemis to lure the twins away to the island of Naxos by promising she would give herself to Otus there. Once there, however, she turned herself into a white doe and ran between the two Giants. They threw their javelins at the animal simultaneously and, of course, hit each other. The prophecy was thus fulfilled, and the rebellion ended.

Since a mountain is a heavy, ponderous object, to put it mildly, to "pile Pelion on Ossa" became a figure of speech for piling one difficulty on top of another, resulting in a morass from which it is virtually impossible to extricate oneself.

See also: Olympian

phaeton: a light, horse-drawn carriage

A phaeton is a light, four-wheeled carriage built to carry one or two people. Drawn by horses, phaetons were a popular means of transportation before the advent of the automobile. They appear frequently in nineteenth-century literature.

The first Phaëthon was not a carriage, however, but the young man who rode to his death in one. He was the offspring of the Greek sun god, Helios, and a nymph named either Clymene or Rhode. Having only one divine parent, he was not immortal, although like most healthy young people he found it hard to believe death could strike him down. When Helios said he would grant the boy anything he wished, Phaëthon asked his father to let him drive the chariot of the sun across the sky. He begged to be allowed, for a single day, to guide his father's steeds over the world from east to west. Knowing that the youth did not possess the strength or the judgment to undertake such a task, Helios tried everything to dissuade him from the reckless endeavor. But his son was resolute, and the god had given his word. As dawn rapidly approached, Helios helped Phaëthon mount the chariot and watched in anguish as he took off. At first Phaëthon was in complete control and felt the exhilaration sweep over him as he rose higher and higher in the sky. But without the weight of their master and his skillful guiding of their reins, the horses of the sun soon went wild. They left the path and pulled the chariot headlong through the sky, crashing into the stars as they went. The panic-stricken Phaëthon dropped the reins, and the car plunged to earth, setting the world on fire. Only the great god Zeus had the power to stop the destruction, and he did so by hurling his thunderbolt at the flaming chariot—knocking it, its horses, and its driver into the river below. The waters put out the flames, cooled the sun's chariot, and gave up the body of the boy who dared too much.

(rise from the ashes like a) phoenix: make an unexpected comeback; rally after a defeat

When Herodotus visited Egypt in the middle of the fifth century B.C., he was shown representations of a mythical bird called the Bennu. Associated with the cult of Ra at Heliopolis, the Bennu was the symbol of the rising sun. Herodotus was told that only one Bennu lived at a time, somewhere in Arabia. Its life span was five hundred years, and when it died its offspring embalmed its body in a ball of myrrh. The young Bennu then carried its deceased parent all the way to Heliopolis, where it was buried in the temple of the sun. Herodotus translated the bird's name as Phoenix, possibly because it was said to nest in the date palm, called *phoinix* in Greek.

Herodotus described the Phoenix as being the same size and shape as an eagle, with red and gold plumage. Later writers embellished on this, saying its feathers were purple and gold, or red, blue, and gold. They also added more details about the death of the parent Phoenix, saying that as it neared the end of its life (which in some cases was said to span 1,461 years) it sat on a nest of fragrant spices, singing as it awaited its death. Soon the rays of the sun ignited the nest and flames consumed the aged bird. A short time later a worm appeared in its ashes. This worm became the new Phoenix, who then made the trip to Heliopolis carrying its parent's ashes as an offering to the sun god.

The idea of the Phoenix dying and being reborn from its own ashes has captured the imagination of people all over the world. In spite of its "pagan" origins, Christians made it a symbol of Christ's resurrection. It has become a universal symbol for immortality. The expression "rise from the ashes like a phoenix" is a popular metaphor for a person or institution that is thought to have passed its prime and become obsolete but is suddenly rejuvenated—making a comeback when least expected. It is also applied in situations where a disaster has occurred and the survivors muster their forces to rebuild their homes or their lives.

In prehistoric times the Salt River valley in Arizona was occupied by Indians, who erected buildings and built a system of irrigation canals before mysteriously vanishing. In the nineteenth century a prospector named Jack Swilling organized an irrigation company, revitalized the canals, and established a village in the area. One of Swilling's associates, English adventurer and scholar Darrel Duppa, remembered the myth of the Phoenix. He predicted that, just as the Phoenix rose from its own ashes, a great city would rise from the Indian ruins in the Salt River valley. The village was called Phoenix, and an ancient Egyptian myth became reality in the American desert.

See also: Phoenix (under "Constellations")

pixie-led/pixy-led: lost; confused

The inhabitants of the British Isles have long possessed legends about "little people." Celtic folklore is replete with stories of small, fairylike beings who interact with humans. Some, like the Irish leprechauns, eschew the company of men and are found only by the sound of their hammering. Others, like the English brownies, keep their distance from us—coming out only while we sleep—but help out around the house, doing the chores we haven't gotten around to.

In contrast to the shy leprechauns and helpful brownies, another group of Celtic sprites, the pixies, has a mischievous streak. In Cornwall, in southwest England, they were believed to pinch maidservants, blow out candles, tap on walls, and kiss girls in the dark. It was said that they loved to dance by moonlight to the music of crickets and frogs. Most of all, they delighted in leading travelers astray. For centuries country dwellers turned their garments inside out and carried bread in their pockets to protect themselves from pixies who would try to make them lose their way.

From these myths we have retained the phrase *pixie-led* to denote someone who acts lost or bewildered, as though a pixie had turned him around in the woods.

The sex of pixies was never clearly defined, but they were often represented with short hair, and from these representations we got the pixie-cut hairdo that remains popular today. We also say a youngster is "cute as a pixie" in the belief that these small creatures were adorable and elfin, in spite of the occasional pranks they played.

Finally, a wonderful adjective, also derived from the confusing effect pixies were believed to have on people, is *pixilated*—*pixie* plus *titillated*—meaning slightly unbalanced mentally, or drunk.

See also: Brownie, fairyland, leprechaun

PLANETS

The name of our home planet, Earth, comes from Norse and Germanic myths. The mother goddess of the Norsemen was called Jord (variously spelled Jordh, Jorth, Fyorgyn, Hloldyn, etc.). Some say the great god Odin was married to Jord before he married Frigga, and that Jord was the mother of the thunder god, Thor. The Germanic peoples called this mother goddess Erda, which evolved into the English Earth.

As for the rest of our solar system, the early peoples of Mesopotamia, collectively referred to as the Babylonians, identified seven moving bodies in the night sky. They were the sun, the moon, and the five planets that are visible to the naked eye. Each of the seven was believed to be a god, and ancient priest-astrologers predicted the future from their movements. Greek and, later, Roman astronomers adopted Babylonian beliefs about the heavens. The Greeks personified the sun as Helios and the moon as Selene; the five planets were associated with five of the Olympian gods. To the Romans the sun was Sol, the moon Luna, and the five planets Mercury, Venus, Mars, Jupiter, and Saturn. In English we retained the Latin names for these planets and added three more Roman gods to the heavens, as additional planets were discovered.

Jupiter: Because it is the largest and most massive of the planets, Jupiter was dedicated to the supreme god of the Romans.

It has sixteen known satellites. The four largest were discovered by Galileo in 1610, shortly after he constructed his first telescope. They were given the Greek names of three of Zeus/Jupiter's mortal lovers—Io, Callisto, and Europa—and of his cupbearer, Ganymede.

See also: jovial

Mars: Red is the color associated with anger and rage, warlike feelings. The "red planet" is appropriately named after the Roman god of war, Mars. The two satellites of Mars, discovered in 1877, were given the Greek names of Phobos (Fear) and Deimos (Dread), after the war god's two sons.

See also: martial

Mercury: The planet closest to the sun, Mercury completes its yearly revolution fastest. It is named for the speedy Roman messenger of the gods, who flies through the heavens on winged sandals.

Neptune: The "blue planet" is aptly named for the Roman god of the deep blue sea. Discovered in 1846, it has two moons. One, Triton, bears the Greek name of Poseidon/Neptune's son. The other, Nereid, is also a Greek name, that of the sea nymphs who attended the god.

Planetoids: There are thousands of minor planets referred to as planetoids or asteroids, in our solar system, most of which revolve in paths between Mars and Jupiter. About eighteen hundred asteroids have been named. The largest of these is Ceres, named in honor of the Roman goddess of agriculture and grain. Nearly all the asteroids bear female names, honoring the goddesses and nymphs of Greek and Roman mythology. Four smaller, well-known asteroids are Juno, Vesta, Psyche, and Astraea.

There is another group of planetoids, which are not found between Mars and Jupiter but which revolve around the sun in nearly the same orbit as Jupiter. These "Trojan planets" bear masculine names, those of characters in Homer's *Iliad*. Both Greeks and Trojans are represented. The "Greek" Trojan planets are Achilles, Patroclus, Menelaus, Nestor, Agamemnon, Odysseus, Ajax, Diomedes, and Antilochus. Those that honor the mythological heroes who fought for Troy are Hector, Priamus, Aeneas, Anchises, and Troilus.

Pluto: The last planet to be discovered, in 1930, was Pluto. Also the smallest planet, its mean distance from the sun is 3,675 billion miles. Revolving on the outer edge of our solar system, its atmosphere is as cold and dark as the Underworld of mythology. Pluto was the Roman name of the Greek god of the Underworld, Hades. This deathlike planet is aptly named for him, and its one moon bears the Greek name of Charon, the ferryman who rowed dead souls across the river Styx.

Saturn: The most distant planet known to the astronomers of antiquity. Saturn is the second largest. It was named for the Roman god of agriculture, who was identified with the Greek Titan Cronus. When he first observed Saturn through its rings, Galileo thought he saw three planets. Later, when the rings shifted and only one mass was visible, he quipped, "Can Saturn have swallowed his children?" in reference to the Greek story that the Titan had swallowed each of his offspring as soon as they were born because he believed one of them was going to overthrow him. Saturn has at least seventeen moons, the largest and brightest being Titan. Among its other satellites are several named for Saturn's fellow Titans—Iapetus, Mimas, Phoebe, Tethys, Dione, and Rhea—and one named for a Giant—Enceladus.

Uranus: After Uranus's discovery in 1781, several names were proposed for the planet, including that of its discoverer, Herschel, but it was finally given the Roman name for the Greek god of the sky. In a departure from classical nomenclature, Uranus's moons are named for fairies and spirits found in the works of Shakespeare and Pope: Miranda, Ariel, Titania, Oberon, and Umbriel.

Venus: The brightest planet, it is called the Morning or Evening Star, depending on when it is visible. Fittingly, it is named for the most beautiful and dazzling of the Roman goddesses.

See also: Verus

PLANTS

The storytellers of ancient Greece invented many myths to explain how certain well-known plants got their names, and several of these popular tales are included below. Many of the common names for plants, which have been used by country folk for centuries, also have their roots in classical mythology. When botanists set about formally classifying our planet's plant life, they too found a great source of inspiration in the ancient myths. Many genus and species names come from those of gods, heroes, and monsters. It would require an entire volume to list all the plants that derive their names from mythology, but here is a sample of the most picturesque.

Achillea: a genus of herbs of the thistle family

Achilles was supposedly taught the art of healing by Chiron the Centaur. One of the most famous myths about Achilles tells how he wounded Heracles' son, Telephus, with his spear and later used scrapings from the same spear to heal the young man. According to other stories, Achilles used plants—including the genus of herbs that includes the yarrow and sneezewort—to heal the sick and wounded. This genus of the thistle family was named *Achillea* in his honor.

anemone: the windflower

The anemone got its name from the Greek word for "wind": *anemos.* Some legends say the flower was sent by Anemos, one of the gods of the wind, as a harbinger of spring. Another myth was invented to account for the blood-red color of many anemones. Adonis was a handsome young man loved by Aphrodite. While out hunting he was attacked by a wild boar, and as he lay dying, the blood from his wounds turned into red anemones. Each spring they bloom in commemoration of his beauty and Aphrodite's love for him.

See also: Adonis

calypso: a bog orchid

There are a number of related orchids, found in bogs, that have white flowers with purple or yellow markings. They were named for the beautiful Calypso of Greek mythology. Like the plants that bear her name, she was a creature of the water—a sea nymph. She lived on an island, and it was there that Odysseus stopped on his way home from the Trojan War, lingering in her company for seven years.

centaury: a medicinal plant of the gentian family

Chiron was the only Centaur of Greek mythology who was a friend to the gods and to mankind. He was said to have taught the art of healing to the legendary physician Asclepius. He was also credited with having discovered the medicinal properties of this plant, called the centaury in his honor.

Daedalea: a genus of fungi

Many fungi have pores instead of gills, and among these there is one genus that has labyrinthiform pores. It has fittingly been christened *Daedalea,* in honor of Daedalus. He was, of course, the evil genius who created the labyrinth of Greek mythology. Wandering helplessly through its convoluted passageways, youths destined to be sacrificed had no way of escaping from the monstrous Minotaur. Theseus finally killed the beast and led them to safety, following the trail of yarn he had unraveled while penetrating the labyrinth.

daphne: the laurel

One of the Greek myths tells the story of Apollo's passion for the maiden Daphne. Overwhelmed by his desire to possess the beautiful young girl, he chases her through the woods. She, however, has dedicated her life, and her virginity, to Artemis. In order to save her from Apollo's advances, the goddess changes her into a laurel tree. To this day, daphne is a common name for the *Laurus nobilis.*

heliotrope: a flower that turns, following the movement of the sun

Helios was the Greek god of the sun. Although he never returned her affection, the nymph Clytie loved him so much that she sat in one place, day after day, turning her head to follow his course in the sky. Finally, the gods took pity on her and turned her into a flower. In this form she lives on, still turning her head to follow the sun's movement all day long. The word heliotrope comes from the name of the sun god plus *tropos,* Greek for "to turn." (Among the early herbalists, all plants that turned toward the sun were called heliotropes, including sunflowers, marigolds, etc. Today, however, the plant most often identified as the heliotrope is the turnsole.)

hyacinth: a fragrant purple flower

There once lived an exceedingly handsome young man named Hyacinthus. He was loved by both Apollo and Zephyrus, god of the west wind. When he chose to devote himself to Apollo, the jealous Zephyrus killed him. From his blood sprang up the beautiful, fragrant flower the Greeks called the hyacinth. (While the hyacinth of the Greeks may have been a type of lily, we now use the name of the unfortunate young man to refer to any member of the species *hyacinthus,* including the common hyacinth.)

iris: a showy plant with sword-shaped leaves and strikingly colored flowers

Iris was the Greek goddess who personified the rainbow. She traveled through the skies wearing a cloak that shone with all the colors of the spectrum. Because its large, showy flowers come in so many vivid and subtle hues—every color of the rainbow—the iris was named for this lovely goddess.

See also: iridescent

Juno's-herb: vervain

Juno was the primary goddess in the Roman pantheon. The plant botanists refer to as *Verbena officinalis* has long had the popular names of Juno's-herb and Juno's-tears in honor of the goddess.

Jupiter's beard: the houseleek

The houseleek is a common European succulent plant with pink flowers, often found on walls and roofs. Its common name—Jupiter's beard—pays homage to the primary god of the Romans. There is also a European evergreen herb (*Anthillis barba-jovis*) and a fungus (*Hydnum barba-jovis*) that share the same popular name.

narcissus: a genus of bulbous plants that includes the daffodils and jonquils

Narcissus was a handsome youth who was loved by the nymph Echo. Unfortunately he had no interest in her—or in any other human being. Narcissus loved only himself, in the form of the reflection he saw in the water each time he leaned over the edge of a pool. When the object of his desire did not reciprocate his feelings—would not speak to him or come out of the water to touch him—he pined away, becoming the beautiful spring flower we know as the narcissus.

See also: narcissistic

peony: a large, showy flower with red, white, or pink blooms

Peonies appear in early summer and are both beautiful and fragrant. At one time they were widely used for medicinal purposes, which is why they were named after Paean, the physician of the Greek gods who is mentioned in Homer's *Iliad*.

Venus's-flytrap: an insectivorous plant

The insect-eating Venus's-flytrap was named for, of all people, the Roman goddess of love. (Misogynists sometimes refer to women as man-eaters, so perhaps the designation was made by a man who had been unlucky in love!)

Many other plants also bear Venus's name, including Venus's-hair (the maidenhead fern), Venus's-basin or -bath, Venus's looking-glass, and Venus's-slipper.

See also: Venus

polypheme: *See: Cyclopean*

priapism: a medical condition in which the penis remains in a state of constant erection

Certain diseases cause the penis to remain in a state of constant erection that is in no way related to sexual arousal. The term *priapism,* used by doctors to describe this dysfunctional condition, is another example of the many scientific and medical terms that can be related back to mythology.

Priapus was generally said to be the son of Dionysus and Aphrodite, and to the Greeks he was the personification of male reproductive power. He was worshiped as the deity who inspired mating and, thus, the perpetuation of the species in plants, animals, and humans. The cult of Priapus began in Lampsacus, on the Hellespont, and during the Hellenistic period spread throughout Greece, to Alexandria, and to the Italian peninsula.

Like Dionysus, Priapus was depicted as lusty and ribald, often drunk and pursuing members of the opposite sex against their will. Artists portrayed him as ugly and misshapen, with an enormous, erect phallus. In fields and vineyards, his statues seem to have served the same function as modern-day scarecrows. They were also placed in gardens, where Priapus held a pair of pruning shears to remind his worshipers of his power over vegetation. Often, he was represented by a simple *herma* or stone pillar in the form of a phallus. So strong was the association of the god with the male sexual organ that the word *priapus* has become an English synonym for penis or phallus.

Priapus continued to be worshiped by the Romans (who sometimes called him Lutinus or Mutinus) and appears in the works of many Roman authors, including Horace, Tibullus, Martial, and Petronius.

Procrustean bed: an artificial standard to which conformity is demanded

Poseidon was the Greek god of the sea. He had a villainous son, Prokroustes (Procrustes in Latin), whose name meant "the stretcher" and who waylaid passersby and forced them to lay down in his iron bed. If the victim was too short, he was stretched until he filled the bed; if he was too tall, any part of him that hung over was lopped off. Needless to say, his guests checked in but they never checked out!

The figurative use of the phrase *Procrustean bed* dates from the sixteenth century, when it came to be used as a symbol for any scheme or pattern into which someone or something is arbitrarily forced. The adjective *procrustean* was also created to describe blanket disregard for individual differences or circumstances.

In the end, you'll be glad to know, Procrustes got a fatal dose of his own medicine. The great Athenian hero Theseus encountered him during his journey from southern Greece to his father's court in Athens. What Procrustes had done to others, Theseus did to him. We don't know whether he was stretched or shortened (probably the latter, since he was a giant), but when Theseus was done with him he no longer troubled travelers.

Promethean: daringly original or creative

The medieval Englishmen who sang the ballads of Robin Hood probably didn't have the Greek Titan Prometheus in mind when they wove their tales, but they might have. The two heroes have a lot in common: Robin Hood, it was said, stole from the rich and gave to the poor; Prometheus, the myths relate, stole from the gods and gave to man. Both were renegades, enemies of the powers that be—as represented by the sheriff of Nottingham and the god Zeus, respectively. And, just as later storytellers maintain that Robin Hood hadn't always been an outlaw but was a fallen nobleman, Prometheus too was once a member of the establishment—a friend of the Olympian gods.

Prometheus, whose name means "forethought," fought on the side of Zeus in his war against the Titans. Hesiod tells us that later, after man was created, Prometheus shifted his loyalty to the new beings. When he was chosen by Zeus to decide how men should offer sacrifices to the gods, he cut up an ox and wrapped the choicest parts in the skin, covering it all with the stomach to make it look unappetizing. He then prepared a second serving, consisting of bones and offal but covered with rich fat. Although Zeus realized that Prometheus was trying to trick him, he chose the latter portion. He got even, however, by refusing to give men fire with which to cook the choice meat they kept after making their offerings to the gods. Again Prometheus took the side of man, stealing fire from heaven so that men might cook their meat and warm themselves. This time Zeus took revenge by sending the first woman, Pandora, to Prometheus's brother, Epimetheus. "Afterthought" ignored the warnings of "Forethought" and married her. She, of course, brought evil into the world of men when she disobeyed the orders of Zeus and lifted the lid of the jar he had given her as a dowry. Having put man in his place, Zeus next punished the defiant Titan for his treachery by chaining him to a rock and setting a vulture on him. Each day the vulture tore out Prometheus's liver, and each night the liver grew back, so his torment was unending—until Zeus finally relented and allowed Heracles to kill the bird.

In later legends Prometheus is credited with having created man or, at least, with having kept Zeus from destroying him.

He is said to have taught mankind how to cultivate the land, tame horses, navigate by the stars, and forge metal into tools and weapons. According to some myths, he invented numbers and letters as well. In honor of the creative, nonconformist Titan, the adjective *Promethean* was created. It means original, innovative, daringly creative—like the Titan who defied the gods in order to set mankind on the path to civilization.

See also: Pandora's box

protean: versatile; always changing

An artist who works in a variety of media could be called protean; so could a politician whose stand on the issues changes each time he or she appears before a different special-interest group. The adjective *protean* means both versatile and adaptable, and constantly changing. Someone who is protean is hard to pin down, just like the Greek god Proteus.

Proteus was a sea god, generally acknowledged to be the son of the Titans Oceanus and Tethys. His best-known appearance in mythology is in Book IV of the *Odyssey,* where Menelaus relates how he forced Proteus to reveal the information the Spartans needed to find their way home after the Trojan War. Homer says that Menelaus and his men had made their way to the island of Pharos, near Egypt, but could not proceed because the winds had ceased to blow. Wondering what he had done to offend the gods and how he could regain their favor, Menelaus was helped by the sea nymph Eidothea. She was Proteus's daughter, and she assured Menelaus that her father—the Old Man of the Sea—could tell him all he needed to know, if Menelaus could capture him. But Proteus possessed the ability to change his shape at will; he would turn himself into any living creature, or any object, in an effort to slip away from his questioners. Armed with this knowledge and determined to make the god talk, the Spartan king and three of his crew tricked Proteus into lying down near them and, as soon as he fell asleep, pounced on him. Proteus assumed the forms of a lion, a snake, a panther, and a giant boar. Through all these metamorphoses, the tenacious Spartans hung on. When he became running water and, finally, a tall tree, they still clung to him. At last the god gave in and consented to answer Menelaus's questions. He grudgingly imparted his knowledge to them, then dove back into the sea, free once more to be whatever he wished.

psyche: the human soul; the self

In Book XI of the *Odyssey,* Homer's hero meets his mother in the Underworld, and she explains to him that when we die our life force (*thymos*) leaves our body and our soul (*psyche*) slips away and flutters on the air. This image gave rise to the portrayal, in Greek art, of the soul as a butterfly and, later, as a beautiful young girl with wings. But the most famous personification of the soul, or psyche, in mythology comes from the Roman writer Apuleius. In the collection of stories called *The Golden Ass,* Apuleius combines elements from the Greek myths and popular Roman tales to create a beautiful allegory.

Psyche is a young woman whose beauty rivals that of Venus. When Psyche begins to receive more attention than the goddess of love, and Venus's shrines are left unattended, the goddess vows to avenge herself. She asks her son, Cupid, to make Psyche fall in love with a monster, but Cupid sees the girl and falls in love with her himself. With Apollo's help he arranges to marry her but visits her only under cover of darkness. Although Psyche soon grows to love him, Cupid refuses to reveal himself to her and warns that she must never try to learn his true identity. But Psyche, like most human beings, cannot contain her curiosity, and one night she lights a lamp to gaze at her husband while he sleeps. When hot oil spills from the lamp and burns him, Cupid flees, leaving the sad and repentant Psyche alone. She looks for Cupid in the palace of Venus, but the goddess refuses to let her see him and consents to her presence only as a servant. She gives the girl a series of seemingly impossible tasks to perform, certain that she will fail at each of them. But the plants and animals take pity on Psyche and help her carry out Venus's tasks. By this time Cupid's burn has healed, and he realizes he cannot live without Psyche. Going to Jupiter, he asks that Psyche be made immortal and that Jupiter bless his marriage to her. Jupiter grants his wish, giving Psyche a taste of ambrosia to make her one of the gods.

A Platonist, Apuleius believed that our souls are intrinsically divine and come from a higher realm. We lose our divine nature during our life on earth and may despair of ever regaining it, but we can do so if we desire it enough to weather the trials and tribulations that come our way, never losing sight of our ultimate goal. Apuleius's Psyche represents, therefore, the spiritual nature of each human being. Later, Christian philosophers saw her as a symbol of the human soul in search of God. In English, the meaning of the word *psyche* has been expanded, and we now use it to mean the whole self: the emotional, intellectual, and spiritual aspects that, when taken as a whole, make up a human being. Our psyche is the seat of our individuality; when we see a psychiatrist, he studies the emotional and mental reactions that are peculiar to each of us.

pygmy/pigmie: a category of size among humans; a dwarf plant or animal

The word *pygmy* comes from the Greek for "fist" and originally meant a unit of measurement equal to the distance from a man's knuckles to his elbow—about thirteen inches. This was purported to be the size of the mythical dwarfs who lived on the shores of the river Oceanus. Homer says that each winter, flocks of migrating cranes besieged the little people, who had difficulty fighting them off. Later writers tell how an army of Pygmies, finding Heracles asleep, attempted to overpower him. The great hero woke up, threw his lion skin over them, and carried them back to King Eurystheus.

Some myths place the Pygmies in India, and others say they lived in Africa, near the source of the Nile. The latter stories may be based on actual encounters with certain tribes of equatorial Africa, whose adults do not exceed five feet in height. These tribes are now generally called Pygmies by English-speaking peoples. In fact, when modern anthropologists classify groups of humans according to size, they designate as pygmies those groups whose males are not taller than fifty-nine inches. A slightly taller group is classified as *pygmoid*.

Among plants and animals, those specimens that are smaller than average members of the species are referred to as pygmies or dwarfs. There are pygmy geese, pygmy hippopotamuses, pygmy hogs, pygmy rattlesnakes, pygmy parrots, and even pygmy sperm whales!

See also: dwarf

R

rankle: make sore or angry

The fantastic monsters we refer to as dragons appear in many mythologies. They are usually a mixture of several creatures, depending on which animals were most familiar to their creators. Reptilian features seem to predominate the world over, however, and most dragons are depicted as huge, scaly, snake-like beasts. Oddly enough, in the Far East they have always been believed to be beneficent beings and symbols of fertility. In China the dragon became the national symbol and was the emblem of the royal family for centuries.

Elsewhere these serpentine creatures were considered to be entirely malevolent, the essence of evil. In Egyptian mythology, Apophis, the great serpent of the world of darkness, was vanquished by the sun god Ra. Large, monstrous serpents appear in many Near Eastern myths. Hebrew serpents or dragons seem to have been patterned on these and were depicted as the source of death and sin, an idea that came down to Christianity and culminated in the stories of St. George and St. Michael battling evil in the form of dragons. Dragons are dominant figures in the mythologies of places as far apart and disparate as Iceland and Hawaii.

In Greece and Rome, dragons were believed to be dangerous but also to have magical powers, such as that of prophecy. The word *dragon,* which we now use to refer to these serpentine creations of early man all over the globe, comes from the Greek *drakon.* Originally, a drakon was any large serpent. *Drakon* became *draco* in Latin, *dragon* in French, and from there entered English.

The Romans created the diminutive *dracunculus,* which literally means "little dragon." It was their word for an ulcer or festering sore, because someone with such an affliction feels as though a little dragon is gnawing away at him. *Dracunculus* became *draoncler* and eventually *rancler* in French. The English verb *to rankle*—to eat away at, making sore or angry—has its roots, therefore, in Greek mythology.

The word *dragon* is also used today as a figure of speech for a violent, combative, or very strict person.

Another word that can be traced back to the drakon of Greek mythology is *dragoon.* Certain regiments of the British Army were so named because they carried muskets ornamented with the head of a dragon, the symbol for war in ancient Britain.

See also: (to sow) dragon's teeth

Rh factor: *See: Rhesus monkey (under "Animals")*

Rhadamanthine: rigorously strict; inflexible

The Greek god Zeus had three sons by Europa: Minos, Rhadamanthus, and Sarpedon. During their lifetimes, Minos and Rhadamanthus ruled over Crete; Sarpedon fought for King Priam in the Trojan War. Most of the myths state that when Minos and Rhadamanthus died they were made judges in the afterlife. Some say Sarpedon was the third judge; others say Aeacus, Zeus's son by Aegina, completed the trio.

In the *Odyssey,* Homer says that, after death, those blessed by the gods go to the Elysian plain, at the world's end, "to join red-haired Rhadamanthus." There the climate is perfect; there is no snow or harsh wind. Only the mild, refreshing west wind blows, and life is easy. Somehow, however, between the time Homer composed his great work and the writing of the Roman poet Virgil, Rhadamanthus became associated not with paradise but with the torments of hell.

In Book VI of the *Aeneid,* the Cumean Sibyl leads Aeneas down into the Underworld. At a certain point the road divides in two, with one path leading to Elysium and the other to Tartarus, or hell. Aeneas hears groans, the sound of flogging, and the clanking of iron chains, as sinners are punished in hell for their wrongdoing on earth. There, the Sibyl tells him, "Rhadamanthus of Cnossos bears rule . . . and his rule is most pitiless. He gives hearing to every work of deceit, and censures each fault. He compels every sinner to acknowledge each act of atonement which he has incurred in the world above, but whose performance he has postponed, blissful in imagined concealment, until death when it was too late."

In this passage and in other, later myths, Rhadamanthus is portrayed as a strict judge of the dead. He allows no sin to go unpunished, accepts no excuses, commutes no sentence. Thus, we have come to call someone who is exceedingly strict or rigid in the enforcement of rules *Rhadamanthine*. The word does not carry the connotation of unfair punishment, for Rhadamanthus was never accused of meting out punishment when it was not deserved, but his refusal to bend the rules has caused his name to become synonymous with inflexibility.

Rx: the symbol for a drug prescription

When we see the symbol Rx we immediately think of a drug or treatment prescribed by a doctor and dispensed by a pharmacist. The sign is an ancient one, used by apothecaries in Rome, where it meant *recipere* (take this). According to *Webster's New International Dictionary, Second Edition,* the sign is reputed to have originally been written ♃, which was the ancient astronomical symbol for the god Jupiter.

Jupiter/Jove was, of course, the leading god of the Roman pantheon and the patron of medicines. Placed at the top of a medicinal formula, the sign was a way of invoking the goodwill of the all-powerful god; it was hoped that he would render the combination of drugs effective against whatever ailments plagued his worshipers. In modern times, Rx has become a common symbol for pharmacies as well as prescriptions, and is also used as a sign for the word *treatment*.

S

sacred cow: someone or something above criticism or change

To Hindus, the cow is a sacred animal, the incarnation of the great earth goddess. Killing a cow is a direct offense against God, which has led to our use of the expression *sacred cow* to denote a person or institution held in such high esteem that it is off limits, i.e., not open to criticism or alteration. What may not be common knowledge, however, is that the Hindus are not the only people who have considered the cow to be sacred. Cows have been associated with life and fertility in general, and the great mother goddess in particular, by many societies.

The Egyptian goddess of the sky was called Hathor. She was depicted as a cow, whose underbelly was the firmament and whose legs separated earth from the sky. Each night Hathor swallowed her child, the sun god Horus, and each morning gave birth to him once again. Another sky goddess, Nut, was also portrayed as a cow on occasion. Isis, the great Egyptian mother goddess, was often confused with Hathor, and the cow was sacred to her as well. Some of the Greek myths say that Zeus was nursed by a cow, and one of the epithets used by Homer to describe the goddess Hera is *boopis* (cow-eyed). The Scandinavians believed that Ymir, the first giant, was nourished by the great cow Audumla, from whose udders ran four rivers of milk. Audumla, by licking away at the ice that covered the world, released Buri, grandfather of Odin, and the Norse gods came into being.

Returning to Hinduism, the *Rig Veda,* the oldest sacred Hindu text, speaks of the goddess Aditi, mother of the world, as "the Cow." A later collection of Sanskrit legends, the *Vishnu Purana,* tells the story of Mother Earth and the monarch Prithu. Prithu tried to exercise his power over Earth so she would yield plants to feed mankind. Earth took the form of a cow and ran away from Prithu. Eventually, however, he caught her and persuaded her to nourish the soil with her milk. As Prithu milked her, corn and other vegetables sprang up, and henceforth mankind never wanted for food. That is why to the Hindus it is permissible to drink the life-giving milk of the cow but not to eat her flesh, for that would truly be biting the hand that feeds them.

See also: Mother Earth

saturnalia: a period or occasion of unrestrained revelry

The Roman god of sowing and the harvest was Saturnus (Saturn), after whom the planet Saturn and Saturday are named. There are many theories as to Saturn's origin, but none has been proven. Ancient writers said his name came from *satus,* meaning "to sow." It is speculated that he was originally an Etruscan deity associated with the clan Satre. Most often, however, he was identified with the Greek Cronus. Cronus, in turn, seems not to have been worshiped much by the Greeks of the classical period, but was perhaps a pre-Hellenic god who was introduced into neighboring countries by early Greek migrants. Cronus was eventually given a role in the classical Greek pantheon, not as one of the Olympians but as an earlier god—one of the Titans—whose son, Zeus, deposed him. Later poets introduced the legend that after he was deposed by Zeus, Cronus/Saturn fled to the Italian peninsula, bringing civilization and a Golden Age of peace and prosperity to its people.

Saturn's temple was on the Capitoline Hill in Rome. His festival, the Saturnalia, was originally held at the end of December, coinciding with the winter sowing season in ancient Italy. It had much in common with the Kronia, the festival of Cronus that was celebrated in Greece. During the Saturnalia slaves were served by their masters—either to commemorate the fact that during Saturn's Golden Age there were no class distinctions, or to emphasize the idea that Saturn himself was once a poor exile. People played games and exchanged presents—wax candles and small clay dolls being the usual gifts—establishing the traditions that continue to be observed during our celebration of Christmas. A kind of Mardi Gras atmosphere pervaded the city, and many of the everyday rules were suspended. "Wine, women, and song" was the order of the day, which is why we use the noun *saturnalia* as a synonym for an occasion of unrestrained revelry. By extension, the adjective *saturnalian* is used to describe riotous or dissolute merrymaking.

It would be natural to infer, then, that a second English adjective derived from Saturn's name—*saturnine*—would have a similar meaning. But, in fact, it means just the opposite: gloomy, grave, morose. Why is this? The answer, it seems, lies in the stars—in the study of astrology, which connected the gods and people's characters with the planets. Although Saturn was associated with fertility and the harvest, and with the halcyon days of the Golden Age, the Greeks and Romans did not forget that he also had a sinister aspect. As the Titan Cronus, he had swallowed his children as soon as they were born. Zeus made him vomit them up, overthrew him, and banished him from Olympus. In Greek mythology Cronus is not a happy, *jovial* figure. Astrologers, remembering Cronus's defeat and exile, believed that the planet bearing his Latin name exerted a depressing influence over people who were born when it was in the ascendancy. They were bound to be saturnine, just as people born under Jupiter were destined to be jovial.

satyr: a lecherous man

Although the Greek satyrs are generally referred to as gods, they hardly fit our modern concept of divinity. These mythological forest deities were followers of the god Pan and, like him, were half man and half goat. (The ancient Italian god of shepherds and the woods, Faunus, was accompanied by fauns, who possessed the same characteristics as the satyrs. Just as the satyrs followed in Dionysus's train, the fauns joined Bacchus in his revels.)

Besides being known for their devotion to the god of wine and his rites, the satyrs had a reputation for unrestrained lust. While most of their cavorting was done with the equally lascivious nymphs, no woman was safe from their advances. The term *satyr,* then, is a fitting one to apply to a lecherous man—one who is always "on the make"—and that is how we use it in modern parlance.

The medical/psychiatric establishment has also drawn on the satyrs' reputation for unbridled lust to define a certain type of human sexual dysfunction. The clinical condition *satyriasis* refers to insatiable sexual appetite in a male, and one who suffers from this problem is diagnosed as a *satyromaniac,* just as a similarly afflicted female is called a *nymphomaniac.*

See also: Hyperion to a satyr, nymph

(between) Scylla and Charybdis: having to choose between two equally undesirable alternatives

English has several colorful expressions to describe a situation in which no matter what choice we make, we'll be headed for trouble: "out of the frying pan into the fire," "between the devil and the deep blue sea," "between a rock and a hard place," etc. All convey vivid images, but none is as terrifying as the one that comes from Greek mythology. To the Greeks, if you were "between Scylla and Charybdis" you were between two monsters, and by avoiding one you were sure to fall into the hands of the other!

Scylla and Charybdis were actually the personifications of two ancient navigational hazards in the Straits of Messina, between Italy and Sicily. On the Italian side a large rock posed a threat to all ships that tried to pass through the narrow channel. In order to steer clear of it, they had to sail closer to the coast of Sicily, but that brought them into the range of a dangerous whirlpool.

In the *Odyssey,* Homer gives an action-packed account of Odysseus's passage through the strait and his encounter with the "monsters." At first, Scylla, a barking creature with twelve feet and six heads, makes herself scarce, hiding inside her rocky cavern. All the crew's attention is directed to the roaring Charybdis, who sucks down the salt water, exposing the rocks and sand at the bottom of the sea. As Odysseus's men try to keep the ship from being drawn into the vortex, Charybdis suddenly spews out all she swallowed, with such tremendous force that the water is flung to the tops of the surrounding cliffs. Scylla, seeing her chance, snatches six of Odysseus's men from the deck. She carries them off, one in each mouth, as they call out to Odysseus for help, but he can do nothing, and must watch in horror as they are devoured one by one.

Before setting out, Odysseus had asked Circe if there was any way for him to "somehow steer clear of the terrors of Charybdis, yet tackle Scylla when she comes at my crew." The enchantress had advised him not to try, saying it would be better to mourn six of his men than the whole crew. The moral of Homer's story, and the point of the expression "between Scylla and Charybdis," is that often, in life, we can't have it both ways. We have to make a decision, whether we want to or not. The only thing we can do is choose the lesser of two evils and get on with our lives.

(in) seventh heaven: as happy as can be; at the height of bliss

A common English expression, "sitting on top of the world," is rooted in the mythological belief that the universe was constructed in layers. This belief figures in the creation myths of several religions, but most prominently in Islam. Sura XLI of the Koran says that after god made the earth, "In two days He formed the sky into seven heavens, and to each heaven He assigned its task." In Sura XXIII, Allah says, "We have created seven heavens above you." Paradise, according to later Islamic doctrine, is located in the seventh heaven or above it. Book

XXIV of the Mishkat tells how Mohammed, during his night journey, passed through the seven heavens, the distance between each being a journey of five hundred years.

Commentators on the Koran elaborated on these passages, making the seven heavens the paths of the celestial bodies and the angels. This is in harmony with the Ptolemaic view of the universe, in which each of the seven heavens contains one celestial body. Their order is generally: (1) the moon, (2) Mercury, (3) Venus, (4) the sun, (5) Mars, (6) Jupiter, and (7) Saturn. In addition, the Greeks after Ptolemy sometimes spoke of the seventh sphere or heaven as the abode of God and his most exalted angels.

sibylline: prophetic; mysterious

Sibylla is not a Greek name; it is probably of Asiatic origin. It first appears as a proper name in the work of Heraclitus of Ephesus (sixth to fifth century B.C.). In Greek legends of this time, Sibylla is depicted as an ancient woman who goes into a trance and utters predictions. She is referred to as having lived long ago, somewhere in Asia Minor.

Sometime toward the end of the fourth century B.C., the legends begin to tell of numerous Sibyls: Sibylla has gone from a proper name to a title. In the first century B.C. Varro listed ten Sibyls: the Persian, Libyan, Delphic, Cimmerian (in Italy), Erythraean, Samian, Cumaean, Hellespontine, Phrygian, and Tiburine. Many others are mentioned in different sources.

The most famous appearance of a Sibyl in mythology is that of the Cumaean Sibyl in the *Aeneid.* After being told in a dream that he will be led to his father in the Underworld by a holy Sibyl, Aeneas sets sail for Cumae. There he looks for the cavern "which is the awful Sibyl's own secluded place; here the prophetic Delian God breathes into her the spirit's visionary might, revealing things to come." Near the temple of Apollo, Aeneas and his Trojans find Deiphobe, priestess of Diana and Apollo. She invites them into the cavern, and Apollo takes possession of her: "Her countenance and her colour changed and her hair fell in disarray. Her breast heaved and her bursting heart was wild and mad; she appeared taller and spoke in no mortal tones, for the God was nearer and the breath of his power was upon her." The priestess ran through the cave, as though trying to escape from the god, but he continued to possess her mind. Finally she gave her prophecy, and "the cavern made her voice a roar as she uttered truth wrapped in obscurity. Such was Apollo's control as he shook his rein till she raved and twisted the goad which he held to her brain."

It's hard to believe and somewhat disheartening, after reading this powerful and haunting passage, that we now give the once-honored title of *sibyl* to modern-day fortune-tellers who ply their trade at carnivals and in storefronts. Happily, the adjective *sibylline* has retained more of the flavor of the ancient myths, meaning mysterious or prophetic, as the Sibyls of old most certainly were.

See also: oracle

siren: a device that gives off a shrieking sound; a temptress

If you've ever heard the high-pitched, unrelenting screech of sirens as fire trucks and ambulances passed by, you may have wanted to plug your ears until they were gone. The inventors of these devices assumed that would be most people's reaction and named them accordingly.

Their name comes from Greek mythology, where Sirens were water nymphs whose singing, while not unpleasant, was a dangerous thing to hear. The Sirens, according to Homer, lived on an island between Circe's home and Scylla. He says there were only two of them, but in later myths there were three: Ligeia, Leucosia, and Parthenope. They sat in a meadow, surrounded by the skeletons of sailors who, hearing their irresistible song and rushing headlong toward it, ran their ships aground, never to sail again.

There were only two groups of seamen who escaped this fate: Jason and the Argonauts, and Odysseus and his crew. The

Argonauts were saved at the last moment when Orpheus, unable to stop his besotted comrades from turning their ship toward the deadly rocks, grabbed his lyre and began to compete for their attention. He played so loudly and so enchantingly that he drowned out the voices of the Sirens, and the ship was saved. Odysseus had more time to plan his defense against the Sirens' songs; he was forewarned by Circe, who advised him to plug his men's ears with wax until the danger was past. If he wanted to hear the singing himself, he could have his men tie him to the ship's mast—where he would have to remain at all costs—as they sailed by the island. Odysseus followed Circe's instructions and safely heard the honey-sweet voices, which promised knowledge of all that was going to happen on earth. No wonder men couldn't ignore them!

While early Greek artists depicted the Sirens as half woman and half bird, their later portraits represent them as all woman, beautiful and alluring. It is this later image that made *siren* a synonym for a woman who tempts men with her beauty, leading them to ruin.

German folklore also contains stories of Sirens. The most famous one sat on the Lorelei rock, overlooking the Rhine, combing her hair and luring sailors with her songs. *Lorelei* is now another English synonym for a temptress.

See also: Orphean

Sisyphean labor: a never-ending task

Sisyphus was a mythical king of Corinth. His name means "very wise" or "shrewd" in Greek, and he was certainly that—at least in the short run. The myths tell us that Sisyphus actually managed to cheat death twice before he was finally condemned to his never-ending labor in the Underworld.

On the first occasion, Sisyphus angered Zeus when he revealed to others that the god had raped the nymph Aegina. To avenge this betrayal, Zeus ordered his brother Hades to seize Sisyphus and take him to Tartarus, where men are punished for their evil deeds. Sisyphus, however, used his wiles to turn the tables on the gods and, instead of descending to Tartarus with Hades, made him his prisoner on earth. With Death in chains, no one—not even those mortally injured on the battle-field—could die. This state of affairs was totally unacceptable to the war god, Ares, and he took it upon himself to set Hades free and deliver Sisyphus into his hands. But Sisyphus had another trick up his sleeve: Before descending to Tartarus, he instructed his wife not to bury him. Once in the Underworld, he approached Persephone and requested that he be allowed to return to earth to arrange for his burial. She agreed, believing his promise to return in three days. Once he was back on earth, Sisyphus refused to return, and this time the god Hermes had to intervene and bring him back by force.

Sisyphus could no longer put off the inevitable. Because he had caused Zeus and the other Olympians so much trouble, he was given a singularly frustrating punishment. He was condemned to spend eternity rolling a huge block of stone up a hill, only to have it topple back to the ground just before reaching the top. Each time it falls back, Sisyphus must wearily retrieve it and begin his exhausting labor all over again. Hence a Sisyphean labor is one in which the toiler never makes any progress and experiences only weariness and frustration.

See also: (to) carry water in a sieve

sphinx: a mysterious, inscrutable person; someone who makes enigmatic pronouncements

We are most familiar with the mythical creatures called sphinxes through Egyptian art. The Egyptians believed the rising sun was the hawk-headed god Horus. As Harmakhis (Horus on the Horizon), the god symbolized resurrection and eternal life and was often portrayed as a sphinx—a creature with a lion's body and the head of a hawk or a ram. Considered to be another incarnation of Horus or Harmakhis, the reigning pharaoh was depicted as a human-headed sphinx. The Great

Sphinx at Giza is one such representation of the living Horus, constructed around 2650 B.C.; its countenance immortalizes the pharaoh Khephren. Aside from being used to represent the god Horus and the pharaoh, the Sphinx figured in no myths in Egypt, and our figurative use of the word *sphinx* to denote a mysterious person or a person who makes enigmatic statements has nothing to do with the sphinxes of Egypt.

The enigmatic Sphinx originated in Greek mythology, and far from being a beneficent god, she was a bloodthirsty monster. Generally acknowledged to be the offspring of the hideous Echidna and her brother Orthros, the Sphinx was a sibling of the Chimera, the Hydra, Cerberus, and the Nemean Lion. She had the face and, according to some, the breasts of a woman, but the body of a lion, the wings of an eagle, and a serpent's tail. Hera supposedly sent her to Thebes to punish its people, and she took up residence on a mountain outside the city. Waylaying those who passed by, she asked each one the same riddle: "What creature walks on four legs in the morning, two in the afternoon, and three in the evening?" When they couldn't answer, she strangled and devoured them on the spot. The murders continued until Oedipus approached and the Sphinx put the question to him. To her great consternation, he replied that the creature was man: he crawls on all fours as a child, walks unassisted in the prime of life, and leans on a cane in his old age. The disheartened Sphinx leaped off the mountain to her death and the Thebans were once more free, but this creation of Greek mythology lives on in our language as a symbol of mystery and the enigmatic.

stentorian: loud; booming

Stentor was the name of the herald of the Greek forces in the *Iliad*. In Book V of Homer's epic, the Greek war god, Ares, takes to the battlefield on the side of the Trojans. As they slaughter one after another of the Greek warriors, the goddesses Hera and Athena can bear it no longer and decide to enter the fight as well. Hera comes down to earth to inspire the

Greeks, and, to insure that all hear her encouraging words, she calls to them, "mimicking the noble Stentor of the brazen voice, who could raise a shout like that of fifty men together."

Just as his sonorous voice echoed through the Greek camp during the Trojan War, Stentor's name continued to be heard through the centuries. In his honor we still call a person with a powerful voice a *stentor* and say he speaks in *stentorian* tones.

Stygian/stygian: dark, gloomy; inviolate

The idea that the souls of the dead must cross a river to get to their eternal dwelling place dates back to at least 2400 B.C., when it was recorded in the Pyramid Texts. When an Egyptian died, his family built a replica of a barge and buried it with him, so he would have his own means of transport to the nether-world. The Greeks were more democratic in their beliefs: Their dead made the one-way trip to Hades in a "public" conveyance.

The Underworld of Greek mythology was separated from earth by several rivers, one of which was the Styx, whose name means "hateful." When a person died, his soul was led to Hades' entrance by the god Hermes. The deceased then had to pay the ancient ferryman, Charon, to row him across the Styx to whatever area of Hades was destined to be his home for eternity. (The family of the dead man made sure there was a coin in his mouth before he was buried, so he would have the "fare" Charon requested.)

For the most part the Greek myths depict the netherworld as a dreary, cheerless place, where the sun never warms the air or lifts the shadows. The waters of the Styx are equally dark and cold. Coined from the river's name, and literally meaning "of or relating to the Styx," the adjective *Stygian* is now used figuratively to describe an atmosphere of extreme gloom and depression.

Stygian also has the meaning of inviolable, as in a Stygian oath. This usage goes back to the myth of the war between the Titans and the Olympian gods. The Titans Oceanus and Tethys had a daughter named Styx, who sided with Zeus when he successfully overthrew the older generation. As a reward for her loyalty, Zeus made Styx goddess of the river surrounding the Underworld and named it after her. According to Homer, the most binding oath the gods can give is one sworn by the water of the river Styx. In Hesiod's *Theogony,* when a god prepares to give his word, Iris brings water from the Styx, over which he must take the oath; if he subsequently breaks his word he is rendered speechless for one year and banished from Olympus for nine.

See also: (give a sop to) Cerberus

sub rosa (under the rose): in strictest confidence

When the Romans held a banquet at which they planned to discuss topics of the utmost secrecy, they hung a rose over the dining table to remind those present that whatever was said in the room was not to be revealed to the outside world. Hence the Latin phrase *sub rosa* (under the rose) came to mean in confidence, or secretly. Oddly enough, the Romans' choice of the rose as a symbol of silence came about through a mythological mistake.

The Egyptians told many stories about the childhood of the god Horus and often depicted him sitting on the lap of his mother, Iris. In some of these portraits he is holding his index finger to his lips. Seeing Horus the Child—whom they called Harpocrates—in this pose, the Greeks erroneously believed him to be the Egyptian god of silence. When the Romans adopted the Greek pantheon, they too assigned this role to Harpocrates, and created the myth that introduced the rose as a symbol of silence. According to this legend, Harpocrates stumbled upon Venus while she was involved in one of her numerous illicit liaisons. Fortunately, her son Cupid also arrived on the scene and, thinking quickly, plucked a beautiful rose that he presented to Harpocrates in exchange for his pledge of silence.

A real flower continued to be suspended over banquet tables in medieval times, especially in France and England. During the Renaissance, sculpted plaster roses replaced the live ones, and they remained a popular motif in dining rooms well into the Victorian era. Countless generations have sat "under the rose" without ever realizing that they were paying homage to an ancient god.

syringe: *See: syrinx*

syrinx: a musical instrument, panpipe

Pan's realm was the forest, where he slept all day and caroused all night. "Wine, women, and song" was the motto of Pan and the satyrs who celebrated with him. They were usually joined in their drunken orgies by equally wanton nymphs, but they were not above forcing their attentions on the unwilling. In fact, the invention of the syrinx, or panpipe, was said to be the result of Pan's attempted rape of a virtuous nymph. As she was being pursued by the lecherous Pan, Syrinx called out to the gods for help and they transformed her into a bunch of reeds. Pan made the reeds into a mouth pipe and became renowned for the sweet sounds he produced from it. The instrument is still being played today.

Syrinx is also the root of the English word *syringe,* a pipe or tube used to inject liquids.

T

tantalize: to tease and invite yet remain unattainable

When something—or someone—tantalizes us, there is the promise of satisfaction, yet it always remains just out of reach. We are left feeling totally frustrated and, perhaps, wondering what we have done to deserve such treatment.

The original victim of tantalization knew exactly why he was being punished: He had offended the Greek gods and was sent to Tartarus to expiate his sins for eternity. Some say that Tantalus stole the food of the immortals and gave it to man; other storytellers accuse him of simply revealing divine secrets. In a particularly gruesome version of the myth, he is also said to have killed his own son, Pelops, and served him to the Olympians at a banquet. Fortunately, most of the gods saw through Tantalus's ruse, but Demeter ate part of the boy's shoulder before she realized what she was doing. Zeus restored Pelops to life, replacing his shoulder with one of ivory, and sentenced Tantalus to eternal frustration. He was made to stand in a pool of water up to his chin, but each time he leaned over to drink, it receded completely, leaving only mud at his feet. When he stood up the water flooded back, and his futile attempts to quench his thirst began all over again. The trees around him were laden with ripe, delicious fruit, but when Tantalus reached for their branches, the wind blew them just out of his reach. And so he remained, eternally deprived in the midst of plenty.

The Greek sinner was, however, an inspiration to at least one inventor. A tantalus is a case or stand that holds decanters of liquor. The bottles are in full view but cannot be removed unless a bar is first unlocked and raised. For the person with the key there is no problem, but all others might as well be in Tartarus with Tantalus!

tartar: a violent, irascible person

When the Mongol hordes swept across China, Persia, and Eastern Europe in the thirteenth century, they left terror in their wake. They arrived in Western Europe around 1240, moving with such speed that there was no way to outrun them or prepare for their attack. Fortunately, they retreated from Germany in 1241, never to return.

They had called themselves Tatars, but the Europeans confused this name of Persian origin with the Greek name for the section of the Underworld in which sinners were punished: Tartarus. To the frightened citizenry, the invaders seemed like creatures from hell, and they became *Tartars*. In memory of their cruelty and ferocity, a violent, bad-tempered person is still called a tartar. The expression "to catch a Tartar" means to attack someone whom you believe to be weaker than you, only to find that he is, in fact, a formidable opponent.

terpsichorean: *See: muse*

thersitical: loudmouthed; scurrilous

In Book II of the *Iliad,* Homer introduces the character of Thersites, the ugliest Greek who had come to Troy. A commoner, he liked "to bait his royal masters, was never at a loss for some vulgar quip, empty and scurrilous indeed, but well calculated to amuse the troops." Both Achilles and Odysseus had been maligned by this agitator, and hated him because of it. When Agamemnon tries to address the assembled forces, he becomes the object of Thersites' invective. Thersites rails against the king, accusing him of greed and selfishness and of sacrificing the Greek troops for his own advantage. He is quieted only by Odysseus, who declares that he has no right to berate his betters and strikes him with his staff.

Poets after Homer continued the story of the Trojan War, including the battle between Achilles and Penthesilea, Queen of the Amazons. In these later tales, Achilles mourns the beautiful woman he has just slain, and Thersites mocks him for it. When he accuses Achilles of unnatural lust for Penthesilea's corpse, his vile insults are more than the hero can stand, and he strikes the jeering Thersites so hard his soul is sent to Tartarus.

Shakespeare included Thersites in his *Troilus and Cressida,* where he is portrayed as a meanspirited commentator on the other characters. His name has been made into the adjective *thersitical,* which means loudmouthed and scurrilous.

throw the apple of discord: start a quarrel

Just as there have always been troublemakers among men, there was one Greek goddess who delighted in setting the immortals against each other. She was Eris, goddess of discord. The twin sister of the war god Ares, she had much in common with him and was hated by her fellow Olympians. They purposely excluded her from their gatherings, having no desire to deal with her or her son, Strife. She was therefore not invited to the wedding of Peleus and Thetis, and she remained outside the banquet hall plotting her revenge for this insult. As Hera, Athena, and Aphrodite stood together inside, Eris threw at their feet a golden apple inscribed "For the fairest." Of course each of the three goddesses insisted it was intended for her, and the squabbling intensified until they prevailed upon Zeus to decide who was the rightful owner. Zeus wisely refused to act as judge and recommended that the Trojan prince Paris, a connoisseur of female beauty, make the award. Not above bribery, each goddess offered Paris a great prize to decide in her favor: Hera promised that he would be lord of Europe and Asia, Athena that he would conquer the Greeks, and Aphrodite that the most beautiful woman on earth would be his. Paris gave the apple to Aphrodite, who led him to Sparta, where King Menelaus lived with his wife, Helen, the most beautiful woman in the world. (In a high dudgeon, Athena and

Hera went off together to plot the destruction of Troy in retaliation for Paris's slight to them.)

Paris proceeded to abduct Helen, and that, say the myths, was the cause of the Trojan War. It was also the origin of the expression "throw the apple of discord" to describe starting a quarrel or trouble between people.

A second metaphor, a "judgment of Paris," which refers to a tough choice—one with which someone is bound to be unsatisfied—entered our language through this story of Eris's revenge and Paris's dilemma.

See also: (a) face that could launch a thousand ships

thunder: a sound associated with electrical storms; a loud, booming noise

Thor was the Norse god of the sky. According to the Scandinavian myths, storms were produced when he rode across the heavens in his chariot, hurling his magic hammer, Mjollnir. The hammer was his bolt of lightning; the rumbling of his chariot was thunder.

Thor was worshiped by the Germanic tribes as Donar, and the Anglo-Saxons called him Thunor or Thonar. In England, *Thunres daeg* was the day of Thunor, which eventually became the modern English *Thursday*. Very little is known for certain about the Anglo-Saxon cult of Thunor, but it seems to have been associated with the oak forests of England. His name survives in several English place names, such as Thunderley and Thundersley in Essex, where it was combined with the suffix *-leah,* meaning a forest clearing. Just as the Germanic peoples represented Donar's thunderbolt by an axe and used stone axes as talismans, tiny hammer-shaped amulets representing Thunor's magic hammer have been found in Anglo-Saxon graves. They were probably placed there in order to invoke the protection of the god of the sky.

The Latin verb *tonare* comes from the same Indo-European root as the names Thor and Thunor. From it we got the

English words *astonish* and *stun* (*ex tonare* means "out of thunder," i.e., to be thunderstruck). In Spanish *tonare* became *tronar,* and the Spanish word for a storm, *tronada,* became our *tornado.*

See also: Thursday (under "Days")

titan: a leader in one's field; someone of great power and ability

Our news media frequently feature stories about titans of industry, sports, politics, finance. They give the title to those whose achievements have put them at the top of their field and who have attained great power and prestige. It's interesting to note that they often describe these individuals as "standing head and shoulders above the crowd" or being "larger than life."

The Greek Titans, after whom our modern-day heroes are christened, were definitely larger than life. According to the Greek creation myths, they were the first and largest beings in the universe. Colossal in stature and in might, they were more like forces than beings, and that is what they represented: the primeval forces of nature that have ruled the universe since its inception. Children of the Earth (Gaea) and the Sky (Uranus), the first generation of Titans is generally numbered at twelve: Oceanus, Tethys, Hyperion, Thea, Crius, Mnemosyne, Coeus, Phoebe, Cronus, Rhea, Iapetus, and Themis. Cronus was their leader; it was he who led them in their revolt against Uranus, after which Cronus became lord of the earth. He and his sister/queen, Rhea, then ruled over the other Titans until their son, Zeus, challenged them.

After losing the war with the Olympians, the Titans were banished to the Underworld. Their reign ended and a new age began, but their might is remembered in the appellation *titan* and the descriptive *titanic,* designating someone or something of enormous size and power, such as the supposedly unsinkable ocean liner that was constructed at the beginning of the twentieth century.

(a) Triton among the minnows: a superior individual; one who stands out

Everyone knows what a minnow is: a tiny fish, usually measuring only about three inches long. Because it is so small it is of absolutely no use to fishermen, except as bait for bigger fish. In fact, it's hard to imagine a more inconsequential sea creature than the minnow. Tritons, on the other hand, were among the most important denizens of the deep. They were actually demigods who, along with the female Nereids, attended the supreme god of the sea, Poseidon.

The first Triton was the son of Poseidon and a Nereid named Amphitrite. He was gigantic and was best known for trumpeting on a conch shell. Virgil tells how one of Aeneas's exiled Trojans, Misenus by name, was drowned by the god when he dared to challenge him to a musical contest on the hollow shells. Ovid, telling the story of the Great Flood in his *Metamorphoses,* says that after the rain stopped, Neptune commanded Triton to come up from the sea, and he appeared "like a tower of sea-green beard, sea creatures, sea shells. . . ." He sounded his famous horn, commanding the waters to recede, and dry land was visible once again.

In later mythology, the proper name Triton began to be used as a generic term for the class of demigods described above. Sometimes sea deities such as Nereus and Proteus were called Tritons as well. The descriptive phrase "a Triton among the minnows" refers to someone who is vastly superior to those around him and who, consequently, is easily distinguished from the crowd. His unique qualities set him apart in the same way a sea god who happens to be swimming along in a school of minnows would never be taken for one of them!

Trojan: someone with great perseverance and stamina

For nearly ten years, the Greeks kept the city of Troy under siege and the Trojans fought them off. When Troy finally fell, it was not due to the Greeks' superior ability on the battlefield but to the subterfuge of the wooden horse, by means of which they infiltrated the citadel and took the Trojans by surprise. But for this strategem of "the wily Odysseus," the hard-fighting Trojans might have won the war, for he thought of it just as the frustrated Greeks were on the verge of packing up and setting sail for home.

The valiant efforts of the Trojans to hold their home against all odds came down to us through the Greek myths and made their name synonymous with perseverance and pluck. A *Trojan* is someone who battles on and on, no matter what obstacles are thrown in his way, to accomplish a goal. The expressions "work like a Trojan" and "fight like a Trojan" give credit to both their stamina and their courage.

See also: Trojan horse, (beware of) Greeks bearing gifts

Trojan horse: someone or something that subverts from within; a deceptive scheme

After laying siege to the walled city of Troy for ten long years, the Greeks began to despair of ever returning home victorious. Many just wanted to return home. At this point, two ideas came to "nimble-witted" Odysseus. The oracles had foretold that Troy would not fall as long as it possessed its Palladium— the sacred image of Athena that protected the Trojans. Odysseus, therefore, crept into the city and, with the help of Diomedes, removed the statue. Step two of Odysseus's plan was to build a huge wooden horse. Under Athena's supervision, the Greek craftsman Epeius constructed it, with a trapdoor in one flank and a dedication to Athena on the other. A number of armed warriors then climbed inside the horse, while the rest of the Greeks put out to sea in apparent retreat. When the Trojans saw that the Greeks were gone, and only a wooden horse remained in their former camp, they went to investigate. Believing the horse to be sacred to Athena, King Priam and others wanted to bring it into the citadel. Others, including the prophetess Cassandra, protested. The priest Laocoön even hurled a spear into it, causing the weapons inside to clash together, but Poseidon sent sea serpents to devour him, ending any further opposition. Then Sinon, the lone Greek who had remained on shore, was captured. He told a tale of mistreatment by his countrymen and maintained that the horse had been made by the Greeks to placate Athena for their theft of Troy's Palladium. When asked why it was so large, he cleverly responded that its size was meant to deter the Trojans from taking it into their city and thus reenlisting Athena's support. That's all the Trojans had to hear! They immediately rolled the horse inside and began to celebrate the end of the war.

After an evening of feasting, the Trojans retired to their beds and slept more soundly than they had in ten years. As soon as the city was still, Sinon crept outside to light a beacon, signaling the Greek ships to return. When reinforcements arrived the infiltrators let themselves out of the horse's belly, opened the gates from within, and began the sack of Troy. By morning the city lay in ruins, its warriors dead, its women enslaved. What ten years of fighting couldn't bring about was accomplished in one night, thanks to the wily Odysseus.

His strategem proved that the best way to defeat an enemy is to get inside his ranks and undermine him from within. The Trojan horse thus became a metaphor for a fifth column—infiltrators who subvert from within—and is also used in a broader sense, to refer to any deceptive scheme.

See also: Cassandra, Trojan, (beware of) Greeks bearing gifts

troll: an ugly person

During the nineteenth century, Peter Christen Asbjørnsen and Jørgen Engebretsen Moe traveled throughout Norway, collecting popular folktales. Their Norske folkeeventyr (Norwegian Folk Tales) was widely translated, and one of the stories it contained, "The Three Billy Goats Gruff," became a classic in children's literature. The villain of the tale is a troll who lives under a bridge and threatens to eat the goats who want to cross over it. Not a very nice creature, was he? But then, neither were the trolls of Scandinavian mythology, who were his progenitors.

The word *troll* is found in Old Swedish and Old Norse, and *trold* was its Old Danish form. The oldest legends about trolls describe them as Jotuns (Giants) who lived in hills and caves. If they ventured into the sunlight they either burst or turned to stone. These giant trolls were immensely strong and blood-thirsty, but they were also quite stupid, and a human being could easily outwit them. Later stories about trolls depict them as dwarfs who, although not endowed with extraordinary strength, were far more intelligent and, thus, more dangerous. While they no longer routinely ate humans, they delighted in stealing women and children. Some of the sagas include stories about kindly trolls, who acted as guardians and even foster parents to humans, but in general trolls were malicious creatures who were best avoided. Enlisting their aid was tantamount to making a pact with the Devil, and most men who did so lived—or died—to regret it.

Besides being unpleasant, trolls as a group were known for their ugliness. The one in "The Three Billy Goats Gruff" is described as "a great ugly troll with eyes as big as saucers and a nose as long as a poker." And he was good-looking, compared to many of the earlier trolls, some of whom were said to have as many as fifty heads! No wonder their name is used when talking about a homely person. The word also carries a connotation of weirdness or lack of personality, which isn't surprising when you think about the way the trolls of Norse mythology acted around people!

(to have seen the cave of) Trophonius: to know what the future holds and be saddened by it

If we really thought about it, how many of us would want to know what the future held—especially if we couldn't do anything to change it? Knowing all the bad things that lay ahead might be too much for us to bear, and, no longer able to remain optimistic about our destiny, we might be plunged into a deep, dangerous depression. That is, in fact, what often happened to the Greeks who went to the cave of Trophonius in search of knowledge about the future.

The storytellers offer many explanations of how Trophonius acquired the power of prescience. According to some, he was an underworld god, a son of Apollo who inherited the ability to predict the future from his father. Others say that Trophonius was a mortal who was swallowed up by the earth and doomed to be a cave oracle in punishment for having murdered his brother, Agamedes. Still others say he was a favorite of Apollo, and that he and his brother built the god's temple at Delphi. In return for his services, Apollo deified him and allowed him to deliver his own messages in a cave at Lebadea, between Athens and Delphi.

The manner in which visitors to his cave received the answers to their queries was unusual, to say the least. Pausanias, writing in the second century A.D., described it at length. The questioner first had to spend several days in a building near the cave, purifying himself and observing specified rituals. Animal sacrifices were made, and the entrails read, in order to determine whether or not Trophonius was favorably disposed to answer the inquiry. If all the signs were favorable, the questioner was then bathed and made to drink the waters of two springs, Lethe and Mnemosyne (Forgetfulness and Memory). This would make him forget everything except what he learned from the oracle. He was then thrust, feet first, into a hole in the wall of the cave. Swept along by an underground river, he either heard voices or saw images that revealed the future to him. When he arrived back at the opening, he was seated on the Throne of Memory and questioned by the priests. A written account was made of his experiences, after which he was free to leave. It was some time, however, before he recovered his senses. In particular, it took a long time for someone who had visited the cave of Trophonius to be able to laugh again. This was not surprising, as the oracle was known for its gloomy and pessimistic predictions.

That is why, when we say someone "has seen the cave of

Trophonius," we mean he or she knows what the future holds and is disheartened by it.

See also: oracle

typhoon: a violent cyclonic storm; a hurricane

Typhon was the name of a mythical Greek monster, the son of Earth and Tartarus. He was the largest monster ever born, with coiled snakes for legs and serpents' heads instead of hands. Typhon's hideous children by the half-woman, half-serpent Echidna included Cerberus, the Sphinx, the Hydra, and the Chimera. The stories about Typhon recount that in revenge for Zeus's destruction of the Giants, he actually launched an attack on Olympus. After terrorizing the other gods and wounding Zeus, Typhon was finally disabled by the thunderbolts the great god hurled at him. By some accounts, Zeus buried him under Mount Etna, where his underground strugglings can still be heard.

The name of this awful monster gave us one word for a violent storm or hurricane: *typhoon.* Interestingly, the word didn't enter English directly from Greek but took a very round-about route, through Arabia and China. During the Middle Ages, Arabs who had heard the Greek tales of the violent fight between Zeus and Typhon, in which thunderbolts were hurled (i.e., a storm filled the heavens), began to use the word *tufan* for a violent storm. They introduced the word into southeast Asia, where it became *tai-fung* and was used to refer to the cyclonic storms that abound in the China Sea. The Portuguese adopted the form *tufaõ,* and the English made it *typhoon.* The name of the Greek monster, like the cyclones he personified, had finally traveled full circle.

U

unicorn: a mythical, one-horned beast, often symbolizing virility and supreme power

The word *unicorn* is not used figuratively in English, but, like mermaids and leprechauns, unicorns are mythical creatures that have become a popular motif in our culture. Those who come in contact with unicorns—shoppers who pick up a decorative crystal unicorn in a gift shop, parents who read their children a story about a unicorn, visitors to New York's Cloisters who marvel at the artistry of the Unicorn Tapestries—may not be aware of how ancient and ubiquitous this legendary creature actually is.

There is a popular Chinese myth about an animal called the Ki-lin (or Ch'i-lin). Emperor Fu Hsi, who ruled China nearly five thousand years ago, was walking along a river when a miraculous animal rose up out of the water. It had the body of a deer, the tail of an ox, and the hooves of a horse. On its forehead was a single horn, several feet long. The strange animal was completely tame, and it knelt down near the emperor, indicating by its gestures that it wanted him to remove the package it carried on its back. He did so and found a map of his empire, with strange markings all over it. The animal then vanished, leaving Fu Hsi with a sample of the calligraphy that became the written language of China. There are many other myths about the Ki-lin, which was one of four symbolic creatures believed to keep watch over the world. It was said to be the noblest animal, and it came to earth only on special missions. (Confucius's mother was said to have seen a Ki-lin just before giving birth to the great philosopher.)

While the Chinese always considered the Ki-lin to be a mythical creature, many other peoples believed that magical one-horned animals actually lived on earth. When the Greek physician Ctesias returned from Persia in 398 B.C., he brought back tales of wild asses that lived in India, "large as horses and larger. Their bodies are white, their heads dark red, and their eyes dark blue. They have a horn on the forehead which is about a foot and a half in length." Ctesias had heard that the horn of this animal was a protection against poison and would prevent certain diseases, such as epilepsy. The stories out of India were probably based on sightings of the Indian rhinoceros. Rhinos, unfortunately, are still being hunted because of the superstitious belief in their horns' curative powers.

Later Greek and Roman writers, including Aristotle, Pliny the Elder, and Julius Caesar, told even more outrageous tales of one-horned creatures—monoceros—that existed not only in faraway lands but in Europe as well. They were usually composites of several real animals: deer, goats, horses, boars, and even elephants. These figments of the imagination eventually found their way into the Greek bestiaries that were later translated and read throughout Europe. The bestiaries reiterated the old tales about the magical powers of the horn of a monoceros (*unicornus* in Latin). They also added the idea that the unicorn was a very fierce animal but that it easily could be tamed by a virgin. During the Middle Ages a whole body of unicorn lore sprang up, and there was a great demand for unicorn horns. What were claimed to be unicorn horns were literally worth their weight in gold and were sold to all the royal families of Europe as a safeguard against poisoning. Filings from them were added, at great cost, to medical prescriptions, and it wasn't until 1746 that the Apothecaries' Society of London removed unicorn horn from its list of effective medications. The unicorn horns for which European royalty and commoners paid so dearly have now been identified as narwhal tusks!

The Hebrew Old Testament included the word *re'em,* which was used when speaking of a certain very powerful animal. The scholars who translated the Bible into Greek in the second century B.C. did not know what a *re'em* was, but they were familiar with the tales of powerful, one-horned beasts. They substituted the word *monoceros* whenever *re'em* appeared in the text. *Monoceros* became *unicornus* in Latin translations, and that is how the unicorn entered Biblical lore. Its appearance in the Bible, its reputation as a noble animal, and its association with a virgin led Christians to make the unicorn the symbol of Christ.

See also: Monoceros (under "Constellations")

V

Valhalla: a place assigned to persons worthy of special honor

The first recorded Viking raid on England occurred at the end of the eighth century A.D., and the invaders seem to have come from Norway. Other raiding parties of Scandinavians—Swedes, Danes, and Norwegians—continued to prey upon the British Isles and Europe, venturing as far south as Morocco, well into the eleventh century. These Norsemen were fierce fighters and put a high value on military might, so much so that they reserved a special place in the afterworld for those who died in battle.

The Norsemen called their abode of the dead Niflheim, and it was there that the goddess Hel presided over those ordinary mortals who had died of sickness or old age. But warriors who had gone to their deaths fighting could not be expected to spend eternity in this dark, cheerless realm ruled by a female! Instead, their souls were taken directly from the battlefield to Valhalla, "the hall of the slain." The Icelandic *Eddas,* in which the Norse myths were first written down, tell us that in Valhalla the fallen warriors joined the great god Odin in his immense palace. There they prepared for Ragnarok—the last great battle with the giants—by jousting violently with one another throughout the day. Any wounds they received in these bloody frays were miraculously healed each evening, before they were seated in Odin's great dining hall. There they feasted on a never-ending supply of pork from the magic boar Saehrimnir and mead from the sacred goat Heidrun.

Due to the exclusive nature of this mythological training ground, reserved for Odin's elite, *Valhalla* has become a figure of speech for a place of great honor. Today any very important person, whether in the military or not, is said to enjoy Valhalla when he or she is set apart and given special privileges denied to ordinary citizens.

See also: hell

vampire: a seductive woman; a person who preys on others, particularly an extortionist

In the early days of motion pictures, everyone in America was talking about Theda Bara, the infamous vamp of the silent screen. A few decades later, a popular song accused "hard-hearted Hannah" of being "the vamp of Savannah." *Vamp* is short for *vampire,* and the term came into use after Miss Bara played a vampire in the 1914 film *A Fool There Was.* The mannerisms and dress she assumed for the role made viewers think of vampires as seductive females who used their charm to lure and destroy men.

The vampires of mythology were neither charming nor seductive: They were the ghosts or reanimated bodies of the dead, who returned from the grave to suck the blood of the living. Such creatures are ubiquitous in ancient legends, appearing in the Sumerian Epic of Gilgamesh; in the character of Lilith in Hebrew lore; as the Greek and Roman *lamia;* the Chinese *ch'iang-shih;* the Indian *vetalas;* etc. Nowhere, however, did these demonic creatures fire the imagination of men as they did in Central Europe.

Vampires abound in the folklore of Greece and the Balkans, all of the Slavic nations, and Hungary. During the eighteenth century vampire mania swept Hungary, and the horrific tales that originated in that country soon spread throughout Europe. Vampires were believed to return night after night, drawing the lifeblood from a human being, until the person died. The unfortunate victim became a vampire in turn and was forced to prey upon others as he or she had been preyed upon. Vampires had the ability to turn themselves into a number of animals, such as cats, bats, and wolves. It was accepted belief that a vampire could be destroyed only by driving a stake through its heart.

In the entertainment world, vamps like Theda and Hannah may be passé, but vampires remain common characters in horror films. The best-known screen vampire is, of course, Dracula. English novelist Bram Stoker based the fictional Count Dracula on the historic figure of Vlad the Impaler, bestowing on him the characteristics of the vampires of folklore. Since his creation in 1897, Stoker's bloodthirsty count has been portrayed by many actors, including Bela Lugosi, whose unparalleled performance resulted in his lifelong identification with the role.

We've also made the vampires of Central European legend part of our language in a figurative sense, calling someone who preys upon others, particularly to extort money, a bloodsucker or a vampire.

See also: vampire bat (under "Animals")

Venus: a beautiful woman

"My Venus in blue jeans is everything I hoped she'd be.
A teen-age goddess from above, and she belongs to me."

The thought of the Roman goddess of love in a pair of Levi's might make a classical scholar shudder, but these lines from a popular rock-and-roll song of the 1950s are a wonderful illustration of how deeply ingrained the ancient myths are in our culture and our language. Even to American teenagers, whose parents often think they speak an entirely different language, the name Venus conjures up visions of a beautiful female. They don't need to have read Ovid's *Metamorphoses* or seen the Venus de Milo; they don't need to understand the concepts of personification and metaphor. They grow up hearing the word *Venus* used as a synonym for beauty, and they use it too, without thinking twice about its origins. If anyone needs proof that the myths of antiquity are alive today, that song is surely it.

Venus was an ancient Italian deity who may have been originally associated with agriculture. There is no evidence of her worship in Roman in early times, but there were many temples dedicated to her in other cities of the Italian peninsula, such as Lavinium and Ardea. Venus was later identified with the Greek Aphrodite, although how she came to be identified with such an important deity is unknown. Since the ancient Italian Venus had no myths of her own, she took over those of the Greek goddess, who was believed to inspire love—and lust—in all living things. At Aphrodite's direction, her son Eros fired arrows into the hearts of men and women, filling them with sexual desire. The Roman counterpart of Eros was Cupid, and he too took on the character of the earlier Greek god of love.

When the cult of Venus was introduced into Rome, the date of the foundation of one of her temples—August 23—became the *dies meretricum,* or "prostitute's day," because Roman courtesans flocked to worship there. Venus's cult grew under the Caesars, who claimed descent from the Trojan hero Aeneas, mythical son of Venus and the mortal Anchises.

Besides entering English as a synonym for a great beauty, the name of Venus can be found at the root of several other common words. *Venereal* describes diseases that are transmitted during the worship of Venus, i.e., sexually. *Venom* comes from the Latin *venenum*—the love potion of Venus that was on Cupid's darts. To the mortals they struck, their effect was as deadly as the bite of a poisonous snake. The Latin verb *venerari* meant "to desire" because Venus inspired desire in men. Now, when we *venerate* someone we may not be attracted to them sexually, but we have ardent feelings for them nonetheless. A person worthy of such deep feelings is deemed *venerable,* which once meant lovable. Finally, the lower portion of a woman's abdomen, just above her genitals, is referred to by anatomists as the *mons veneris,* or "mount of Venus," in deference to the goddess's control over our sexuality.

See also: aphrodisiac, (struck by) Cupid's arrow, Venus (under "Planets"), Venus's-Flytrap (under "Plants")

volcano: a vent in the earth's crust through which steam and molten rock issue

Volcanoes abound in the Mediterranean region. Vesuvius, Etna, Stromboli, and Vulcano are four of Italy's largest, but there are many smaller ones as well, and some of them have been active for thousands of years. The Latin-speaking inhabitants of ancient Italy named these vents in the earth's crust after Vulcanus, the god of fire. As Vulcanus Quietus and Vulcanus Mulciber (fire allayer), he was invoked to protect his worshipers from the destructive aspects of fire, such as the rivers of molten lava that sometimes ran down the mountainsides or the conflagrations that broke out from time to time in populated areas.

This indigenous Italian deity eventually came to be identified with Hephaestus, whose cult came from Asia Minor, through Greece, to the Roman Empire. Hephaestus was first worshiped in areas such as Lycia in southwest Anatolia and on the island of Lemnos, where deposits of natural gas often caught fire and escaped through the soil. By the time his cult reached mainland Greece, myths had arisen that made Hephaestus the son of Zeus and Hera. He was said to be lame and to be the often-cuckolded husband of Aphrodite. He had no equal, however, in the art of metalworking. He created such masterpieces as Zeus's thunderbolt; Achilles' armor; and the first woman, Pandora. A hole in the earth through which fire came out was, of course, the site of one of the fire god's forges and was called a *vulcanus* by the Romans. This became *volcano* in Italian and in English.

The Roman god of fire also lives on in a technical term coined for a process developed by Goodyear in 1839: *vulcanization,* the strengthening of crude rubber with sulphur under heat. A chemical treatment of rubber at room temperature to obtain the same effect was later developed by Alexander Parkes and is called cold vulcanization, which to anyone familiar with the Greek and Roman myths is a definite contradiction in terms.

W

werewolf: a man who periodically turns into a wolf

Like vampires, werewolves are popular subjects of horror films. In the familiar story line, the werewolf is a normal human being by day, but as night falls—and especially if there is a full moon—he takes on the shape of a wolf and is filled with bloodlust. In his beastly form he rushes out into the night, chasing down human and animal victims and tearing out their throats. At dawn he returns home, exhausted and with no memory of his gruesome nocturnal deeds.

Shape-shifting is a common theme in many mythologies: in Scandinavia and Russia, people were believed to turn into bears; in Africa, hyenas and leopards; in South America, jaguars; and in the Pacific Islands, sharks. The Persians believed in creatures who could turn into camels; the Icelandic *hamrammrs* were people who became whatever animal they ate, and acquired its strength; the Haitian *loup garou* and the Indian *rakshasa* could assume any form they wished.

Our literary and screen characterizations of werewolves are based, for the most part, on European folklore, in which the most common form of shape-shifting was from man to wolf. According to the popular tales, a person usually became a werewolf by being bitten by one. However, it was possible to fall victim to the affliction by making a pact with the Devil or if someone put a curse on you. Our English word *werewolf* comes from the Anglo-Saxon *were* (man) and *wulf* (wolf). Its synonym, *lycanthrope,* is derived from the Greek *lykos* (wolf) and *anthropos* (man). The most familiar lycanthrope of Greek myth was Lycaon, a king of Arcadia. There are many versions of Lycaon's story, but the one that was most often repeated says that he served Zeus a meal of human flesh, knowing that only a god would be able to detect the trick. Not only did Zeus detect it, but he did not appreciate it, and he showed his displeasure by killing Lycaon's son with his thunderbolt and turning Lycaon himself into a wolf.

Today, besides meaning the study of werewolves, *lycanthropy* is the clinical term for a form of insanity in which the patient thinks he is a wolf.

wheel of fortune: popular symbol of luck or chance

> "Round and round it goes.
> Where it stops, nobody knows."

Those are the words recited by carnival barkers as they spin the popular attraction we call the wheel of fortune. The lucky person on whose number the wheel comes to rest receives a prize, but there's no way of knowing in advance who will be the winner and who will come away empty-handed. The ancient Romans were also familiar with such a device, but they called it the wheel of Fortune, with a capital "F." Their wheel was an attribute of the Roman goddess Fortuna, and when she spun it she could grant a mortal all his wishes or take away everything he held dear. As the personification of the concept of chance, she could "turn the tables" on anyone, at any time.

Originally, Fortuna (sometimes called Fors or Fors Fortuna) was an indigenous Italian fertility goddess. From the earliest times she was worshiped as the deity who insured the fertility of the soil and of women. As such, she was associated with the changing seasons of the year rather than the vagaries of chance. It was only after she began to be identified with the Greek goddess of fortune, Tyche, that her followers looked to her for happiness and material wealth. She was still depicted carrying, in one hand, the cornucopia from which she distributed the earth's bounty to man, but in the other hand she now held a wheel or a rudder to control the course of human events. Sometimes she was portrayed standing on a ball or globe, to symbolize the changeability of fortune.

Fortuna's ball was probably inspired by that of Tyche, who

was said to carry one, which she constantly juggled, making men's fortunes go up and down whenever she wished. Fortuna's wheel may have come, however, from Nemesis, the Greek goddess of retribution. It was she who monitored the actions of those on whom Tyche had bestowed her favors. If they abused their position, or became greedy or presumptuous, she could always spin her wheel, sending them from the top back to the bottom.

Of all the Roman gods and goddesses, Fortuna was the one most spoken of during the Middle Ages and the Renaissance. Her constant turning of the wheel, causing the ceaseless rise and fall of men's fortunes, was an extremely popular theme in art and literature. The wheel of fortune continues to be a ubiquitous motif in our society, appearing in songs, at parties, and as the title of the most popular game show in television history.

See also: nemesis

Z

zephyr: a gentle breeze; a piece of lightweight clothing

In ancient Greece the god of the west wind was called Zephyrus, and he was often depicted partially unclothed, carrying flowers in his robe. He was the husband of Chloris, goddess of greenery and flowers.

The allegorical meaning behind this myth is obvious: It is the mild west wind that is the harbinger of spring, supplanting the cold northerly winds that prevail in winter. Each year, with this shift in wind comes the rebirth of vegetation: The earth once more wears a mantle of green; crops spring up; flowers bloom.

It is through this ancient allegory that we have come to call both a mild, gentle breeze and a light, gauzy piece of clothing (appropriate to wear only after winter's winds have subsided) a *zephyr*. The adjectives *zephyrean* and *zephyrous* (like or suggesting a light breeze) are also derived from the Greek god's name.

Zephyrus was called Favonius by the Romans, and his name is the root of another English adjective, *favonian,* meaning mild or favoring, like the west wind.

See also: aurora

zombie: a strong rum cocktail; a person who acts as though in a trance

After drinking a few zombies—cocktails made with several kinds of rum and fruit juice—a person will probably end up acting like the reanimated corpses of the same name, who are dreaded figures in West Indian mythology.

The people of the West Indies, particularly the Haitians, have long believed in supernatural powers or essences that enter the body of a dead person and cause it to come back to life. The result is a zombie; a walking corpse that has no will of its own but follows the orders of the spirit that has taken over its mind and soul. In Kongoese, the language of the Bantu tribes of the African Congo, the word *zumbi* means "fetish." Brought to the West Indies as slaves, these tribesmen soon developed their own religious beliefs and traditions, which became West Indian voodoo. Followers of voodooism believed wholeheartedly in the existence of zombies and greatly feared them. Their fears may have been exploited by unscrupulous voodoo priests who created their own zombies by administering a drug that gave the appearance of death. The priest would officiate at the public burial of his victim and then, several hours later, secretly dig up the comatose person and revive him with an antidote. Still suffering from the stupefying effects of the first drug, the victim would be able to move only slowly and hesitantly. He would follow the priest's orders unquestioningly and could be exhibited as proof of the existence of zombies.

This image of a half-dead being, plodding along in a trance, has given us the slang word *zombie* for a person whose senses are deadened and who shows no initiative.

♂, ♀: scientific symbols for male and female

These two symbols, now used by biologists, medical practitioners, and botanists all over the world, are derived from Greek mythology. The first represents Ares, the god of war: the circle and arrow stand for either the helmet and plume or the shield and spear worn by Greek warriors who invoked his name as they charged into battle. The second sign is that of Aphrodite, goddess of love: the circle with the cross beneath it is believed to represent her looking glass or hand mirror.

These symbols were first used by ancient astronomers to represent the planets we know as Mars and Venus. Until the twentieth century, war was the exclusive domain of men, and warriors strove to emulate Ares' aggression and virility, so his symbol was naturally deemed an appropriate one for the male sex. On the other hand, women traditionally were thought to occupy themselves primarily with their looks, using them to attract the opposite sex, just as Aphrodite used her beauty to dazzle gods and men alike. Men, therefore, chose the astronomical symbol for the planet Venus to represent the female of the species.

With increasing numbers of women serving in the armed forces and more and more men pursuing modeling careers, the symbols are no longer as appropriate as they were when the scientific community adopted them. They've become so universally accepted, however, that it doesn't seem likely they'll be replaced by anything more in keeping with contemporary sexual roles.

BIBLIOGRAPHY

American Heritage Illustrated Encyclopedic Dictionary. Boston: Houghton-Mifflin, 1987.

Apollonius of Rhodes. *The Voyage of the Argo: The Argonautica.* Trans. E. V. Rieu. Baltimore: Penguin Books, 1959.

Apuleius. *The Golden Ass of Lucius Apuleius.* Trans. William Adlington. New York: Hogarth Press, 1924.

Asimov, Isaac. *Words from History.* Boston: Houghton-Mifflin, 1968.

————. *Words from Myths.* Eau Claire, Wis.: E. M. Hale, 1961.

Ayto, John. *Dictionary of Word Origins.* New York: Arcade, 1991.

Barnet, Sylvan, Morton Berman, and William Burto, eds. *Eight Great Tragedies.* New York: New American Library, 1957.

Barnett, Lincoln. *The Treasure of Our Tongue: The Story of English from Its Obscure Beginnings to Its Present Eminence as the Most Widely Spoken Language.* New York: Knopf, 1964.

Barnhart, Robert K., ed. *The Barnhart Dictionary of Etymology.* New York: H. W. Wilson Co., 1988.

Bennefoy, Yves, comp. *Dictionnaire des mythologies et des religions des sociétés traditionelles et du monde antique.* 2 vols. Chicago: University of Chicago Press, 1991.

Brandon, Samuel G. F., ed. *Dictionary of Comparative Religion.* New York: Charles Scribner's Sons, 1970.

Bulfinch, Thomas. *Bulfinch's Mythology.* New York: Modern Library, 1970.

Ciardi, John. *Good Words to You: An All-New Dictionary and Native's Guide to the Unknown American Language.* New York: Harper & Row, 1987.

————. *A Second Browser's Dictionary and Native's Guide to the Unknown American Language.* New York: Harper & Row, 1983.

Claiborne, Robert. *Loose Cannons & Red Herrings: A Book of Lost Metaphors.* New York: Ballantine Books, 1988.

Corsini, Raymond J., ed. *Encyclopedia of Psychology.* 4 vols. New York: John Wiley & Sons, 1984.

Craigie, William A. *The Icelandic Sagas.* Cambridge: The University Press, 1913.

Dawood, N. J., trans. *The Koran.* 3d rev. ed. Baltimore: Penguin Books, 1968.

Deutsch, Babette. *Heroes of the Kalevala: Finland's Saga.* New York: Julian Messner, 1940.

Dudley, Donald R. *The Civilization of Rome.* New York: New American Library, 1960.

Encyclopaedia Britannica. 24 vols. Chicago: Encyclopedia Britannica, 1971.

Euripedes. *Three Great Plays of Euripides: Medea, Hippolytus, Helen.* New York: New American Library, 1958.

Evans, Bergen. *Dictionary of Mythology, Mainly Classical.* New York: Dell, 1972.

Funk, Wilfred J. *Word Origins and Their Romantic Stories.* New York: Wilfred Funk, Inc., 1950.

Funk & Wagnalls Standard Dictionary of Folklore, Mythology and Legend. Vol. 2. New York: Funk & Wagnalls, 1949.

Giblin, James. *The Truth About Unicorns.* New York: Harper Collins, 1991.

Graves, Robert. *The Greek Myths.* 2 vols. London: Penguin Books, 1955.

————. Introduction to *New Larousse Encyclopedia of Mythology.* New York: Putnam, 1968 [c. 1959].

Gray, Louis H., ed. *Mythology of All Races.* New York: Cooper Square Publishers, 1964.

Hamilton, Edith. *The Greek Way to Western Civilization.* New York: New American Library, 1948.

————. *Mythology.* New York: New American Library, 1942.

————, trans. *Three Greek Plays: Prometheus Bound, Agamemnon, The Trojan Women.* New York: W. W. Norton, 1937.

Haviland, Virginia. *Favorite Fairy Tales Told in Norway.* Boston: Little, Brown, 1961.

Herodotus. *The Histories.* Trans. Aubrey de Selincourt. Baltimore: Penguin Books, 1954.

Hesiod. *Theogony; Works and Days.* Trans. Richmond Lattimore. Ann Arbor, Mich.: University of Michigan Press, 1959.

Homer. *The Iliad.* Trans. Emile V. Rieu. Harmondsworth: Penguin Books, 1950.

————. *The Odyssey.* Trans. Emile V. Rieu. Harmondsworth: Penguin Books, 1946.

Hughes, Thomas Patrick. *A Dictionary of Islam: Being a Cyclopedia of the Doctrines, Rites, Ceremonies, and Customs, Together with the Technical and Theological Terms, of the Muhammadan Religion.* 2d ed. Clifton, N.J.: Reference Book Publishers, 1965.

Interpreter's/*The Interpreter's Bible: The Holy Scriptures in the King James and Revised Standard Versions with General Articles and Introduction. Exegesis, Exposition for Each Book of the Bible.* 12 vols. New York: Abingdon Press, 1952–1957.

Ions, Veronica. *Egyptian Mythology.* London: Hamlyn, 1965.

King, Cynthia. *In the Morning of Time: The Story of the Norse God Balder.* New York: Four Winds Press, 1970.

Lass, Abraham H., David Kiremidjian, and Ruth M. Goldstein. *The Facts on File Dictionary of Classical, Biblical, and Literary Allusions.* New York: Facts on File, 1987.

Limburg, Peter R. *Stories Behind Words: The Origins and Histories of 285 English Words.* New York: H. W. Wilson Co., 1986.

Liungman, Carl G. *Dictionary of Symbols.* Santa Barbara, Cal.: ABC-CLIO, 1991.

Loomis, Roger Sherman. *The Development of Arthurian Romance.* New York: Harper & Row, 1963.

Menzel, Donald H. *Astronomy.* New York: Random House, 1975.

Mercatante, Anthony S. *The Facts on File Encyclopedia of World Mythology and Legend.* New York: Facts on File, 1988.

Molière. *The Dramatic Works of Molière.* Trans. Henri Van Laun. 3 vols. New York: Worthington, 1880.

Morris, William, and Mary Morris. *Morris Dictionary of Word and Phrase Origins.* 2d ed. New York: Harper & Row, 1988.

Murray, James A. H., et al., eds. *The Oxford English Dictionary: Being a Corrected Re-Issue with an Introduction, Supplement, and Bibliography.* 13 vols. Oxford: Clarendon Press, 1961.

Ovid. *The Metamorphoses.* Trans. Horace Gregory. New York: New American Library, 1960.

Partridge, Eric. *Name into Word: Proper Names That Have Become Common Property.* New York: Macmillan, 1950.

————. *Origins: A Short Etymological History of Modern English.* 3d ed. London: Routledge & K. Paul, 1961.

Ridpath, Ian. *Star Tales.* New York: Universe Books, 1988.

Shipley, Joseph T. *Dictionary of Word Origins.* Totowa, N.J.: Littlefield, Adams, 1982.

Shakespeare, William. *The Complete Works*. Eds. Stanley Wells and Gary Taylor. New York: Clarendon Press, 1988.

Skeat, Walter W. *An Etymological Dictionary of the English Language*. 4th ed. Oxford: Clarendon Press, 1963.

Sophocles. *Oedipus the King*. Trans. Bernard M. W. Knox. New York: Washington Square Press, 1959.

South, Malcolm, ed. *Mythical and Fabulous Creatures: A Sourcebook and Research Guide*. New York: Greenwood Press, 1987.

Stein, Jess, ed. *The Random House Dictionary of the English Language*. New York: Random House, 1983.

Tennyson, Alfred. *Idylls of the King*. New York: Bantam Books, 1965.

Thompson, Stith. *Motif-Index of Folk-Literature: A Classification of Narrative Elements in Folktales, Ballads, Myths, Fables, Mediaeval Romances, Exempla, Fabliaux, Jest-Books, and Local Legends*. 6 vols. Rev. and enl. ed. Bloomington, Ind.: Indiana University Press, 1955–1958.

Tuleja, Tad. *Namesakes: An Entertaining Guide to the Origins of More Than 300 Words Named for People*. New York: McGraw-Hill, 1987.

Urdang, Laurence, ed. *Picturesque Expressions: A Thematic Dictionary*. Detroit: Gale Research Co., 1985.

Virgil. *The Aeneid*. Trans. William Francis Jackson Knight. Harmondsworth: Penguin Books, 1956.

Warner, Rex. Forward to *Encyclopedia of World Mythology*. New York: Galahad Books, 1975.

Webber, Elizabeth, and Mike Feinsilber. *Grand Allusions: A Lively Guide to Those Expressions, Terms and References You Ought to Know But Might Not*. Washington, D.C.: Farragut Publishing Co., 1990.

Webster's New International Dictionary of the English Language. 2d ed. Springfield, Mass.: G. & C. Merriam Company, 1934.

Webster's Word Histories. Springfield, Mass.: Merriam-Webster, 1989.

Weston, Jessie L. *From Ritual to Romance*. Garden City, N.Y.: Doubleday, 1957.

Word Mysteries & Histories: From Quiche to Humble Pie. Boston: Houghton-Mifflin, 1986.

Wyld, Henry Cecil. *The Historical Study of the Mother Tongue: An Introduction to Philological Method*. London: John Murray, 1931.

Zim, Herbert S., and Robert H. Baker. *Stars: A Guide to the Constellations, Sun, Moon, Planets, and Other Features of the Heavens*. Rev. ed. New York: Golden Press, 1985.

ABOUT THE AUTHOR

The author is a native of New York City who studied language and literature at NYU's Washington Square College and Graduate School of Arts and Science. She and her twenty-one cats now make their home in the foothills of the Adirondack Mountains.